The Dead Living Mummy

An epic story of a lost city that ended with a lost mind

by

K.J. Goss

The Dead Living Mummy
Copyright © 2020 by K.J. Goss
All rights reserved

ISBN Number: 978-0-9960140-9-0

As always none of this would have been possible without the encouragement of my wife and her patience with me for all the time taken to pursue my dreams.

Contents

The Dead Living Mummy

The Dead Living Mummy

Part 1

Chapter 1

I had always read about and was told how hot and miser-able the Yucatan could be but I was still not prepared for what I was facing now. Coming from New England we had a few hot spells but they never lasted very long. I have been here at the Hotel Juarez for two days now and I don't think the thermometer has varied by more than one degree, night or day. I just wasn't used to one hundred and six degree readings with what seemed like four hundred percent humidity, but a job is a job and I had been waiting for just such an opportunity like this for a long time.

As an outdoor and wildlife photographer this was like a dream come true. For a crack at ancient history Eric Dexter could put up with a little discomfort. I was to meet with Frank Thurber, an archeologist from the University of Pennsylvania, who had just recently uncovered what could be another lost Mayan city.

I was anxious to get moving but there was a message waiting for me when I arrived informing me that Frank would be delayed a few days. I managed to get my film supply into the hotel's cooler which gave me one less worry, at least for the time being. Surprisingly the hotel food was quite good and the beer was cold.

The town of Oxtec was small, with two rundown cafe's, a larger, what appeared to be a general store, and sundry souvenir shops to capture the tourist dollars. In other words, there was nothing to do. I had checked my equipment countless times, so much so that I was afraid I was going to wear it out before I actually got to use it.

One of the few pleasures I discovered was an

afternoon siesta. It was a small but pleasant escape from the oppressive heat of the afternoon There was no air conditioning in the room but I did have a slow moving fan directly over the bed. That coupled with stripping to my shorts made the afternoon tolerable.

Chapter 2

It was day number four at the Juarez Hotel when I finally saw Frank Thurber checking in at the lobby desk. Boy, was I happy to see him. We exchanged pleasantries and he apologized for his delay. He finished signing in and I followed him to his room for a beer and he went right to outlining his plans and what equipment we would need, at the same time trying to keep it minimal because of weight restrictions. Having previously been here he already had a guide and porters lined up. Frank figured we only needed a day to get everything together, then we would be on our way. That was wonderful news to my ears. I was tired of watching the grass grow.

We spent the rest of the day acquiring the necessary supplies, food and equipment. The day was topped off with a great dinner, a few glasses of wine then we headed for our respective rooms in hopes of a full nights rest.

Chapter 3

Full sun, mosquitoes and a cool ninety eight degree day greeted us as we exited the hotel. Three porters and our guide, all locals I guessed, met us just outside the door. The equipment was divided up and our party of six headed for the river about a half mile away. A crude flat bottom boat, that looked like an oversized John boat, with an old outboard motor awaited us. We were barely settled as the boatman shoved away from the broken down dock. The motor was surprisingly quiet for its obvious age.

Eight hours later put us quite deep into the jungle looking at another broken down dock. Thirty yards or so away stood our hotel for the night. A roughly put together, weather worn, boarded structure with a tin roof. This was to be the end of our creature comforts for a while, if that's what you call creature comforts.

It was good to stand and stretch after being cramped in that boat all day. No sooner had we unloaded our supplies when the boatman turned and sailed back down river again. As quiet as that old outboard had been the sound of silence really set in as soon as he was out of sight. At least I thought it was silent. Not having spent any time in a jungle before, I never realized just how much sound is generated by the unseen inhabitants. The quiet noise was not at all stressful as a busy city would be. It was more like a symphony os sound. Each note individual while blending for a chorus of nerve soothing natural music. I was suddenly aware of just how relaxed I felt. I smiled to myself thinking just how naive and silly I must look to others, but right now I didn't even care.

Every one turned to in setting up a quick camp. At least for tonight tents were not needed, only our cots and mosquito netting. Frank and I reviewed some maps while we still had some daylight and our guide and crew prepared dinner. We swapped some stories during and after dinner and again hit the sack early. I lay awake for a while listening to nature's nighttime symphony. It was different than music of the day but just as captivating.

For whatever reason I was the last to get up the next morning. The cleanup had already taken place, some breakfast had been put aside for me. I just had to take my bunk down. Today would be another day by water. Just as I finished securing my cot away, two large dugout canoes arrived. From here on the river was too shallow to accept the motor traffic. We loaded our gear in short order and were soon on our way with the rhythmic swish of paddles. Because we were moving somewhat slower than yesterday I managed to take some great photo's of nature that few people ever get to see. The colorful bird life alone was worth the trip. The Caymans also are interesting in their own right. Most people know them as alligators but down here they call them Caymans. The power they possess is awesome and should command anyone's respect.

By mid-afternoon the dugouts beached at a large clearing. This would be our departure area. From here on our trek would continue on foot following our GPS. Frank decided that since we still had some daylight left we should take advantage of it and start into the jungle. Within minutes the sun was no longer directly visible. The jungle canopy provided an almost impenetrable roof. I thought that without the direct sun it would be cooler, but that same canopy prevented all air movement which made the heat seem even more oppressive.

After three hours of hacking a pathway we stopped for the night. We had only gone about a mile and a half. Now I understand why expeditions always took so long. With all of today's travel conveniences the only way to cross the jungle was just what we were doing. We set up camp and once I had my mosquito netting in place I fell exhausted in my bunk. I noticed the local chaps rigged up hammocks in the lower trees, netting and all. It certainly appeared to be a lot more comfortable. Tomorrow, I thought, I would ask about the hammock. Perhaps I could try that myself. I closed my eyes and let the orchestration of sound lull me off to sleep.

I awoke the following morning to a very different, yet as pleasing serenade. The jungle was a never ending supply of music. One surly did not need a radio for entertainment. Surprisingly I was the first one up. I stoked the fire and put the coffee on. I was rested and raring to go. Breakfast was some sort of flat bread and fresh fruit which was quite filling. I inquired about the hammock and it was agreed the porters would show me how to hang it tonight. With renewed enthusiasm we set out on our quest for this new lost city.

The jungle is certainly not user friendly. At least not to a suburbanite like me. Almost every step is hard earned with the aid of the machete. I always thought I was in pretty good shape but this jungle sure makes you reassess what being in shape is. Nevertheless we forged on.

I learned to follow the others, that made it a little easier. At the end of the day I surprised myself with how well I had held up. I actually felt good. Not too tired and not too achy. Dinner was good. I don't know what we ate but it was filling. I almost don't want to know what we ate.

After dinner I learned to hang a hammock and netting. Frank and I then relaxed as he discussed what he hoped to find. I must admit I myself was anticipating great things. The day's trek was catching up to all of us so we called it a night. Again I drifted off to the songs of the forest.

As we started the next morning, Frank mentioned that two more days would possibly put us there barring any unforeseen circumstances. I was feeling the excitement of a kid at Christmas. I couldn't believe how anxious I had become.

Each day seemed to be a repeat of the day before. Nothing new, but everything new. I was actually enjoying myself. I would stop now and then for what I thought was an irresistible

photo op. I got so carried away one time that I suddenly found myself completely alone. For some reason or other I wasn't alarmed. I probably should have been but I was having too much fun to think of my own safety. I put my camera away and ran as fast as best I could to catch up. The path was obviously easy to follow. It's not like there are many people using machete's to blase a trail.
I finally caught up to the group. Frank, of course expressed his concerns and suggested the next time I feel so inclined that I keep the guide or one of the porters with me. I agreed with him and we continued our pursuit for the lost city.

Around six o'clock we stopped for the night and I managed
the hammock by myself under the watchful and smiling eyes of my teacher Diego. Dinner again was pleasant and Frank was extremely animated while talking about tomorrow's journeys end. His anticipation was contagious.
I could feel my own anxiety building. We hit the sack in hopes of getting an early start for the final leg. I think I was the most enthusiastic of us all. I had never seen an ancient Mayan city before, not even one that had been excavated. To be present at the discovery or the uncovering of something that old was the dream of all dreams for me. I could not imagine what was in store for me. I felt like running the whole way just to get there to discover things for myself, though I really knew I couldn't do that. I was very familiar with methods of archeology and of course there are certain procedures to follow. That not with-standing, I still couldn't wait to get there.

Frank stopped a little after two with the announcement, "We're Here."

I looked around at nothing but jungle and unconsciously said, "We're Where ?"

"The lost city." he answered. "You're standing in the middle of it."

I gazed around at thick jungle. Thicker than we had encountered before. I guess my confused look gave me away. Frank spoke again.

"Look around. Look carefully." he said.

I slowed my mind down and realized what they mean when they say, *"You don't see the trees for the forest."* I let my eyes wander slowly and then there it was. A small pyramid. So taken with this image, my eyes began to tear and my body trembled slightly. The facade was so overgrown with vines, roots, leaves and trees it was barely visible. But here it was right before me. I didn't move for what seemed like hours. I could feel the city filled with people, moving to and fro, busy with their daily lives. Frank's voice shook me from my revery. He was staring and smiling.

"I know how you feel." he said. "It struck me the same way when I first encountered it."

Turning to our four guides he continued.

"Okay, let's set up camp right here. I know there's some water about a hundred yards or so over there." he said pointing easterly.

I was already shooting some pictures. Addressing me like one of his students, Frank pointed out.

"There will be plenty of time for that later. We all help set up house now. This will be our permanent base for a while."

Feeling slightly embarrassed, I knew he was right. Reluctantly I put my camera away and joined the others with the work at hand. It took the six of us almost two and a half hours to clear an area and put together our semi permanent home. Tents and tarp's for shelter from the rain and storage for equipment and supplies. Frank and I continued with equipment checks while our four local helpers disappeared into the jungle in search of dinner. Although we were more than busy with our tasks I could not help but sneak peeks now and then at the wonderful structure before me. I was anxious for a closer inspection, but I knew it would have to wait. I guess after all these centuries, this magnificent building was not going to disappear over night.

The work of setting our base camp was more tiring than I thought. There were more details involved than I ever could have imagined.

It was a welcome pleasure to sit down for dinner and rest. Dinner also turned out to be a surprise. At least to me it was a big surprise. I had never eaten monkey before. I was a little hesitant at first but after a few tastes I decided it really wasn't that bad and I ate heartily as the rest were doing. They all politely pretended not to notice my earlier discomfort at the start of the meal.

It was almost dark now and relaxing with a full stomach and a second cup of coffee we continued into an impromptu bull session discussing our plans for the work ahead. This is where I found out that Mateo, whom I thought was just a guide, was more than just a guide. He was an accomplished Mayan historian. A keeper of oral history dating back centuries. Years of practical study taught him to read and interpret Glyph's and writing. His own ancestry dated back to an unknown past. As he spoke, the pride in his people was obvious. He seemed to know how special they were based on the depth of their knowledge long before that of the Europeans.

As fascinating as our discussion was, we all were tired and
agreed to call it a night. I climbed into my hammock, listening to the music of the night and let my mind wander into the past.

Chapter 4

The aroma of fresh coffee tickled my senses as I slowly became conscious of the world again. I was comfortable and content and did not want to leave my world of peaceful dreams. The low voices of Frank and Mateo did manage to invade my private space and prod my mind awake. I swung out of my hammock and happily realized I did not have to take it down today since this was home for a while. I finished my wake up job with some water on my face and followed the coffee smell. The work table, under a canopy, was covered with maps and other assorted papers as Frank outlined our days activities. We were to work in three teams of two, for obvious reasons, each man equipped with a hand held GPS.

After breakfast we were to fan out from our camp center to see what else, if anything, could be found. Carlos, one of the porters assigned to work with me was also a surprise. He was locally educated in his cultures archeology and was well versed in his own oral history. I was beginning to feel like, and actually was, the neophyte of the group. It didn't really matter though, I felt my excitement and enthusiasm could make my contribution worth while.

Carlos and I headed out in an easterly direction and had not yet gone a hundred yards when we came upon rectangular blocks almost flush with the ground. A more careful examination revealed a regular pattern of these blocks. We carefully walked the outline, along with photographs and GPS readings. Much to our surprise we were uncovering a large rectangular plaza which stretched before us back to our campsite and the vine covered pyramid. We would ascertain an accurate measurement after our findings were plotted on the maps but I guess it to be about fifty yards by one hundred yards. To me, in my uninitiated capacity, this indicated possibly a major city since we already had a large pyramid structure and now a huge plaza. I was excited to plot our find but was reminded by Carlos we were not to meet back at camp until mid-afternoon.

We finished the complete plaza outline then continued in our easterly direction. We cut through another twenty five or so feet and were stopped by a wall. A man made block wall. We spent the next couple of hours doing a preliminary clearing of vines and underbrush exposing mire of our wall, recording our slow progress with photographs. We guesstimated it to be about twelve foot high but its length was still undetermined.

We finally called it quits around three in the afternoon. I was physically tired but my mind was still in overdrive. I can't ever remember when I was this stimulated about anything. Luckily it was a short walk back to base on an already cleared path. I was too exhausted to do much more hacking.

We arrived back to find the other four already enjoying a leisurely sit while being refreshed by fresh fruit. We collapsed into our portable deck chairs excitedly telling of our find. Feeling somewhat renewed we all migrated to the planning table and recorded our GPS information. Frank had discovered two small pyramids a few hundred yards away while Mateo and Mario had uncovered a large living complex, probably of the more common people. The area was approximately two hundred yards square. Proud of our day's accomplishments, we all showered, (*these portable showers are great*) and relaxed over dinner. Dinner was a choice of MRE's (meals ready to eat) but under the circumstances it felt like a feast. After dinner Frank had a surprise for us. He had secreted away in his pack a bottle of Remy Martin Cognac. We all had a shot in celebration of our fruitful day. We relaxed for a while longer letting the cognac do its job and finally drifted to our respective sleeping area's. I comfortably lay there for a while

allowing the sounds of the night work their magic on my overactive
brain.

Chapter 5

       The next morning Carlos and I headed east again back to the wall. Another hours worth of hacking at vines proved fruitful. We came to a portal that appeared to be about eight feet wide and seven feet high, the top arched and key stoned. I stood there marveling at the engineering feat when I noticed carved inscriptions along the top of the arch. I could not get to my camera fast enough. I needed to capture this before they disappeared. There I was being silly again. Why was I worried after they survived all these centuries.

       I checked with Carlos about translating, but he was not sure and would leave that up to Mario. Feeling that we wasted enough time already on our admiration of the magnificent entrance way we stepped through. Inside, were of course, more jungle vines, but not so the tall trees.

Looking ahead and up, directly aligned with the portal we sighted the flat top of an extremely large pyramid. I judged it to be approximately five hundred feet away and well over fifty feet high. Snapping myself out of a trance I again reached for the camera. Carlos busied himself recording GPS numbers of both the wall, Its opening and was headed directly for the pyramid. We realized then we were walking on another plaza. Down on our hands and knees we clawed away at some dirt and grasses. Sure enough the same large, rectangular, flat stones came into view matching those of yesterday's plaza. I raised my head to speak to Carlos but didn't utter a sound. Looking behind and past him, I spied another smaller pyramid. I finally managed to get the words out and as Carlos looked up e he said there was also one behind me. I snapped my head around and there it was. Both these smaller structures were peaked although they really weren't that small.

By now my head was spinning. I almost could not believe what I was seeing. I wondered if Frank was having as much luck. Remembering some past readings the layout of these structures appeared to be classic in design.

The plaza, large and small pyramids, and miscellaneous structures all on some planned celestial alignment. I made a mental note to check on the alignment and compare it to other known cities.

Carlos continued with his GPS recordings while I went camera crazy. We alternated our information gathering with more attacks on vines and grasses not even stopping ti eat. At around two in the afternoon, energy drained and soaked in sweat, we called it quits. We rested in silence for a while before returning to base camp. The grandeur of the place just seemed to require stillness and respect.

We were first to arrive back to camp and were in the middle of plotting some of our GPS readings when Frank and the others returned. As a greeting Frank started right in, excitedly, about his finds that day. There was obviously no interrupting his enthusiasm until he drained his head of all that he encountered. Carlos and I looked at each other smiling. We were listening to exactly what we ourselves had uncovered. Frank, half out of breath, reached for a cup of water which gave me a chance to tell our story. He was totally elated and speechless by the time I finished.

The next few hours were occupied with our plotting's and

recordings. This was turning out to be the find of the century. From the looks of it, it might even be the largest city found to date.

That evening after dinner, Frank and the others made journal entries, as I busied myself cleaning my camera and equipment, and storing away the exposed film. A quickly made up double lined box worked just fine to keep my precious film out of the excessive heat and harms way. Satisfied with the safety of my livelihood, I retired to my hammock and let my mind wander centuries back.

-15-

Chapter 6

      We awoke the next day to a jungle rain. The thick canopy protected us somewhat from the heaviest of the rain but regardless of this small gift everything was drenched. I patted myself on the back for having the discipline of taking care of my film last night. The tarp's we erected over our work tables were doing their job well. The up side of the rain was that it gave us a day off so to speak. We all enjoyed the break and leisurely worked individually and collectively in updating our records and information. The rain let up early afternoon but by then we were all pretty much in a siesta mood.   Carlos and the other porters, Diego and Mario, took advantage of the rainless afternoon to go in search for supper with fantastic results, returning with fish which they then willingly prepared and cooked. During our relaxing evening repast, Frank out lined the next day's plan. To determine the full extent of our new found city, we were to fan out in all directions to try and set a size for this metropolis.   Once that was accomplished we could then concentrate on some more detailed work. That was like music to my ears. I had always wondered what it would be like to be the first to enter such an ancient dwelling. I went to sleep that night thinking of just that. The jungle orchestrations highlighted my dreams further.

Chapter 7

Yesterday's rain only caused more humidity and discomfort.
A quick breakfast and we were on our way. We had no idea how much territory we would have to cover today but we were anxious to get going. Compass directions were assigned and safety instructions were reviewed. It was hoped we could at least maintain visual contact. Just before eight AM our machete's were in action. I was happy to be in another direction thinking it would give me a greater chance of discovering something new.

The vines and undergrowth severely hindered our line of sight so periodic shouts were employed as a means of staying in touch. It was slow going, but necessarily so in order to be vigilant and not miss anything.

I was swinging away with my machete at an unusually thick clump of vines when suddenly I hit stone about three feet above ground. My arm went numb and my hand stung as I dropped the blade. I muttered a few expletives as I looked around to make sure no one heard me. There I go being silly again as if someone was going to be there. When I got feeling back into my hand and arm again I picked up the big knife noticing a nice sized chunk missing from what was once a sharp edge. I more carefully finished what I had started and to my delight was faced with a stelae. It stood approximately six foot high and twenty inches at it's widest. Of course I could not read it's message, but who ever it was dedicated to must have been very important fore it had Glyph's carved on all four sides. I recorded it with both GPS and film. I knew this was an important find and I'm sure Frank would be overjoyed.

As fascinated as I was with the stelae, I dared not delay any longer. I heard a signal shout and answered even though they were becoming more distant. My trek continued for what seemed like hours. Actually it was hours. By three o'clock it was obvious that all around me was just jungle. There were no signs of the slightest hint of previous occupation. It felt good to be returning to camp. I was hungry, tired and my arm still ached from the argument I lost to the stelae.

So much for what I thought was being thorough. In my trek back to base camp I came across what was possibly a small living area. I don't know how I missed it the first time. I took some quick readings of the location and the usual accompanying photo's. I noticed a few piles, somewhat buried in the undergrowth and vines, of small statuary broken and discarded. Perhaps this living area was for special artisans, but not being the expert I would have to discuss my idea with Frank.

Still deep in thought over my artisan theory, I was startled by Diego calling my name. Since I was long overdue at camp he was sent out to look for me. I indicated the find that was holding me up and he sort of confirmed my idea of artisans being special, and living away from the common man. I spoke of my discoveries as we made our way back to camp and he too appeared as excited as I was. It seems everyone had a run of good luck today and there would be much to discuss and chart tonight. We reached base and shelter just in time fore the rains started again.

Dinner was the quick and easy MRE's again as we had much work to do. The meal hit the spot as far as I was concerned. I found it quite good and filling and there was always plenty of coffee. Between the hard work and exercise along with the unwelcome regulated diet there would no longer be any worry about my growing waistline. I felt I had already lost five pounds in the last few days. Oh well, that's just the way it goes.

Due to all the successes of the day the energy was running high although there was a much relaxed atmosphere in camp tonight. We were all working but not very hard. It was more interesting to continue our conversation from dinner. Mateo was anxious to see the stelae I found because of the Glyph's. Even though I had thoroughly photographed all four sides he said he would shoot some Polaroids to give him time to study the writings. He was also going to attempt some tracings. I thought that was a great idea considering we did not have an artist as part of our expedition as so many in the past have had. It was then I found out I was wrong again. Diego was an accomplished artist and also had taught art and Mayan art history at the University of Mexico. He shared with me some of his sketches that evening. The detail he captured with just pencil and paper could have passed for photographs. I almost felt embarrassed thinking he was just a mere porter here to carry equipment.

A while later I had the opportunity to talk quietly with Frank. I asked him about Mario, the only one left I didn't know anything about yet. Sensing my embarrassment, he smiled and apologized. He was in such a hurry to get started when we first met at the hotel introductions had slipped his mind. As it turned out Mario was a language and calender expert with numerous publications to his credit. I was truly the ignorant one in the group, although thankfully no one treated me as such.

The rain continued and our extremely physical day caught up with us in spite of our enthusiasm. We all agreed to call it a night. As I lay in my somewhat dampish hammock my mind drifted back home. Everything seemed so distant and unimportant. There was only the here and now. I felt a contentment with what I was doing I had not experienced in years.

I awoke the next morning to the extreme humidity the rain left us with. I was fully rested and anxiously awaiting some new discovery. Frank was already at the planning table with his coffee. I filled my mug, grabbed a piece of flat bread and joined him. Staring at the area map for the first time in days it was then I realized how large our new found city was. I let out a low whistle as I looked for a scale measurement. Sensing what I was searching for, Frank volunteered.

"Three kilometers across, so far. I have a feeling we're looking at something even broader in scope."

"Is this what you expected ?" I asked.

"I expected a new find, but not something of this magnitude. I believe we may have to extend our search even further out than we are now." he answered.

"Too bad you didn't have some aerial photography of the area. It might make this a little easier." I returned.

Smiling, Frank wandered over to his pack, retrieved what he was looking for and threw on the table before me a stack of nine inch by nine inch aerial photo contact prints.

"These are really useless, there's just too much jungle to see anything." he muttered. "This is the latest overflight I obtained from the government mapping department." he added.

"I don't suppose you have any stereo glasses." I inquired.

He smiled again and dug in his pack a second time and threw me a small leather case.

"I think you're wasting your time, but have at it." he said still smiling. "Everything is all the same, jungle and more jungle." he continued.

"It's worth a try." I responded. "I was trained in the military in aerial photo interpretation, and quite successfully I might add. I have also been part of quite a few civilian endeavors using this expertise."

Getting more serious than I should have, I started mentioning various nuances of interpretation, such as spectral reflectance, foliage densities and colorations and so on.

"Whoa, slow down Eric, you're way over my head now. I bow to your judgement. Perhaps you can find something." Frank interrupted.

Laughing apologetically I said I would sit at the corner table and ply my trade.

"Who knows." I mumbled, and just left it at that. I suddenly felt pretty good about myself. Perhaps I could contribute something to this endeavor besides my photography.

After clearing the table, I first plotted the structures we already found. Now for the more difficult task of making comparisons and foliage studies. Alignment patterns also showed themselves. An hour and a half later I returned to the plot map Frank was working on with six probable locations. His earlier guess also seemed to be correct. These locations were all beyond the area we had already inspected. Frank looked at the map, then at me with a very doubtful expression.

"Okay my friend, let's go have a look."

Leaving Mateo and Mario at camp, we remaining four took our compass heading from the master map, a GPS fix on the closest site and off we went. Frank was giving me constant good natured jabs about how we needed a walking exercise anyhow. I made him promise that if we were successful I would get another shot of cognac tonight. The deal was agreed upon as we hacked our way through the undergrowth. Every now and then we would come upon areas that were more open then the others as if something hindered tree growth.

Carlos took to his hands and knees and started digging through the grasses. Turning his head up towards Frank with a big grin said.

"Looks like you're going to lose some of your precious cognac tonight."

Frank, with a befuddled expression questioned.

"What do you mean by that ?"

"Well, if I'm not mistaken this is the remains of a roadway, a very old roadway." answered Carlos.

Now all four of us were on hands and knees scratching at the grass. A half hour passed and we stood back and gazed at our labors. We had cleared a stretch about eight feet wide and ten feet long. There was np mistake about it. This was the remains of a classic Mayan roadway, gravel, stones, cut blocks and all. Frank and

I were both beaming right now.

"**But !**" Frank said, "The bet was finding a structure."

I returned his look and countered with.

"**Lead on McDuff.**"

We refreshed ourselves with some fruit and water before continuing.

We hacked away for another forty five minutes and as I checked on my GPS I heard Diego shout.

"**Look ! Look over there.**"

We all turned where he was pointing. About twenty yards ahead, entangled with vines was a small pyramid with a pointed top. Frank, smiling, almost laughing, asked if I wanted my cognac direct from the bottle or served in a glass. We started to clear some vines as I answered with great delight.

"**In** a glass and served on a tray please."

Everyone chuckled including Frank.

We continued to go through the routine recordings, measurements and photo's which kept us there for a while. Realizing there would not be enough daylight left to attempt a second site we returned to base. Our mood was light and jovial with Frank commenting.

"**And** to think for my whole career I've been doing it the hard way."

To make him feel better but still pleased with myself I said that this could have been just dumb luck.

"**Perhaps** my friend, but we still will hold that decision until we check another site tomorrow." Frank answered.

Mario and Mateo had planned a wonderful fish and fruit celebratory dinner, after which I received my cognac on a hastily made tray with much pomp and circumstance.

We made plans and chose a new site for tomorrow's search. Mateo and Mario chose to stay in camp again to continue working on the translation of the stelae Glyph's. It had been a wonderfully relaxed evening but I could feel the tired's coming on so I retired to my hammock I finally felt good about being able to contribute something tangible to the expedition. I then lost myself in the all familiar symphony of the night.

I slept well and was fully refreshed the next morning. I couldn't believe how rested and invigorated I was. Secretly I hoped we would have as much success today as we did the day before although I was confident that we would.

We left camp a little earlier today knowing we had a further distance to cover. Our enthusiasm was high and because of that the jungle trek did not seem as difficult. We reached our destination around one in the afternoon, and yes there were two almost perfect pyramids connected by a causeway between them. They were also walled on three sides. This struck everyone as something different that no one had seen or read about before. Some serious study would have to take place to determine its actual use. We had a quick lunch then routinely did our measurements before starting for base. The main topic of conversation on our return was speculation of this new structure. Of course nothing would be answered without extensive study.

It was almost cark by the time we reached camp and again Mario and Mateo had supper waiting for us. The evening bull session was stimulating. Apparently the home-body's had made some headway on the decipherment of the stelae but felt it a little premature to disclose anything yet.

Diego suddenly remembered something that had been haunting him all day. A drawing he gad seen a long time ago done by Catherwood in the eighteen hundreds. It was of two small structures connected by a causeway and partially walled in. This opf course piqued everyone's interest. Further details would have to wait until our return to civilization and the university's library. It was later than usual when we all turned in for the night. It started to rain again and the soft noise lulled me right into dreamland.

Chapter   8

The rain persisted for almost forty eight hours. We were obviously experiencing a tropical storm from the gulf. The winds, which usually do not affect us, were now a concern. We worked fortifying our camp, securing everything possible. All we could do was wait it out. Our work went on only at a slower pace with a few more siesta's thrown in. We had rigged up a double walled sleeping area which turned out to be quite comfortable and quiet. We enjoyed the forced rest but were really anxious to move on to hopefully new finds. Everyone shared their fields of expertise in such a way that we all benefitted from a new perspective of the whole. Frank even caught on to the use of the aerial photo's.

On the third day we awoke to a literally steaming jungle, the humidity was so thick it was like fog. Nevertheless plans were made for checking out a third site I had determined from the air photo's. I had volunteered along with Carlos to be the camp watchers this time. We both welcomed the empty quiet camp and kept ourselves busy wit what seemed like menial tasks, but were still important to the overall mission.

Late afternoon we started preparing dinner and none too soon either. Our weary searchers wandered into camp excitedly talking about another large pyramid they found. This one was about two hundred yards off from where I had indicated but it still confirmed my location technique. Frank was slowly being convinced that aerial photo's were certainly not the complete answer but had its advantage as an additional tool that could possibly save field time.

Chapter 9

Rain again the next day forcing some more rest time. Although the downtime was welcome, it did put a damper on our averall enthusiasm of new finds. Mario and Mateo continued working tirelessly on the stelae translations. Lately though, they seemed more animated than usual. We all could tell something was up but they chose to remain secretive. When asked, Mario would answer that he wanted more tome to confirm or shoot down his suspicions. We all respected his expertise and thereby left him alone. We knew when the time was right he would let us all in on his findings.

Frank, as planned suspended our jungle treks for a while and was making arrangements for some preliminary excavation. It was just a matter of deciding what and where. Of course we all were allowed our input. Carlos and I both thought a good place to start would be the complex we came across by the archway. It seemed to represent a place of importance. At least it had that feeling about it. By the end of the day the consensus was also aligned with us.

Sometime during the night the rain ceased and we awoke to a much clearer day. The temperature had dropped to a cool ninety six degrees. We took this as a good sign as we prepared for an exciting day. At least exciting for me. I had never participated in a Mayan excavation before. Mario and Mateo chose not to join us on this first preliminary try but did travel wit us for a while. Their plans were to visit the stelae again foe some further confirmation of something or other. Details were still not forthcoming. Our journey seemed easy today and eventually the two Glyph experts parted company taking a heading for the stelae.

Approaching the archway and the complex it protected, we all became silent. It seemed the right thing to do in reverence for the secrets not yet revealed. Frank was wandering around making mental notes and checked some note book now and then. I occupied myself by taking a few more detailed photo's rather than the general area I covered last time.

Frank, in a soft voice, broke the silence.

"This is it. This is where we start our cleanup."

He was standing in front of the large flat topped pyramid. He turned around checking the alignment with the archway. Satisfied, he made some notes in his journal, then indicated we all get busy clearing vines and grasses.

After nearly two hours of backbreaking labor we took a break and stood back to view our progress. WE were stunned by what we had accomplished. This structure was more magnificent than we had hoped for. The front facing the archway was stepped up to the flat top, while halfway up was a smaller flat area, guarded on two sides by intricately carved figures, half animal, half human. Set back in this alter area was a sort of portal, also intricately carved. I concentrated my lens on these figures to capture this wonderful detail. Diego, too was busy sketching away.

Carlos and Frank were discussing interpretations of some Glyph's carved above the portal. After some animated bantering back and forth, Carlos climbed up a few steps and carefully edged his way over until he was above and in the middle of the portal. Ever so slowly he reached his hand down and grabbed a small protruding center stone, almost losing his balance.

"Wait a minute." cautioned Diego. "I'll give you a hand."

Diego also climbed the steps until he was above Carlos. He managed a firm hold on Carlos's waist belt then said.

"Okay, now give it a try."

As if they were a professional mountain climbing team, Carlos, with added confidence again reached for the protrusion. With some applied force the stone turned slightly and pushed inward. He quickly pulled his hand away, so as not to get caught and we all listened to a slow growling rumble as the carved door, slowly inch by inch moved outward allowing a two foot opening behind the door. All movement stopped, including our own. Double checking their footing Diego and Carlos climbed down and joined Frank and I in front of the door. I looked at Carlos and he must have read my questioning eyes before he softly answered.

"I remembered an old story passed down through oral history. Because of my modern university training I never put much stock in it. From now on I'll have more faith in my ancestors."

The smell of stale air emanated from inside the tomb. It

wasn't just stale air. There was another acrid odor mixed in. None of us could identify it. It was like a chemical smell of some kind. Whatever it was it was strong We hesitated entering, then decided to wait a while longer. After ten minutes or so the acrid odor dissipated. We wet our bandana's and tied them around our faces covering nose and mouth. Jesse James and his gang could not have looked any worse.

Since this was Frank's expedition he was first to enter. Each carried a battery lantern with wide angle heads. The light chased the darkness of who knows how many hundreds of years. Not a word was spoken as we entered what appeared to be an anti chamber. The walls were painted with muted color depicting various actions, one of which was a beheading. We assumed fir now, it was an enemy warrior. There were two stone benches flanking another large stone door. Glyph markings edging both sides and top. I know I should have been taking pictures but I was mesmerized by what I was seeing. Photo's would have to wait. Frank indicated with a nod of his head that we should try and enter. All eyes turned to Carlos, who was already studying the portal. A few minutes passed which seemed like hours, then Carlos carefully ran his fingers up and down the outline of both sides of the door. Making a choice he moved to the left side and putting his hands near the seam, gave a slight push. Nothing moved. With an obvious more exerted effort he pushed again, which produced a low sound of stone on stone, but not much movement. His next effort was to put his shoulder against the stone and use his body weight. The large stone indeed started to move but with much resistance. Diego quickly threw his shoulder against the stone and with a great effort by both of them the door slowly opened. It pivoted on a center point and opened like a vertical louver. Again the stale acrid smell rushed out to greet us. Stepping back we turned away from the odorous attack. Once the air stabilized we returned our attention to the doorway with Frank leading the way. This room was considerably larger, which I judged to be about forty foot square. Our attention immediately went to the center of the room. On a rectangular stone pedestal was a mummified body. All time stopped.

We silently stood in awe, our minds working overtime processing what was before us. Diego was the first to move closer. As if it were a signal we all followed. The body was adorned with a cloak of feathers of many colors, although red was predominant. There were many strands of gold and jade around the neck. Bracelets of jade and other polished stones occupied both wrists. His right hand held a scepter of some kind, a design of which I had never seen, not even in books. A large feathered headdress encircled his head, highlighted also with jade. The facial expression was majestic and peaceful with closed eyes. There did not appear to be any sign of age as you see with so many mummified remains. Even the hands did not show aging.

Finally remembering my camera I recorded for posterity this magnificent figure from another age. Still not a word passed among us. I noticed the expressions of both Diego and Carlos had changed to sincere reverence and adoration. This was obviously one of their ancient rulers, and even after all these centuries they felt the need to subjugate themselves to his authority. It was fascinating to watch this transformation take place. Un seen hereditary knowledge took charge over their twenty first century behavior.

The room itself was exquisitely decorated with all the finery befitting a king. The walls were painted with all sort of life's scenes apparently indicating major events in this man's reign. Some were freestyle paintings, some stylized drawings filled with unimaginable color. Carved Glyph panels stood from floor to ceiling, which was about ten feet high. Even the ceiling was painted with the colors of the night, depicting celestial events and planet movement. One could read individual events, yet all blended together as one never ending sky, representing the infinity of the universe they seemed to understand. The pyre on which the body rested was carved on all four sides in stylized Glyph's, which we later learned from Mateo, depicted calender dates.

There were six stone benches scattered about the room, all strewn with finely woven, multi colored fabric. Woven baskets and stone chests occupied one corner, filled with objects of pottery and statuary, large and small figurines of all shapes, some definitely human, others half human, half animal. The animal figures were mostly identifiable while others defied interpretation, at least to us at this moment.

Children's wheeled toys were in a basket by themselves. This seemed incongruous to their lifestyle. The mayan were known for their great roadway system, yet they did not possess draft animals or the wheel except on toy's.

Again this would require extensive study and research. It appeared as if the whole of Mayan history was shown here in one form or another, pre-classic through post classic. We were looking at a span of perhaps fourteen hundred years.

Chapter 10

For the first time in my career I actually ran out of film at a shoot. What we were looking at was beyond expectation. I would have to postpone any further documentation until I retrieved more film from our home base. Up to this point a word still had not been spoken by anybody. Almost two hours had passed before anyone realized the time of day. Frank, after checking his watch, spoke in a soft, almost undetectable voice.

"It's time we left if we want to make it to camp before dark."

We slowly exited the room feeling in "I don't want to leave the party." kind of mood. Carlos and Diego automatically pushed the door closed. It appeared as if Frank was going to say "Don't bother" but I guess thought better of it. After all, this was their history not his.

Conversation was light on our return to base camp. Mostly "Did you see this or did you see that." The magical influence of the tomb still held sway over our thoughts.

Dinner was ready as usual upon our return. Mateo and Mario were acting like children with a big secret to burst out. Up till now we four had not spoken of our find except that we had an interesting day. Halfway through dinner Mario could no longer contain himself.

"We have something very important to tell you." he blurted out.

"I was going to say the same thing." Frank threw back.

The table was all smiles now.

"You go first." Frank and Mario said simultaneously.

Mario did not politely wait any longer and proceeded with his story.

"It's about our translation of the stelae." He hesitated a moment as if thinking of other things. "We weren't trying to be secretive by not saying anything before this, we just were not sure of what we were reading. Now I think we are."

"**A**t least we feel ninety five percent sure." interrupted Mateo. "The Glyph's as far as we can discern, are speaking of some very high ranking personage. Perhaps a king,----a very old king."

Mario picked up from there again.

"**T**he dated Glyph's we are looking at are written using the long count. This is a rare use in classic and post classic times."

"**W**e won't go into detail now." said Mateo. "But this person we are talking about is probably from pre-classic times. Exactly how old we don't know yet, however he is very, very old."

Mateo joined in with.

"**I** have never come across this age before. It may even be the beginning."

Looking around the now quiet table all faces were sober. Frank's eyes were sparkling now as he took over the conversation. Gazing directly at Mateo and Mario he announced.

"**I** think we found your king. It fits, it all fits. We opened a tomb today.   The one we agreed upon the other day. It was a tomb like I've never seen or heard of before. In side is the mummified body of what appears to be a king or very high ranking ruler. There are markings on the pedestal that we could not read. You must come with us tomorrow. Gentlemen, we may be looking at the find of the century."

Everyone started talking now, each remembering something specific that stood out in their minds. We were all excited beyond our dreams. Frank retrieved the cognac bottle once more to toast our success. Carlos suggested we make journal entries individually of what we observed. A combined story could be put together at a later date. Mario and Mateo could do the same after they witnessed the tomb. It started raining lightly, though no one seemed to notice. The excitement and postulating carried on well into the night. I slipped away unnoticed and retired to the luxury of my hammock. I let my mind relax with the patter of the rain and drifted off to space unknown.

Chapter 11

I was up early and alone. I was actually pleased to be alone. I needed the time for my mind to settle and slowly accept and put in order all that had recently transpired. I mindlessly went about making coffee and other morning chores and finally sat down to relax in my portable deck chair enjoying my heavy black liquid and suddenly realized it was still raining. This was a good thing I thought. It would give us all time to settle and collect out thoughts. My own thoughts wandered away from the tomb and into the surrounding jungle. How cruel and hostile this environment could be and at the same time be so beautiful and luxurious. Micro ecological systems surrounded us at all levels, yet co-existence and dependency prevailed to make this one of life's greatest wonders. Right now I did not try to understand any of this, I just accepted and enjoyed where I was and what was around me. The gentle voice of Diego shook me back to reality.

"It is beautiful, isn't it." he said reading my thoughts. "Where ever I have traveled observing the wonders of our modern world, nature itself is still the most beautiful."

He filled his mug with coffee, joined me in a deck chair and we both listened to the noise of the silence.

Slowly the others drifted into states of consciousness and congregated around the coffee pot. The rain was actually welcome which allowed for additional planning. Frank suggested we set up camp at the tomb site to make things easier, which brought up another logistics problem. Our present camp was centrally located for our area of interest as far as the extent of this city was concerned. Setting up by the tomb would mean extra and inconvenient travel for boundary research, though it would allow for more hours of study at the tomb. A compromise plan was finally decided upon in early afternoon. We would split into two camps, leaving the present site as our main base. We would then set up a satellite base at the tomb to maximize our hours of study. Alternating people between sites to maintain a fresh approach was Diego's idea and well accepted by all.

     By the end of the day Frank was riding high anticipating the research we would accomplish considering our small compliment. Mario and Diego set aside the necessary resources to set up out tomb side campsite if the rain ever ceased.

Chapter 12

Two more days of rain had us all itching to be on the move again. It had been decided how a basic rotation was to work between the two camps and I was lucky enough to be included in the first shift at the tomb. This would allow me to finish my initial photos. The rain had given me time to reorganize my equipment and film supply. From here on my shooting would have to be more selective in order to guarantee not running out of film all together. I knew I could manage this although it would prove difficult at times. Once my film and camera had been double checked I again turned to the air photos. I found three more tentative locations that might prove fruitful. Of course they were in three different directions dictating three separate searches. Our city would now cover many miles of never before known area.

After five days we had our first reprieve from the rains as we awoke to a steaming jungle. By mid-day the first shift for the tomb camp departed. Frank, Mateo and myself, fully loaded, happily took to the trail. Carlos was to follow in short order with the balance of our supplies. Tomorrow, Diego and Mario would resume the search for new sites based on the aerial photo information.

We reached the tomb with about an hour and a half of daylight left and chose a spot just inside the archway to set up camp. There were no large trees to hang a hammock from so we had to resort to fold up cots with air mattresses. I was still working the foot pump filling the mattresses when Carlos joined us at the compound. By actual darkness we were pretty much finished with our camp layout and finally settled for some dinner around a small fire. The atmosphere around the fire was more somber than it had been for the last few days. Anticipating tomorrow one could feel the influence of the kingly figure casting his spell over us into the mysteries of the past. I for one could not wait to get back into the tomb to pick up where I left off with my photo documentation.

Supper was quick and we all turned in for the night. As I lay on my cot listening to the jungle I realized the sounds were different. Just as beautiful, but more serene as if they too were under the influence of the principal resident here. Sleep easily overcame me as my mind blended with the surrounding music of the night.

I was startled awake by a human cry only to find out Frank had just tripped over some vines and twisted his ankle. Luckily it was nothing serious as he apologized for waking us all. A quiet day was before us with traces of sunlight dappling through the overhead canopy. It almost felt cooler but I know that was just my imagination. Breakfast was light and none of us could keep our eyes from the tomb entrance knowing what awaited us again. Finally the moment arrived and with lanterns in hand we moved to the entrance to another world. I worked with Carlos to open the door just as he and Diego did days before. The escaping air was not as potent as the first time so we did not use our bandana's though we did have them at the ready. We allowed Mateo to be first to enter, to behold what we had already seen upon our first entrance.

Again silence prevailed out of respect for the surroundings. I was last to enter and was captivated by Mateo's frozen stance in front of the mummified king. So much so that it was the first photo I took. I then turned my attention to the other areas where I had run out of film. The four of us sort of did our own thing for a while with a few soft words mumbled here and there. My wanderings and shooting soon found me back at the pedestal of the king. I had not captured the carvings or Glyph's on the base yet and was about to set up to do just that when something caught my attention. Looking at the body before me, something was not right. I could not quite put my finger on it. I repeatedly scanned the figure from head to toe. Nothing appeared to gel. I finally dismissed it as my imagination again and returned to my camera.

I set up my tripod at a measured distance to the pedestal. This way I could move the camera parallel to my subject shooting at a set distance to attain overlapping exposures that could then be viewed in stereo at a later date. Very much absorbed in what I was doing, out of nowhere an image popped into my head. An image of the scepter by the mummy. I stood gazing again at the stately figure. I stared at the scepter but nothing registered in my mind. After a few minutes I shook my head to clear the cobwebs and returned once more to the camera.

I completed my task of recording in stereo the marking on all four sides of the pyre. I did not realize how much time had elapsed until my stomach reminded me it was being ignored. I broke down my tripod, gathered my equipment and stacked everything by the entranceway, exiting the tomb.

As fascinating as the kings room was it was good to view daylight again and breath some un-stale air. Carlos was already rummaging for lunch so we both settled for some fresh fruit we located just outside the wall. Reseated back at the table Carlos looked a bit preoccupied. We ate silently for a while, then looking directly at me he spoke hesitantly.

"This may sound silly, but there is something about the mummy that just does not sit right. I can't put my finger on it."

Half smiling I answered.

"I'm glad to hear you say that. I thought at first it was just my wild imagination. The same thing has been bugging me all morning. I keep having these thoughts about the scepter and I don't know why."

Quietly shouting excitedly, he jumped up.

"That's it ! The scepter, that's got to be it. Come on." he said as he headed back to the tomb.

I quickly followed nearly knocking Frank and Mateo aside as we rushed through the door.

"What's going on." Frank yelled as we passed.

"Don't know yet." I yelled back. "That's what we're going to find out."

Frank and Mateo retraced their steps joining us at the pedestal. Carlos and I were studying the mummy. Minutes passed without a word when Carlos finally spoke in a somewhat subdued tone.

"You were right ! It is the scepter. The other day it was in the right hand."

"And look here." I interrupted. "The dust in the folds of the cloak has been disturbed."

Frank and Mateo looked at each other and then at Carlos and as if we were crazy.

"Are you trying to tell us that after two thousand years this thing is alive."

Mateo and Carlos snapped their heads towards Frank, a hurt look in their eyes. Catching their meaning of this instantly, Frank recovered with.

"No disrespect meant."

I quickly answered to cover Frank.

"**W**e don't know Frank. I'm not even going to speculate on that. All we're saying is that something is different. We both felt it this morning. The scepter was in his right hand, and now sas you can see for yourself it is in the left. If I had the film developed from the other day it would bear out what I'm saying."

All was quiet once more as the four of us stared intently at the body before us.

Frank quietly mumbled, "I hope this is not some kind of joke you're pulling because right now I don't think it's very funny.

Understanding his confusion I assured him this was not a prank.

The four of us went outside and back to the planning tables and sat silently while munching on some fruit. You could almost hear our four minds working to make sense of this. Frank sounding slightly annoyed questioned.

"**A**re you certain of what you're saying. This makes absolutely no sense at all."

"**H**onest Frank." I answered. "I'm not pulling your leg." I then continued in a more serious tone. "I'm a trained professional Frank. It's part of my job to pay strict attention to details. Little things out of place could either make or break a photograph." I paused for a moment, then added, "I'm quite confident and positive, Frank, that the scepter was in the right hand the other day. Carlos even bears me out on this."

Frank's tension eased a bit and his body relaxed somewhat. He turned and looking directly at me, said;

"**I**'m sorry Eric. I'm not doubting what you are saying, it's just that this whole thing comes as quite a shock. I've never had an experience like this before."

"**I** think this is quite a shock for all of us. You're not alone in this." I returned.

Mateo, who had been staring at the tomb entrance, slowly and quietly inquired.

"**D**id any body leave their lantern on in the tomb ?"

Everyone automatically checked for their own lantern. We each had ours with us. Turning our attention to the opening in the pyramid, a faint flickering light and shadow could be seen.

"Is it just me or do I see moving shadows ?" Mateo asked.

He was right. You could see slight shadow movements. We kept looking at each other and then back at the entranceway, each trying to figure this out in his own way.

"Perhaps Mario and Diego decided to join us." suggested Frank.

"I don't think so." Carlos replied. "They were heading in the exact opposite direction this morning."

Well there's only one way to find out." Mateo said already on his feet walking towards the Pyramid. The rest of us followed single file. I was the last in line preparing my camera as we went. The closer we came the mare distinctive the shadow patterns became. This was not the light of an electric lantern. It was obviously the flickering light produced by some sort of torch.

Mateo, upon reaching the door did not hesitate, but continued right inside. We three followed after him. It wasn't until we were all completely in that we stopped, eyes wide in disbelief. An empty pedestal before us and standing just beyond that, his back to us was the king. Apparently hearing us enter he slowly turned and seeing us quietly uttered some unintelligible word. Carlos and Mateo immediately dropped to their knees bending forward at the waist, faces to the ground and arms outstretched. Frank and I looked at each other in a quandary. The stately figure before us again grunted the same word staring at us. Mateo quietly mumbled,

"I would strongly suggest you both bow to keep him calm until we can make some intelligible contact."

We did as requested although this was not really my thing. You know what I mean- - - - *bowing to another person..* But considering the place and present situation, I went along with it for safety's sake. The ruler, king, or whatever he was grunted again and Mateo and Carlos stood up. Frank and I followed suit.

Without making any deliberate moves I slowly aimed my camera in the direction of the speaker and pushed the shutter button hoping the focus would be okay. Not wanting to push my luck I refocused my attention to the king. He was an impressive figure I judged to be about six feet tall. His chiseled features just added to his regal appearance. The most distinctive feature I found was his complexion. It was not bronzed color that we know of today. It seemed to be more Caucasian white. Whether or not that was because of the mummification process I could not ascertain as of yet. He just did not fit the mold of Maya.

Carlos took th lead in trying to communicate with him with limited success. Luckily for us our king was a very patient man. It was almost as if he knew the time difference between our two worlds. In my opinion he showed his wisdom in that patience. After a few minutes of bantering back and forth with Carlos and Mateo and their limited language skills, the king held up his hand as a command to cease talking. Frank and I instantly prepared for the worse, but much to our surprise he smiled slightly and walked to a bench and sat down. Using his scepter to point he indicated that Mario and Carlos should sit on the floor before him. When they were seated he looked directly at Frank and I, and again with his scepter waved us towards a bench on the opposite wall. It was obvious we were not of the same heritage. Satisfied that we were all settled, and ignoring Frank and I, he resumed the conversation with Carlos with much difficulty. This word exchange went on for one half hour with a mutual recognition every now and then. I was totally lost by then. They could have been speaking Martian for all I knew. I did, however, manage to get a few more shots with my camera. This time I was sure of the focus.

With the kings assent Mateo stood and walked over to Frank and I. He looked both anxious and frustrated. Speaking just above a whisper he asked that we go to get Mario. The king agreed to wait for the next sun to grant us an audience again.

Carlos had made some headway but Mario was the language expert.

We stood slowly, not wanting to startle the king and headed for the entrance. It was only mid-afternoon, which meant ample daylight to get back to the main camp. Frank was not to eager to leave. He was completely taken in by the unbelievable scene that was unfolding before our eyes. Although I was feeling pretty much the same I agreed to make the trip alone. I realized it was risky to go alone but the trail was well marked and I felt confident I could make it safely. I passed through the archway and broke into a slow trot knowing Frank had already returned to the tomb.

Chapter 13

I surprised myself by running most of the way. I didn't think I had it in me any more. It's amazing what exercise and a healthy diet can do to a man who had become too used to the luxuries of urban suburban life.

I approached the campsite at the same time as Diego and Mario who were more than surprised to see me. Relaxing with some fresh water I told my story of our encounter with the mummified king. Naturally neither wanted to believe it but both were drawn in by its incredulous nature. Mario was all for leaving right then but it was already twilight and better judgement ruled for an early morning start.

We three had dinner while I continued to answer questions. Supplies and light packs were readied before we turned in for the night. The feel of the hammock was good for my weary bones as I was lulled to sleep by familiar sounds.

We were on the trail just as the first light dripped through the trees. We made good time on the now well worn path. Mateo had only asked for Mario but Diego was not to be denied. If what I told was true, it was a first and he wanted to be included. I didn't blame him, I certainly didn't want to miss last night although we were obviously summarily dismissed by the king. Oh well, I guess it was more important for Frank and the other scientists to be there.

It was just after ten AM when we walked through the archway. We were in luck. Frank and the others had not reentered the tomb yet. There were smiles all around and of course more questions and few answers. Carlos immediately huddled with Mario discussing the language constraints. Mario, as if expecting this kind of encounter, reached into his pack and retrieved a small note book. He thumbed through the pages excitedly, stopping about half way, ran his finger down the page and then grunted some sounds. Carlos, eyes aglow, jumped up almost shouting.

"That's it ! That's it ! That's what he was saying."

Mario tugged at his arm to get him back in his seat and to quiet him.

"This is definitely early Yucatecan. Probably from between one thousand and two thousand BC It most likely has not been spoken for some two thousand years on a regular basis. Frank, his attention caught by Carlos's outburst, questioned.

"Can you converse with him ?"

"I can try." was Mario's answer. "I have been doing a lot of research lately on old original stems of the language. If this king is authentic as you seem to believe, then I think we can communicate. Enough at least to get his and give our stories.

"Great !" responded Frank enthusiastically. "Now we just have to wait for his excellency's invitation to go back in there."

"I'm glad you're waiting." Commented Mario. "Long ago, as best I can figure out, there was a great deal of protocol and formality involving the "CHOSEN ONES". With this particular situation we sure as hell don't want to upset or piss off the Chosen One. I think the first thing I would like to try is to establish his name and tie it to a calendar date. That way, perhaps, we can fill in some blanks in our history."

Mario mentioning "Our History", showed his great pride in his heritage.

You could tell the waiting was beginning to get to everyone. Nervous chatter was interrupting the quiet of the jungle. Diego had begun the makings of coffee when we heard an authoritative command echo from the tomb. Mario understanding the command said.

"That's our call." then looking at me added, "By the way Eric, bring your camera with you but don't attempt any shots until I can establish an explanation of that little black box."

I appreciated his warning. The last thing I wanted to do was to screw up this never before and probably never again opportunity.

We filed into the great room of the pyramid. Our four Mayan friends immediately bowed, and with the king's eyes on us, Frank and I soon followed suit. Mario was the first to stand and uttered a few words. As I said earlier, it could have been Martian he was speaking for all

I know, but what ever it was it registered with our host. A hint of a smile could be detected as he studied Mario and slowly answered.

With definite waves of his scepter he motioned Mario forward and the rest of us were relegated to the stone benches along the back wall. We sat silently and listened to the conversation that was beyond our comprehension. The slow exchange of words went on for almost an hour and then an abrupt lull. Mario turned and signaled for me to come forward much to the dismay of Frank. He actually looked hurt.

I approached cautiously not knowing what to expect. Mario whispered for me to bow as I neared the king, which I did, which obviously pleased the king. His eyes dropped to my camera as he pointed to it with his free hand while mumbling something quietly to Mario.

I snapped my head around to Mario in disbelief as to what he just asked. Yes, I did have a back up camera but to turn over an expensive piece of equipment to a two thousand year old mummy who had no idea what it was, was out of the question. Why that was like committing heresy. That was like asking me to cut off my finger and give it to a head hunter as an appetizer.

Mario, staring at me with serious eyes, said.

"Don't let him think you mistrust him. Just give him the camera. Please !" I did as much explaining as I could. Trust me, he will not hurt it."

He repeated the "Please" again.

I hesitantly slipped the strap off my shoulder and begrudgingly extended my arm towards the king. He reached out his hand, smiled and made a sound, I guess of approval, and accepted the black box from me. He then proceeded to put down his scepter and looked at the camera from all sides. I was surprised at how gently he handled it. I almost felt guilty about the way I was acting a few minutes ago. He looked at me, made a motion, grunted a few words and handed it back to me.

"He wants you to show him." Mario said quietly.

I looked at Mario, surprised again. I carefully took the camera, removed the lens cap, put the viewer to my eye and focused on the crew sitting behind us. I then offered it to the king, indicating that he also look through it. He accepted it back and drew it to his eye, but only for a few seconds. Suddenly he pulled his head back and looked with his naked eyes at Frank and the others. Returning to the viewer again he looked longer this time, a slight smile crossed his lips. He removed his eye from the camera, pointed to the four in the back and made a motion with his thumb and forefinger indicating a small size. I smiled and shook my head in the affirmative. The king now proceeded to look at everything in the room through the viewer constantly. He viewed his scepter up close, pulled his eye away with a confused expression and shook his head. I realized it was out of focus and offered my hand for the return of the camera. Putting the viewer to my eye I turned the lens barrel to refocus on the scepter and returned the black box to the king. He gazed at his scepter again and then back at me smiling. He then proceeded to go around the whole room viewing and focusing.

He came back to me after a few minutes, mumbled a few words again and opened a small chest at the foo of the pedestal. Reaching in he retrieved three emeralds, each about the size of a silver dollar across and handed them to me. I took them hesitantly and looked to Mario for an explanation.

"He is giving you a gift in trade for your camera." he replied.

"But my film, the shots that I already took. He can't take my camera." I pleaded.

"I'm afraid you can't refuse him." said Mario. "Let him have it for now. Perhaps we can work something out later. Besides, from the look of the size of those emeralds you can buy ten camera's just like it and then some."

"I know." I returned, "But that's my pride and joy, I don't want to give it up."

"I'm afraid you don't have a choice right now. I think you have just secured his full cooperation for us." Mario replied.

From the back of the room, Frank added,

"Let it go. You can use your spare camera for now. If this gives us an in with the king it will be worth one hundred cameras."

I knew he was right but I still felt like I just lost my best friend. Oh well, the advancement of science comes first I guess.

The king was acting like a kid with his new toy. So much so that Mario was having a hard time getting his attention again. It took a while but he did manage to settle him down and they spoke for about another hour. This session also allowed Frank to join in with questions. The king finally picked up his scepter and waved it indicating the end of our visit. We were again dismissed. As we filed out of the tomb the king

touched my arm and nodded as if to say thanks, but we were definitely
dismissed.

Chapter   14

Once back outside at our hastily made campsite, Diego finished making the coffee he started hours before. Mario now became the center of attention. We all sat comfortably in a circle recording in our journals our own version of what had transpired that day. Mario commented that he felt at ease with the king and that further conversations should prove fruitful. He did not yet learn the name or time period of the king, only that it was very early Mayan. He also felt that tomorrow would tell the how and why of him still being alive.

The balance of today's in depth discussion was mostly about the king's people, their benefits and their future. How they once ruled the existing world and how they would again some day. This caught everyone off guard. No where in the history books does it say anything about Mayan rule of the world.

Mario went on to explain that the way the king used the word rule did not mean as a regency or government, more like an influence on culture and knowledge. He spoke of his people as advanced in what we would call the sciences. According to the king, people in other lands grew up in ignorance. It was the beneficent influence of the Maya that brought them out of the darkness.

Wow ! I thought to myself. Talk about egocentric. He spoke as if the world revolved around the Maya and their predecessors. Then again, who was I to criticize. All the history I was taught growing up was from standardized texts. It wasn't until I was an adult that I realized a lot of what I learned as a child was not necessarily true. It was history as some self chosen people wanted it to be. Especially early history where we did not have the instant communication systems we have today. So much for getting lost in my own thoughts. Mario was still talking and I was missing some important information.

Frank wanted to know when he could actually meet the

king, as we referred to him. Mario thought that would also be tomorrow, for the king also asked about Frank and I. I assumed that was because of our skin color and facial features. This pleased Frank and he now sported a large smile. I really feel Frank thought he was being left out considering this whole expedition was his idea.

The conversation then turned to questions and suppositions whose answers we would not know till our next audience with our strange new friend. I removed myself from the group, again lost in my own thoughts. I found my pack and dug out my backup camera, loaded it and proceeded to check it out by snapping a few shots of the crew still talking.

Still involved with my own thoughts I almost failed to notice our old friend Mr. Rain stopped by for a visit. Safely covering my camera I joined the others in quickly setting up some tarp canopies. It's amazing how fast things go once you get used to doing them. In short order all was comfortably sheltered and each of us relaxed in his own way. Mine was to let my mind drift to the sound of the jungle rain as I stretched out on my cot.

Chapter 15

I awoke to the smell of warming MRE's. It was still raining and darkness had settled in but I felt unusually content and at ease. I had slept a dreamless sleep for over two hours and was totally refreshed. I joined the others for supper and accepted the light chiding I received for such a long nap. It was a much relaxed atmosphere tonight even though we all looked forward to tomorrow. Diego was occupied with some pencil and charcoal drawings while Mateo continued on Glyph translations. Carlos and Mario studied more of the old language in order to formulate questions in a more understandable way. That left Frank and I to work on the map plots. Diego and Mario did find another small pyramid the day before, which meant I was batting a thousand so far with my air photo interpretations.

Frank could not be happier. If we could tie all these finds together some how it would mean this truly was the largest community ever discovered. This we knew would take many years to excavate and record the discoveries found.

Now that Frank had contributed questions to the king he no longer seemed upset and we speculated some more on what else we could learn from him. I think what intrigued me the most was not who he was or where he came from but how it was after two thousand plus years he came back to life. Frank sort of agreed with me but was still more interested in the past history of the Maya and what led to their advanced knowledge. We kept our fingers crossed and hoped we would get both answered in further sessions with the king.

The hour was growing late and one by one the team turned to their sleeping areas. Even Frank said his goodnights. I remained alone by the fire light still feeling refreshed from my afternoon nap.

Gazing over at the entranceway to the tomb I noticed a flickering light and moving shadows. I sat there mesmerized, my thoughts going wild. Curiosity overcame my better judgement. I knew I shouldn't go over to the tomb but I felt this strange magnetism I could no longer resist.

Leaving my lantern on the table I cautiously made my way through the dark toward the pyramid. Even the jungle was suddenly silent, warning me to stay away, but still I could not comply. Reaching the outer door I inched my way in as quietly as I could. The torch was flickering but I no longer could detect moving shadows. I hesitated, knowing I should not be doing this. My actions could anger the king and blow the whole mission. Frank would also undoubtably be upset no end. Should I listen top myself. Hell no and I moved forward, once more being drawn by the a power my conscience could no longer fight, or did not want to, which was probably more the case.

I paused at the inner portal, my whole body shaking, not knowing what to expect. I could feel beads of sweat forming on my brow as I moved my head to the edge of the entrance. The pedestal was empty and I could not see or hear the king. Forcing myself further through the doorway I could see the flickering light of another torch which drew my attention to a section of wall that was opened. I hesitated again. Hearing nothing, I moved towards this new door ever so slowly. Finally able to see in to the anti chamber, the king was seated, his back to me, reading a scroll like document. The room was full of these scrolls. It was a library, I thought. Who knows what history it contained. I froze as the king reached for another document. He settled again, his back still to me. Somehow I felt he knew of my presence but showed no physical signs of this. I retraced my steps to the exit, my heart pounding like a base drum.

Once again outside, I carefully made my way to my cot. I lay there shaking with excitement, not only from my discovery but from the adrenalin rush to get to the discovery.

Now I thought, do I admit my infraction to the others or do I retain my secret for a while. Rationalizing my thoughts I chose to keep quiet about my night time prowl until such time I found it necessary to expose myself. My breathing returned to normal and I drifted off to sleep once more to my jungle music.

Chapter 16

A late and leisurely breakfast served us all well. A restful night and we were all ready to go. In between light conversation my thoughts kept going back to last night's intrigue.

"I wonder if we'll get to see that library ? I wonder if we'll get any answers at all ? Why was I having sudden doubts about this whole thing ? Was this some kind of practical joke ? Whoa boy, slow down. Why are you letting yourself go on like this. Get a hold of yourself."

I suddenly realized some one was calling my name. Mario repeated his call.

"Where are you Eric ? You seem to be somewhere in outer space. Come back and join the living, my friend."

"Oh - uh Mario. I was just thinking - -uh - -uh, thinking about my camera." I answered.

"I know it meant a lot to you, but giving it to the king meant even more to this project." Mario remarked.

"I know that now. Let's hope it really pays off in that we can learn some unknown secrets of the Maya." I replied thinking of last nights wayward adventure.

"That's what we are all hoping," he answered.

Apparently no one heard anything last night so I was able to relax somewhat.

We all went about our individual work with nervous energy waiting for the kings call which for some reason didn't come until very late morning. As before we filed silently into the anti chamber awaiting the kings direction. He indicated with his hand for us to look around.

I moved to the wall where I saw the door last night trying not to look obvious. Searching closely as I dared I could not detect the slightest hint of the opening. Suddenly feeling self conscious as if I was being watched, I turned toward the king and found him staring at me. He smiled, almost imperceptibly and nodded his head.

*"**D**id he suspect anything."* I wondered. *"I think he most likely knew of my presence last night yet indicated nothing. For some reason I felt more relaxed now."*

Raising his scepter the king summoned me. Now all eyes were on me. As I drew near his smile broadened and he pointed to the camera that hung from my neck. He continued smiling as he reached down to the bench beside him and picking up the camera I had given him yesterday acknowledging that they were similar. He called Mario over to us and spoke to him. Mario relayed the kings message.

"**G**ive him the camera."

I was shocked again which I'm sure showed on my face. I started to protest but was interrupted as the king spoke again.

"**N**ot to worry Eric, he said he just wants to look at it." said Mario

Quite relieved, I took the strap from around my neck and offered the camera to the king. This was a different make and possed a different viewing system. I flipped open the top to reveal the square glass viewer and removed the lens cover.

The king seemed to know what to do after that and just like yesterday proceeded to look around the whole room with both the camera and the naked eye. After some five minutes or so he gently returned it to me smiling and nodding his head in thanks. While I was closing it up and returning the strap around my neck the king was saying something to Mario that made him look confused and surprised. The king faced the others signaling them to be seated as Mario whispered to me.

"**I**'ll talk to you later. The king just said something that really puzzled me."

I nodded in agreement, and took a seat with the others and returned my attention to our host who was looking at the wall where I saw the door last night. He then looked at me and tipped his head slightly. *"He definitely knows."* I thought feeling guilty again. *"I guess I'll have to wait this one out."*

The king, as if holding court, opened up the question and answer period by indicating that Mateo should start. He approached the king, bowed and then produced some Glyph tracings and through Mario asked some questions as to their meaning. Receiving answers that obviously pleased him he returned to his seat all smiles and happy.

Carlos was summoned next and he too returned to his seat quite satisfied after his session. Diego's interview was much shorter but he did receive permission to sketch a portrait of the king which he began immediately.

Mario and the king then spoke at length leaving Frank and I anxiously waiting. You could sense Frank's irritation which he was unsuccessfully trying to hide.

A little over an hour later Mario announced to us all that the king felt we should take a break and take some sustenance. He then bid Mario to fetch a basket of fruit from under the bench and pass it around. When all were served, indications were made that we should eat. Where he got the fruit from was a complete mystery, but then there was a lot of mystery surrounding this man.

Our rest period was over an hour which did nothing to sooth Frank's nerves. There was not much conversation during lunch which seemed to be the kings wishes. More than once the king made direct eye contact with me but for some reason it did not make me uncomfortable. In fact it was just the opposite. I could feel a growing connection to this man. What the common thread was I did not know but it was almost like a kindred spirit meld.

A wave of the scepter let us know the rest period was over. When the king settled on his bench his raised scepter finally pointed at Frank. In trying to play it cool he almost tripped over himself in getting to the king. Mario was already in place and so the questions began. Frank was taken completely by surprise for it was the king who was asking the questions. They were talking quietly so we really could not get the gist of the whole conversation. We did, however, catch the king's question of where did Frank come from. Was it across the sea to the east. Taken aback by this, Mario tried to explain North America. He was waved silent and told the king knew all about the land to the north because he had been there before, but the people there were primitive and lacking culture. The king further questioned Frank's ancestry. AS it turned out he traced his heritage back to England. Late comers to the world of culture according to our Mayan celebrity. The king then went on to say he knew about the light skinned people from over the sea to the east. He further stated they were late learners of the arts and culture. He was referring to the sciences when he used the word culture.

Frank was becoming irritated, not a good characteristic for a professional man. The king sensed this and allowed him to ask a question.

His first question was not a good one I thought. It was too challenging, however I was not the one asking.

"What do you mean when you say these people were late learners ?" Frank asked.

Even our four Mayan friends stiffened at the question.

The king settled back considering the inquiry as if it had been asked by a child. He was trying to find the right words to answer the child. Showing his wisdom and patience the king slowly smiled and spoke in a quiet and reserved tone.

"Let me give you an example. There are a few pyramids on the south continent over the eastern sea. We, indicating himself as all the Maya, taught them how to build them. Ours, waving his arm to show the surroundings, were here before they were children."

He continued to smile and stare directly at Frank, who suddenly seemed humbled. He knew he had been bested and realized his attitude had been too pushy. Instantly back peddling he assumed a proper demeanor for a professional scientist. The king in turn picked up on this and adjusted himself to reflect his acceptance of Frank as a scientist.

"I know you have a lot on your mind." remarked the king, "I hope we can come to a mutual understanding on some answers."

"I wish that also." answered Frank. "You seem to be aware of the world as we know it but where did you yourself come from ?" he continued.

"I thought you would get around to that." the king smiled. "My world was once the center for all culture. Knowledge of the stars and planets we inherited from those who went before us. We learned to meld with the creatures who did not speak. We learned to work with the growing earth and seas, not control it. It cannot be controlled, they will always return to their original form. Universal powers beyond our limitations and comprehension have set things in motion that must play out on its own accord. There were those from my world that sought to control and thus brought on their own destruction. Eruptions from within the planet caused the seas to engulf the land and swallow it forever. I and others alone were allowed to escape so we could teach the ways of culture and live with the land."

We were all hypnotized by his words like children hearing

their first fairy tale. I have to give Mario credit for his translation efforts of the king's words I don't imagine it was easy deciphering phrases that were thousands of years old.

I guessed he was talking about a legend and myth that has survived for eons but no one really believed. Anticipating our thoughts the king said the magic word.

"My world was called Atlan. After its upheaval we few came here and so started our new world. Over the centuries we traveled the planet enlightening peoples as we went. However, here is truly my home where the land provides all needs that matter."

Standing, scepter in hand, he announced,

"I must rest now, the air grows thin and I must rejuvenate."

We all knew dismissal was at hand and even Frank accepted this although a thousand more questions were begging to be asked.

As we were leaving our king spoke softly to Mario. The words could not be heard but I did see Mario glance at me and nod affirmatively to the speaker.

We left in an orderly procession quietly contemplating what we had just witnessed. No one spoke as we assembled around our all but dead fire. Carlos poked the embers and added kindling. Diego took advantage of the new flames to reheat our now cold coffee.

Before I sat down Mario drew me aside and whispered that the king wished to see me later tonight, alone. I attempted an explanation to Mario but he just smiled and said he didn't want to know. I then changed thoughts and asked Mario what he meant when he said earlier that he would tell me later.

"Oh that." He answered, now using a regular speaking tone. "The king said something to me referring to the cameras. He was describing to me that long ago he saw an image projection through a hole in a wall in a reduced size, only it was upside down."

I was both shocked and elated on hearing this. Mario looked at me curiously.

"What did he mean by that ?" he inquired.

"This is unbelievable if it's true. What he was describing was probably the first discovery of light characteristics that would later become lenses and then cameras. He may have been present at the first demonstration but that took place thousands of years ago."

Mario interrupted with, "He did say it was on the southern land mass across the sea to the east."

"I can go into detail later if you want." I answered. "But right now this is definitely journal information."

Joining the group near the fire they were already occupied with that very task as had been our habit. Mario and I started our own entries.

Paper work temporarily done with we moved to our debriefing phase while eating our standard MRE's. Apparently Mateo's preliminary decipherment of the stelae's Glyph's were correct as confirmed by the king. They referenced an extremely early date, what Mateo called the pre-pre classic period. It was definitely using the long count and was most likely highlighting the beginning. Naturally it was decided a greater and more detailed study of the stelae would be done to try and fix the age of the carving and thus date the stone. Here is where my stereo pictures would be of value.

Carlos admitted the king shed a great deal of light on previously unknown history. He said we Maya have even more to be proud of than before. Carlos hoped to be able to gather more history if he could speak with the king again. It seems that's what everyone wants, more time with the king.

Diego acknowledged his interview was brief but received what he wanted most, permission to do a portrait of the king. He passed around hie preliminary sketches. They were extremely life like and captured everything that was the king. I only hoped my photos would be that good.

Mario took his turn at debriefing. His discussion with the king was naturally centered on language and the history tied to it. He admitted that he himself would now have to do further study. The growth of the Mayan language encompassed many stems from middle eastern and far eastern nations. They were mixed and bastardized over the millennia into something unrecognizable even by the original language the stems were derived from. The king was most cooperative and helpful though and taught him many things regarding language decipherment.

Apparently finished with what he had to say the king turned his eyes to Frank. We all followed his glance. Frank appeared to be deep in thought still digesting the kings words. Finally realizing we were waiting for him, he spoke humbly.

"There's no need for me to say much right now. You all witnessed my exchange with the king and I really don't have anything to add. I gather by listening to this session that you all garnered some valuable historical information. Let's just hope the king will continue to enlighten us before we awaken from this dream come true. I guess we can go back to our journals. WE must record as much and as accurately as we can."

Just then a call emanated from the pyramid. It rang out a second time clearly understood by Mario who instantly took off running for the entranceway. The rest of us remained by the fire, curious.

Not even ten minutes passed when Mario returned. Looking directly at me but announcing aloud.

"The king wants you Eric, in about an hour. He also wants me along to translate. Oh, and bring the camera."

"I guess it's your turn Eric." Frank said not looking too upset, then went back to his journal.

Mario was not the only one intrigued by the night time visit. I do believe he suspected something between the king and myself, but also respected my personal space. I decided I would explain what I knew to Mario when I got the chance later.

It was now eight o'clock and almost dark as Mario and I walked to the great room and the king. He was waiting at his usual bench, scepter and all. Mario and I bowed in respect which visibly pleased the king. He briefly spoke with Mario, who in turn faced me;

"He wants you to explain how the camera works. He is very astute and quick to understand. I have been dismissed but I will return with pencil and paper for you to illustrate with."

"What do you mean you've been dismissed. How do I talk with the king without you ?" I questioned.

"He said the two of you could manage. These are his wishes. I'm afraid it's out of my hands." answered Mario. "I'll see you in a few minutes." and off he went.

There I stood, not knowing what to do next while in the back of my mind I also felt for some reason that the king and I could manage without a translator.

The king waved his hand, motioning me to sit down on the same bench as he. I was a bit surprised by this but did as requested. He reached down under the bench and brought up the camera I so reluctantly gave him. He made a gesture toward the one I had around my neck indicating I should open it to show. I lay the case aside and removed the lens cap just as Mario returned. He bowed to the king, handed me the pad and pencil and retreated without a word.

I heard the king let out a small sigh, relieved that we were now alone. He held the camera to his eye, made a motion with his finger as if clicking the shutter, smiled and pointed to the pad and pencil. It was obvious to me that Mario must have been doing some preliminary instructing.

I hesitated, well not really hesitated, I paused collecting my thoughts. I never before taught someone who did not understand English. Finally deciding on a starting point I held the camera in one hand and with the other pointed first to my eye and then to the camera lens. Drawing a lens representation on the pad, I then pointed to the opposite wall and made a line on the pad away from the lens figure. I drew another line, smaller and closer behind the lens. The king was watching intently. My next step was to connect the two lines through the center of the lens, top of one to bottom of the other and visa - versa. The king was then all smiles, as he pointed to the opposite wall then turned his head as upside down as he could. He straightened up and looked at me questioningly. He pointed to the wall again, then touched the back of my camera. I smiled, almost in disbelief, and nodded affirmatively. Mario was right, the king understood completely and instantly. I wish my other students over the years caught on as quickly.

What to do next stumped me and I could see the king anxiously waiting. Then it dawned on me. My wallet, I had pictures in my wallet. I dug it out and removed three different ones to show as samples. A portrait of an old girlfriend, A vase from Mesa Verde and a landscape scene on the back of some ones business card. One by one I went through the motion of pointing to an object, clicking my camera, then holding the picture at the back of the camera. Again the king smiled broadly pointing to the wall, the lens and the photo. This was almost too easy I thought but we were getting along fine.

Questions and answers were becoming complex but overall it was still easy teaching. He understood before I was halfway through the answers. An hour had whizzed by unnoticed. The king hand signaled to put the camera down and follow him. He moved to an earthen chest by the pedestal and retrieved some fresh fruit.

"How does he do that and where does it come from." I wondered.

We ate silently both feeling at ease.

~ ~ ~ ~

Now refreshed, he bid me to follow him as he moved to the wall that opened. Indicating that I should close my eyes, which I did, I then heard stone moving on stone. I light tap on my shoulder told me I could open my eyes. There before me was the library. There had to be thousands of scrolls on the shelves os stone and sticks of a type of wood could not identify. I turned to the king who was smiling knowingly.

"He knows." I thought. *"Of course he knows stupid, but for some reason trusted me not to have told the others."*

I nodded to him letting him know I understood. He also nodded slightly in return. It was amazing how well we understood each other with a span of some two or three thousand years between us.

The king chose two scrolls from different places and returned to the big room. He stretched them out side by side on the bench. Employing hand signals again, he made it clear one was very old and the other from when he lay down on the pedestal. Now it was my turn to interrupt him, which I did not feel uncomfortable doing. I raised my hand to halt him, and he nodded approval. I returned to pencil and pad again and between that and hand motions I managed to get my questions across, which was basically;

"How was he still alive all these years on the pedestal sealed in."

It took a while but he did comprehend what I was asking. He smiled again touching my shoulder as if patting it. Taking my pad and pencil he drew two suns and then quite distinctly said "Mario". Then making three lines he pointed to the first, then to himself, the second he pointed to me, finally the third and said again Mario. Nothing could be clearer; in two days the three of us would meet and my question would be answered. I shook my head yes.

The king, very unceremoniously, put his arm around my back and gently guided me back to the library. He bid me wait there as he returned to the great room. Twenty seconds later he reappeared with my camera. He said a few words, which of course I did not understand, but simultaneously employed hand signals. Opening a scroll flat on a stone, he aimed my camera at it, made the motion of clicking the shutter then with one of the photographs I had showed him went through the act of removing it from the back of the camera. Holding the photo in an out stretched arm

-56-

to no one, said "Mario".

Not knowing whether to laugh or cry I looked at him, shock I'm sure showing on my face.

"Was he saying what I think he was saying." I wondered aloud.

The king was looking right into my eyes showing a quiet smile and as if anticipating my thoughts said in clear English, "Yes."

I repeated his motions with my camera and photograph including the act of handing it to Mario, and in answer the king again said yes.

My mind started spinning a million miles a minute. What a find ! What a discovery ! To be able to copy all these scrolls for later study. How much time would it take ? I don't have that much film with me. Which do I copy first ? How do I get more film here ? How long will it take not only to get the film but to actually shoot each and every scroll ? Can I start now ? Can I come back at another time ? Will they still be here? Will the king still be here ? Do I stay here ?

The questions in my head were coming so fast I could not even fix on one when it was forgotten and replaced by another.

I felt the king's hand on my arm as he led me to a bench and made me sit. By his own example he had me breath deeply to relax. He sat down next to me, the low smile still fixed on his face. It took a few minutes, but I did calm down somewhat, even though the excitement was overwhelming. Lost in my thoughts again I was not aware my new friend left the bench and closed the wall to the scroll chamber until he returned and was standing before me. Handing me my camera and papers he looked to the passageway out. Our session was over. He placed his hand on my shoulder and proudly said yes again as we walked to the door. A few feet from the opening he stopped as I continued towards the outside.

The night was pitch. Thank goodness for the glow of the fire embers to lead me back to my cot. The others were asleep. Checking my watch as I fell to my bed, it was three forty in the morning. I started to review what had just happened but everything went black from exhaustion.

Chapter 17

The heat was intense as the flames engulfed the pyramid. So much so that the stones themselves were melting. I ran to the telephone booth only to find it occupied by some woman gossiping with a friend.

"Please get off the phone." I yelled, "this is an emergency."

The woman ignored me and turned her back to me. I banged on the glass of the door to no avail. Then I heard a voice behind me.

"Nothing doing pal, you're not jumping ahead of me, I'm next for the phone."

"But this is a real emergency. Can't you see the whole jungle and pyramid are in flames." I pleaded.

"So, what's that got to do with me." Was the answer I got.

"No ! No 1" I screamed. "This can't be happening to me." I ran over to the bird bath, tried to scoop up some water when I felt a hand on my shoulder and my name being called.

"Eric, Eric." Diego's voice said softly. "It's okay man, you must have been having one hell of a nightmare."

I looked into his eyes and could feel my body shudder as it slowly came back to life. I sat up feeling a little woozy.

"Take it slow man." Diego said, "I'll get you some coffee."

"What was that all about." he inquired when he returned with the coffee.

"I'm not sure I even know myself." I lied, a little embarrassed. "I don't remember much at all."

"Probably from staying out carousing all night. I understand the night life around here is pretty hot." Diego chided.

"Where is everybody." I asked looking around.

"Frank and Mario were summoned to the king, and Carlos and Mateo went fishing for supper." Diego said. "Frank and Mario have been gone since eight o' clock."

I looked at my watch. I couldn't believe it said almost ten thirty. I guess all that excitement of yesterday plain wore me out. I walked around a bit looking for something to eat when I heard Diego say.

"What do you think." Referring to a charcoal drawing at his table.

I wandered over and was stunned. This man was truly an artist. I thought his preliminary sketches were good but this was the king himself ready to step off the paper.

Mario and Frank walked toward us looking quite pleased. Seeing me led to remarks about sleeping late and staying out late.

"By the way Diego, you and I are to return to the king this afternoon, and bring your art work." commented Mario.

Frank, a bit more serious now questioned politely,

"I understand you have something to share with us ?"

Mario added, "It's okay Eric, the king said he shared something with you that you are, in turn to share with us."

Smiling myself now I said I was very anxious to give out my information, but in all fairness I would like to wait for the return of Mateo and Carlos. Frank reluctantly agreed but was obviously a little annoyed.

"By the way." he asked. "How did you manage with the king not knowing the language at all."

"I've been asking myself the same question. I don't really know. We just seemed to have a mental connection. It's almost like we can read each others thoughts. Trying to switch back to a lighter note I commented.

"You're really going to like what the king shared with me. Oh, and while we're waiting, did you learn anything new today ?"

"As a matter of fact we did." smiled Frank. "Thanks to Mario's translations we learned some interesting history about our new found city. Apparently this was a central repository for knowledge."

These words of his triggered an internal smile in me.

"Only the very elite resided here. Knowledge, or culture as the king says, and governing emitted from this very temple. This particular pyramid housed the highest authority of all. So our king may be

"The King" and so far everything points in that direction."

"**H**ey! Look at that, our party boy is finally awake." joked Carlos.

"**D**on't talk so loud." joined Mateo. "He may have a hangover."

All five joined in the ribbing for the next few minutes. There was not much I could do but take it and smile and accept it the way it was meant.

"**O**kay you guys if you don't knock ot off I won't tell you my secret." I threatened.

Frank took over from there explaining to the others what the king said and how I was to share the news. All eyes were on me now. I took a swig of coffee and was about to start when Mario interrupted,

"**W**hoa, wait till I take care of these fish."

He held up a catch of four good sized fish I dared not ask the name of. Within five minutes he was back as attentive as the others. So I began my tale of the camera and library.

"**W**here is this library and how do we get to it." inquired Frank.

"**I** know where it is but how to get into it I have not been made privy to. At least not yet. But, and this is the crowning jewel, he said I could use my camera and copy all the scrolls for future study, but they can not leave the tomb."

Every one was stunned to silence, even Frank. Then as if it was ice melting smiles began to appear. Mario was the first to speak.

"**I** guess I have my life's work already planned for me."

This drew a few chuckles. Questions poured forth from all five at the same time.

"**O**kay guys, slow down." I asked. "Yes, I have been in the library, and yes I have seen the scrolls. There must be thousands of them. From what I can gather from the king this is history going back before what we know of as recorded time."

"**T**his will be the biggest breakthrough since the Codex. Even bigger then the Codex." stated Mario.

This could possibly rewrite history itself." said Carlos.

Eyes fell to Frank.

"**I**'m thinking of the papers, books, appearances: this may be a hard thing to sell. No one likes to think that the history we have known for centuries is wring. These scrolls may be the truth, but the establishment minds are not going to change over night just because we produce a few scrolls. Especially only photographs of them. They are going to fight and question everything we may say."

Right now who cares about them. Let's just do the job we are all trained to do and do it to the best of our ability, gathering help and support as we go and let the pieces fall where they may." Preached Mateo. "Fearing something that has not happened yet will only hinder our work. Let us accept this gift and educate ourselves."

Silence reigned for a time while each digested Mateo's words. All agreed and all were happy again. Frank came over to shake my hand.

"**I** don't know how or what you did Eric, but history, myself and all the Maya will thank you and will be grateful for all eternity."

I thought this was going a little overboard but I accepted his thanks and was glad there were no hard feelings between us.

Chapter 18

Mario's name was being called.

"Oh geeze ! I almost forgot. Come on Diego, grab your stuff and let's go." rushed Mario's words.

The pair arrived at the great room to find the king all smiles. They started to bow but the king bade them stand up. They looked at each other questioningly. Then in total surprise the king said to them, still smiling,

"Come sit." as he pointed to the bench. Have you made any progress with your art ?"

Diego unrolled his charcoal portrait proudly. The king moaned a sigh of approval. Mario and Diego stared at the two drawings side by side. They were almost identical. The king still showing his approval said something to Mario using words of the Long Count time. Translating for Diego he said,

"His portrait is just over three thousand years old. It was done by one of the court artisans as a present for him. He also asked if he can keep the one you did after you sign it and date it."

Not wanting to part with his work, he also felt honored, so Diego agreed reluctantly.

"I can always do another." he mumbled.

The king picked up the camera he had and pointed to the outside asking for a name of the other man.

"Eric." answered Mario.

"Eric." repeated the king quite correctly. He then continued to say that Eric can copy both portraits with his camera.

Explaining this to Diego resulted in a broad smile. The king then took them around the whole room describing the events the wall paintings depicted. Stopping at a blank space about five feet wide he turned to Diego saying,

"This is for you."

At first Diego did not understand. Mario then explained that the king wanted Diego to draw this event for posterity, just like the others.

Diego was humbled, yet overwhelmed with emotion. He bowed in thanks. The king touched his shoulder, smiled and said,

"Yes."

Diego was instructed to start tomorrow early and for now they were both dismissed. As they were leaving the king handed Mario the pictures from Eric's wallet he had left behind.

Outside it was raining heavily and the pair made a dash for the tarp shelter. Relaxing out of the wet Diego related his encounter with the king and his commission to draw this event on the wall.

Mario spoke with me about shooting both portraits with my camera.

This expedition was turning out to be a huge success. Much more than was anticipated. The evening turned into a mini celebration along with the fresh fish dinner.

Later, lying in my cot, I could not believe my good fortune. I smiled to myself and let the rain lull me to sleep.

Chapter 19

       Diego, not wanting to go against the kings wishes was up early and out on an expedition of discovery of his own. Luckily for him, his knowledge of prehistoric art and study of Mayan art gave him a firm basis of what natural ingredients he needed to make the colors he would need for his wall art. He wanted to keep in the tradition of his ancestors and match as close as possible the already existing art work. By noon time he was satisfied with what materials he found to fulfill his needs.

       He and I had a quick lunch out of necessity and excitedly walked to the pyramid. The king was waiting and acknowledged our presence without words. He pointed with his scepter and Diego went to his assigned wall and immediately got lost in his own world.

       The king turned to me smiling, put his arm around my shoulder and led me to the already opened library vault. Leading me to a back corner I interpreted his motion to mean this was the beginning. I was almost afraid to touch the scrolls for they seemed so fragile and delicate. He encouraged me to proceed as I slowly and gently extended my hand to touch one. I was surprised and amazed to see how sturdy they were. Whatever their process was for producing this parchment like material, it was light and appeared extremely strong. Gaining confidence because of this I lay it on the flat surface provided by the king, ans secured it with long flat stones. I set up my camera on my light weight travel tripod and snapped my first exposure. The torch light in the room burned with an amazingly bright light that almost had a blue white hue to it. It was well suited to do the work ahead of me. I was soon into a regular step by step routine of copying these priceless treasures. Apparently the king had complete trust in me as I soon found myself alone with these priceless treasures. No matter, I was too thrilled and involved in what I was doing to really care or even notice.

       In the meantime the other four members of our team had been summoned and a history question and answer period had begun. As usual Mario had been invaluable. I found out later it wasn't just Mayan life being discussed, but the king seemed to have extensive insights into other parts of the world of old.

   Afternoon arrived sooner than expected and I was instructed by the king that my time was up for the day as it was also for Diego. I wanted to keep going but I knew better than to counter the kings wishes. I packed up my equipment and joined Diego in the great room. We bid our farewell and headed for the exit.

   It was only mid afternoon and both Diego and I were disappointed about leaving early. The others were also surprised to see leaving the tomb. Our usual debriefing took place with everyone more than satisfied as to how the day went. The chat was short and all took to doing their own thing. Frank was well buried in his journal, Diego was mixing more color while I was doing a film count. Mario and Carlos were playing a game with small pebbles, an old Mayan game I assumed, which caught my attention but I did not have the time right now.

   Supper was light with everyone just sort of picking at whatever was available. The conversation was light also, mostly speculation on what do we do next. Everything seemed to be working out so well. Too well I thought. Something started nagging at the back of my mind. I couldn't quite put my finger on it. I just felt like the bubble was going to burst any minute now. I kept these thoughts to myself because the others appeared to be taking everything in stride. I did, however. Enter these doubts in my journal as a foot note. I could always scratch them out later if nothing came of it. Remembering tomorrow was a special day, the king was going to reveal his secret of staying alive. I reminded Mario, who was also anxiously awaiting.

   Finishing up with my camera equipment faster than I expected sort of left me hanging without anything to do for that particular moment anyway. Everybody else was otherwise occupied so I decided to take a walk. I grabbed my camera, made my intentions known to Diego and left the compound through the archway.

   Once outside I turned left for no particular reason. I lazily followed the compound wall though I was at a distance of thirty some odd feet. Enjoying the dappled light and thinking of nothing in particular, a sudden sound caught my attention. It was not the usual jungle sound. I froze, listening, remembering that there are large jungle cats that appear now and then. I stood silent for at least three minutes not hearing a thing. Deciding to dismiss the whole thing, I took a step and heard the noise again. I froze again and could feel my nerves tense and tingles run down my back.

"I should not have come out alone." I thought. I didn't even have my knife with me. "Stay calm." I repeated aloud to myself. I heard it again, this time behind me. Trying not to move too fast I slowly turned my head. Standing there was the king. A slight smile crossing his lips. My whole body instantly relaxed although my breathing was still a little rapid. I bowed my head in recognition, the king returned the nod. It was obvious he saw the question on my face as he reached down for a basket by his feet filled with a variety of jungle fruit. He turned away from me but signaled for me to follow. WE had walked about a hundred feet when he stopped at a large boulder. It moved exposing an opening that revealed steps leading underground. I followed blindly as he descended. I counted ten steps, then a narrow passageway about twenty feet in length, then again tan steps up which opened to the great room. The wall door swung closed, again leaving no trace of seam. Once closed, the king turned to me sporting a large smile. He seemed to sense my curiosity. He pointed to the wall that was no longer and shook his head in a negative manner. To me the message was clear, don't tell anyone about the rear entrance. I confirmed what he had said and took my leave, questions filling my head. That uneasy feeling was there again.

"**W**hat was wrong with this picture ?" I kept asking myself. "Perhaps there will be some answers tomorrow."

Back at the campsite, I mentioned nothing to the others of my encounter with the king although I still had uneasy feelings about what was happening lately. I settled in a seat away from the others, journal in hand. I opened the now dirty book but did not see the pages. My mind was preoccupied in another zone.

As much as I liked the attention from the king, there was a disturbance there, a gut feel if you will, that was very unsettling. Was this all a hoax ? Some kind of big joke ? Could the king really have been asleep all those years ? Was he really a king ? Who was he and where did he come from ? More importantly, why ?

I was startled back to the present by Diego who was handing me a cup of coffee.

"**W**hat a great day this has been." He said cheerfully. "I can't believe our good fortune."

I smiled and agreed with him, trying to hide my real

feelings of disturbance. We chatted for a while about his art, particularly what he was doing now at the tomb. I was happy for him but still plagued by uneasiness. For Diego's sake I hoped my feelings were wrong.

Darkness was fully upon us and Diego said good night. I moved to my cot and welcomed the night and the chance to be alone again.

Chapter 20

I awoke to a relatively bright day. At least it was not raining and I wasn't feeling too bad but I remained a little apprehensive about yesterday's darker shadows that had crossed my mind. I made a conscious decision to dismiss those feelings as best I could.

Breakfast was fruit and coffee and fun conversation. Everybody was in an upscale mood. I was with Frank when the king's call came summoning Mario and myself.

"**T**his is it." I said to Frank. "Perhaps we can get some answers now."

I grabbed my camera and met up with Mario and started for the pyramid.

Once inside, the king as usual, was seated in the same spot. Next to him on the bench were a few scrolls and an earthen cylinder of sorts. The king indicated, with his ever present scepter, a nearby bench. We settled ourselves while the king spoke a few words to Mario. He then looked at me and nodded. There seemed to be a twinkle or sparkle in his eye divulging a hidden secret between us. His gaze did not go unnoticed by Mario who looked at me with a half smile.

As the king spoke, Mario translated.

"**S**o, my friends, you want to know how I came to be here. If I did not know the things I know, I would be curious also. I like that in a person. Since you are curious I'm guessing you do not have too advanced a knowledge of the sciences as of yet. I would have thought that by now you would have learned of such things."

Mario and I looked at each other a bit bewildered. Here we thought we were so advanced only to be politely criticized by someone who was over two thousand years old.

The king smiled at us and continued,

"**T**hese scrolls here." as he reached for one, "Tell of the preservation process and the need to do it."

Again Mario and I looked at each other questioningly. What did he mean by *"The need to do it ?"* I thought. As if reading my thoughts again, the king pressed on.

"**O**ur scholars realized long ago the need for the preservation of our scientific knowledge. Many of our ambassadors traveled to distant parts of the world meeting peoples of all kinds and knowledge. We determined the necessity of collecting this world wide learning and having it repose in one place. We also determined it would be up to us to keep this history because the other societies around the globe were not stable enough to maintain them without destruction. A man called Alexander, a long time ago had the foresight to try this only to have his storage place destroyed by short sighted peoples. This act only confirmed what we already knew and further cemented our resolve. The future of this cosmic orb is on shaky grounds at best, more so now I'm sure than the last time I walked the nations. Even our own people were destroyed by those who thought themselves superior when if fact their knowledge of the sciences was lacking to the point of destruction of others and eventually their own self annihilation. We, on the other hand, have managed to endure through our use of the sciences in a way they were meant to be employed."

The king paused here and refreshed himself with a vessel of water. He ignored us while he reread the scroll in his hand. He put it aside and reached for another. We watched a tear form in his eye as he read this second scroll. We were anxious for more of this tale but dared not disturb him. Finally looking at us he made no excuses but continued as if there had been no interruption.

"**I** and others like me were put into a preservation state throughout the world, each of us a keeper of the collective sciences. Whether or not the others have survived is yet to be determined. That will be my quest once I have found persons responsible enough to handle this knowledge of the sciences. I only pray that I am not too late."

I looked at Mario who appeared to be shaken as he finished translating the last few words. Gazing back to me Mario said,

"**I**t's obvious the king does not know the state the world is in today."

"**Y**ou mean because of the wars, pollution and greed that controls the planet today ?"

"**E**xactly." he returned. "Do we dare tell him."

Turning again to the king and noticing his expression as he listened to us and said.

"**I** think we just did."

The king waved us silent, and ignoring our interruption, continued his discourse.

"**T**his," again indicating a scroll, "Contains the secret of our preservation. When you opened this resting place of mine you most likely detected an almost unpleasant odor. This was not just stale air of long ago. It was a gaseous substance that kept us in a suspended animation state for later discovery and release. You have triggered my release so that I may hopefully continue my work os sharing our long collected knowledge. A goal that is only meant for the good of all peoples, not the destruction and control. These scrolls in the wrong hands could mean the ultimate annihilation of the living things of this planet as has happened so many times before."

The king paused again letting us digest his words. The silence was frightening as our minds and imagination worked on what we just heard.

Then came the question.

"**C**an you be the keeper and the teachers of this collective information and not let its power influence you to control others ?"

This wasn't just a question, it was the question of all time.

How does one person, or even a few people maintain such a wealth of knowledge and not be tainted by its power ? How does one protect this knowledge to be used for good against those who would use it for world domination ? How does one protect himself against others who would destroy life itself to gain access to such knowledge which in turn is power of control ?

The questions were without end. The answers were not forthcoming. The king obviously knew this as he watched both of us struggling, knowing he put our minds in turmoil. Neither of us spoke for quite a while because there was probably no real answer. It was a question that has plagued mankind since the beginning of intelligence. I began to doubt there even was an answer. I suddenly decided I needed more information. Here we were contemplating the future of all mankind but still did not know the scope of the sciences the king referred to, so in my innocense I asked directly.

"**W**hat exactly is it that we do not possess that you feel would corrupt and destroy us."

The king nodded his approval of my inquiry. Directing our attention to the scrolls he answered.

"This is the knowledge that can change the future for all persons from all nations. It is beyond the comprehension of most but the discerning few."

I immediately pictured in my mind Steven Hawking. A mind beyond most now residing in a physical host which was of no value to him in the way of movement. I pushed my inquiry further stating.

"I understand what you have just said but that does not tell me what that knowledge is specifically. Can you give us an example of what you are referring to. A demonstration if you will. I find it difficult to make an intelligent decision on something I have no knowledge of."

I hoped, deep inside, I did not offend the king with my directness but I felt we were being taunted with riddles. The king paused considering my request. Fearing I pushed things too far I was about to rephrase my question when the king extended his hand and retrieved his ever present scepter. Now staring directly at Mario and I he moved his arm outward away from us all and appeared to squeeze the trunk of the scepter. The room was instantly filled with a blue white light. It was almost blinding and at the same time was soft and very acceptable to our eyes. Daylight had been duplicated in the room. There was no noise or heat from the light source. Mario and I were stunned into silence, in awe as to what was before us. The king spoke calmly and matter of fact, without emotion.

"This is an unlimited and unrestrained power source. It can be used to power anything at no physical or monetary expense. It is all but harmless, however, with a slight modification it can destroy instantly all matter. This entire planet could be vaporized in a matter of seconds. Does that answer your question, my cautious friend ? This is only one of many things these scrolls tell of. So I will ask again. Can you be the keeper and teacher of this collective information and not let it's power influence you to control others ?"

I felt as if the weight of the world was just dumped on my shoulders and I'm sure Mario reacted the same. Finally finding courage I answered the king.

"I think I or we could be the keepers." I pointed out to Mario, "But I feel that once the secret of this power source was known we would most likely be in great danger, and that is something I don't know if

I can handle or would want to handle. I don't know what you remember of your time before on this planet but today's world is not an ideal situation."

"I'm sure you are right my friend, the paths that some men follow are not always the right ones. This has always been the nature of man. Now you know why we have kept this collective of knowledge, hoping some day it could be used to benefit all peoples. It could provide unlimited heat to those who live in the dark frozen lands, power water pumping for those in the dry lands, cooling in the heated jungles. But by what you are saying though, the same mind set that existed thousands of years ago, still exists today. If that is truly the case then I can understand your hesitation. But being of positive thinking and attitude is what has kept us going as a people. We have always known that we were advanced beyond all others but were willing to hold ourselves back in order to bring others out of the dark. Our willingness to wait these few thousand years has not been totally in vain. I have encountered the two of you and Diego. This has given me much hope. Perhaps, before I go further with this gift of knowledge you could enlighten me on the scientific status of your world today."

The king paused a moment obviously contemplating before he went on.

"As anxious as I am to learn this information, it shall have to wait another sun. I am growing weary as I know Mario is also from translating for both of us."

I put up a mild protest, but to no avail which is what I expected. Talking to the king was sometimes like watching a seriasl movie when we were kids. Just when things got exciting it was continued next week. In all fairness though I knew Mario was getting tired. It was quite a struggle at times for him to find the right words in translation to make sense of the Old Mayan words or phrases.

"You may send Diego to continue his art. He will not disturb me."

We knew we were dismissed. Bowing respectfully we left the king and once again entered the daylight. It was early afternoon and the air was very refreshing. We drank deeply of it hoping to clear our minds. Mario and I lingered just outside the tomb doorway both mentally reviewing what had transpired with the king. Mario spoke first, echoing my own thoughts.

"I don't think we should tell the others all that we heard and saw. At least not yet."

"I agree." I answered, "What we just witnessed was almost too much to believe."

"That scepter thing I found downright frightening." replied Mario.

"Yes it was a bit scary." I said. "I wonder though, was it real or just some kind of trick. Do you really think that it is some kind of energy source ? If it was its potential is unbounded."

I gazed at Mario who had an expression of disbelief on his face that I could question something the king had presented.

"Don't get me wrong Mario, but before I believe everything completely I think I would like more information and further demonstrations. If this source is what he says it is, it's way beyond any technology that we possess today and yet it is thousands of years old. How can this be ? What happened to man all those years in between. We, or at least what we know of history, were still throwing rocks when your ancestors had this potential to change the world. This is what I find so questionable. The fact that this potential is now being offered to us, I find downright frightening. How do you go about using this for all mankind when there will be those who would kill and destroy to possess and control ? What safeguards will we have against such movements ?"

Mario continued to look at me though acceptance of what I was saying could be seen in his face.

"At least we have time now to reflect on what we have learned so far." I continued. "Perhaps we will know more tomorrow. Please go with me on this Mario, this is far too important to make hasty decisions."

He smiled in answer as we walked to the others.

Frank was the first with questions as we neared the group. Mario and I explained the gaseous preservation state but avoided anything more. Frank was pleased with the information we gave him but you could tell he wanted more. He seemed annoyed that he could not have more direct contact with the king. He was even a little jealous of Diego having more time in the tomb. I had a lot of respect for Frank as an archeologist, but he was one of the people I had in the back of my mind when I spoke of control. He would not mean to control on purpose but I could see it happening, especially under the influence of others. I did not want to bring this up even to Mario because loyalties can make unsuspecting bedfellows. Mario relayed the kings message to Diego who happily gathered his art materials and was on his way whistling cheerfully.

Questions having been answered somewhat satisfactorily I wandered back to my cameras. I needed time to think. Too much was happening too fast and it all had to be sorted out. I cleaned my lenses and cameras, sorted out my film and performed other meaningless tasks almost as an involuntary action while my mind was mired in the clutter of the last few day's events.

For the rest of the day I tried to keep to myself as much as possible. I really needed the alone time. Diego returned just before supper, his usual happy self, Frank instantly cornering him, but to no avail. He had no new information. In fact he said he had not even seen the king until he was dismissed. Frank was becoming impatient and everyone knew it. After a quiet dinner he joined me at my sleeping area. Trying to act nonchalant he asked,

"So Eric how goes the picture taking ? Do you have all the scrolls copied yet. ?"

"Hardly." I lied, "It's not as easy as it sounds. They have been rolled so tight for so long they have to be handled with kid gloves." I exaggerated. "It's going to take a lot of time, if I even have enough film."

"I know, I know." He answered. "I'm not rushing you, I was just being curious. Tell me, when you talk with the king do you get much information from him." he pried. "I thought for sure, once we met him that we would have all the answers to a lot of old mysteries. I have to admit I feel disappointed so far. I feel like I'm back in Anthropology 101. We sure could use a break with some new historical documentation about now."

"Boy, if he only knew." I thought to myself. Pretending to be interested in what he was saying, I sympathized with him and counseled him with the fact that it has only been a few days and that we should give him time to learn to trust us. Surprisingly, this appeared to make him feel better. We continued with some polite chit-chat and he finally said good night.

I was happy to be alone again but was not happy or pleased with myself for withholding information the way I did. I rationalized my feelings by telling myself all will be disclosed soon enough. I soaked my head with some water and lay down looking forward to my night time symphony.

Chapter 21

It was a restless night. Even the jungle orchestrations would not sooth my troubled mind. Each time I would start to doze off I was taunted by the kings words. *"Why me ?"* I kept thinking. *"Why is the king favoring me to be the keeper of his secrets ? I am not a scientist or a political leader or statesman. I have no influence on world happenings."* My thoughts returned to my earlier doubts. I believed the king, yet I didn't believe him. If he has all this power and knowledge let him use it himself. Suddenly it dawned on me. Perhaps he can't use it. Perhaps his time is limited because of the preservation technology. Perhaps even his sciences have limitations. I started racking my brain for a candidate to be the keeper of this future world. No matter how hard I tried, the answer always came up the same. *"No One."* The few that would even be close that I could think of would easily be overcome and destroyed by the greed and power hungry many who existed in today's world. The responsibility is far too great for any one man, or for any one group for that matter. The king seemed to be referring to an ideal world. I personally don't know if that could even really exist. Knowing the world as it exists today to me would make it an impossibility.

My next question for the king is how extensive is the science he is referring to. Maybe it's just another form of control that has reared its ugly head time and time again through the centuries. What ever it is I feel it's beyond my capabilities, or am I just making excuses for fear of failure. Failure of what though ? Now I know I'm thinking in circles. For all I know the king may not even be thinking of me as a successor. Perhaps he is just using us to lead him to the right person. Now I feel I'm back ti where I started from. Suddenly my head cleared and the only thing I heard was my favorite night time serenade. I could feel the stress leaving me as I let myself be drawn into the music.

Apparently I slept. I don't really recall when I dozed but

the smell of coffee tickled my nostrils enough for me to open my eyes to daylight. I sat up shaking off the cobwebs of the night. Carlos was the only one awake and he greeted me with a salute with his coffee mug. I nodded in return, still not quite awake myself. I made my way to the coffee pot and drank deeply of the hot black syrup. I was really becoming addicted to the black stuff. I breathed an unconscious sigh as the coffee went down and Carlos laughed quietly.

"It does get to you after a while doesn't it."

I just smiled in answer and sat down at the table. Carlos sat across from me and after the time of day pleasantries he became more specific.

"I've been meaning to ask out of curiosity, since you seem to have spent more time with the king, has he ever mentioned possessing powers that were beyond the understanding of most men ?"

"Why do you ask ?" I questioned in reply not wanting to divulge any information just yet. He took another swig of coffee and quietly responded.

"Well, I recall years ago reading a report by an archeologist , I can't remember his name ay the moment, who had been doing some Mayan research and mentioned just such a thing. Supposedly he had found a letter in some church archives in Spain, written by a missionary who came over with the early explorers. Remember, one of the purported missions of Spain at the time was conversion of all the heathens to the Catholic faith. Anyway, in this letter he talks of a scroll he had seen with some strange markings, almost like writing. It was translated for him by one of his local converts, talking of this power. Of course this priest dismissed that such a thing could exist, but nevertheless he did mention it in his letter to the Spanish home church. He also reported that he had that scroll in his possession. What has since happened to it is anybody's guess. It was reported the priest was working in the Uxmal area well north of here."

"That's quite a story. Do you think that letter still exists today ?" I asked.

"I really couldn't say." Carlos replied. "The archeologist's report was from the early nineteen hundreds, so I guess it's possible that it still resides in the archives of the church of Spain. Which particular church and where would have to be determined."

I was excited by what Carlos had told me but did not want to reveal anything yet.

"**I** had not heard any stories like that so far but perhaps I could ask the king if the opportunity arose.." I responded. "I wonder what this so called power was." I said rhetorically.

"**I**'ve wondered about that for years but I must admit I never pursued it any further. Maybe I should have." Carlos answered.

Mateo was now awake and after filling his mug with coffee joined us at the table. He spoke of going fishing for dinner again and I was glad for the change of subject. After a few minutes I excused myself, returning to my cot. I sat down fumbling with my camera so I could reflect on the conversation with Carlos. This information shed new light on what the king said. Perhaps he wasn't totally out to lunch. It was known that some of these old missionary's were extremely reliable in their reporting, and tolerant and understanding of the people they had conquered. I will definitely mention this to Mario. Hopefully we can talk with the king about this power, or knowledge as he calls it, again. Not this soon though, I thought. I still need time to collect my thoughts.

By now everyone was up and our little camp was bust with routine activity. I had already made arrangements with Mateo to go fishing in the afternoon. This was the perfect excuse for me not to see the king today. I found Frank at his writing table and convinced him to see the king. I could tell he was excited with the thought even though he did not pre-arrange the meeting. I was also counting on the king's hospitality and congenial nature not to turn Frank away.

Right after a light lunch Mateo and I started off for the river, fishing gear in hand, while Frank and Mario headed for the tomb. Diego was already there working on his event mural. Carlos was now alone working on his writing which I'm sure he was happy with the alone time. I know I would be.

Learning new ways to fish from Mateo was a welcome relief from the pressures of my visits with the king. No mention at all was made of our searching expedition, just light conversation of river fishing techniques entertained us both. It was like a day off and a very welcome one.

Late afternoon and a bakers dozen large fish to our credit, Mateo and I returned to camp. Frank and the others had been dismissed an hour or so earlier by the king. I braced myself for a scolding as I noticed Frank walking towards me.

"**I** see you had a good day also." he said indicating our

string of fish.

"Yeah, we did pretty good." I replied.

"My day was great." Frank said excitedly. "I'm glad you urged me to go. I have a lot to share with everybody."

"Can it wait until supper Frank ? I promised Mateo I would help clean the fish and do the cooking tonight."

"Sure thing Eric, I want everyone to hear it at the same time anyway. I'll catch you later."

That being said Frank turned and went back to his table. I sighed quietly to myself. *"That's a relief."* I thought *"I guess he had a good time with the king. I wonder what little tidbits he learned to make him so happy. The fact that he's happy again is the important thing. Now perhaps he won't bug me for a while."*

Feeling better myself now I cheerfully attacked the task of fish cleaning while Mateo prepared the fire.

As it turned out I wasn't the only one affected by Frank's good mood. Everyone benefitted and the atmosphere at dinner was light and jovial. Frank, of course, dominated the conversation with a few fill ins by Mario. The king shed some new light on not only this city but others as well. This was actually the oldest, though not the most elaborate in design. Why this had not been discovered before was a puzzle to all. He pointed out that some of the engineering and art work, as good as they were, were not as advanced and sophisticated as in other temples and cities. Frank went on for what seemed like an hour. The fish dinner, by the way, was as good as his new information. With dinner finally over and the stories at an end everyone drifted to their journals to log the day's activities.

Mario joined me shortly thereafter.

"The king was not happy with your absence." he said. "He is not accustomed to being put off by one of his subjects."

I think Mario anticipated my reaction because he instantly put his finger to his lips in an attempt to quiet me. I understood his meaning and looked around to make sure I had not disturbed the others with my sudden outburst. Lowering my voice I ranted at Mario, who politely listened, that I was not one of his subjects. My tirade finally over Mario spoke calmly.

"I'm just the messenger Eric. I understand how you might feel. You must remember though, the king is from another era when things were different."

I looked apologetically at Mario and replied.

"I'm sorry my friend. Forgive me for making you the blunt of my anger and you are right, the king is from another time. I think we both have a lot to learn from each other."

Calm having returned, Mario finished his message that the king wished to see me the first thing in the morning. I looked directly at Mario and said.

"Check with me in the morning and I'll tell you then if I am going to comply with his wishes."

Mario agreed but I could see he was disturbed by my answer. I think he also knew it was useless to continue any further discussion. He politely said good night and left me alone with my thoughts. As I watched him walk away I realized I was no longer upset, in fact I felt rather pleased with myself and sat down with my journal before going to bed.

The next morning our old friend Rain was back. A good reason not to get out of bed. As I lay there listening to the rain I started thinking about the king's proposal. In my mind we seemed to be pretty well advanced. That is the collective we, of course. Yet the king spoke as if we were almost primitive. It dawned on me then that this should be my next discussion with the king, to let him know just how advanced we are. After all, not being around for the past few thousand years, I'm sure he has no idea. This trick he performed with the scepter could have been just that. A trick, something to keep the masses in line. But then again I shouldn't judge without all the correct information, nor should he. I decided then to see the king again. We must have this discussion. I don't know how long I lay there thinking but the sound of voices mingled with my thoughts, enough to realize that the others were up and about. I dragged myself out of my cot, washed and headed for the coffee pot. Mario was already there and showed no signs of anger from yesterday. I was thankful for that. I mentioned about seeing the king and why, which pleased him. We had a quick breakfast, notified the others of our intention and took off for the tomb.

As we entered the outer room we caught the king, as the expression goes, with his pants down. Apparently not expecting us this early, he was finishing up his morning toilet. Dressed only in a sort of loin cloth, his torso was a surprise to us both. He was sinuously lean, with muscles that seemed to dance with his every move. The skin was taut without an ounce of fat to be detected. I judged him to be about one hundred and eighty pounds on an almost six foot frame. He reminded me of a sleek panther when he moved. The whole scene just added to the confusion in my head as to how he could have maintained such physical shape while having been asleep for two thousand years. I did note that the scepter, as usual, was not far from his reach. I made a mental note to investigate this further at another time.

The king did not appear to be annoyed or distressed at all by us seeing him this way. In fact, I think I detected a show off quality in his behavior that may have been meant to intimidate us. I filed tahe away in my mind also for possible later use.

The king maintained his usual reserved friendly smile while his eyes continued a non-readable look. His ever present mysteriousness remained. Mario and I bid our good mornings and proceeded on to the larger chamber while the king finished dressing. We took seats in our usual place not saying a word to each other. A few silent minutes passed before the king joined us, scepter and all. As he seated himself on his chosen bench he looked directly into my eyes, a half smile on his lips, almost a sneer, as if to say, *"See, you did come at me bidding."* but at the same time I saw a glint of respect which I assumed was because of my refusal to appear the day before. I think we were both finally on the same page and on equal standing. He was not my king and we both knew it.

Once we were all comfortably settled I wasted no time in starting the conversation and I spoke rather bluntly and direct without being completely disrespectful.

"You seem to think of us as primitive by comparison. Apparently you are not aware of our scientific accomplishments over the last several thousand years."

Without letting him interrupt I went on to list the most startling of these breakthroughs. Astronomy, Gunpowder, Mathematics, Internal combustion, Flight, Under water travel, Engineering, Space travel, Nuclear power, communications and finally Computers.

The king listened patiently, his demeanor being quite calm. I finished with a few minor discovery processes and sat back feeling quite proud of myself in the game of one upmanship.

The king, without showing any signs of distress, reached into his ever present basket and handed each of us a piece of fruit. He also served himself and proceeded to eat quietly. His silence was agonizing but I let him have his time. When he finished eating he wiped his hands on a cloth, sat back and spoke my name aloud in perfect English. He smiled slightly as if proud of himself and I smiled back in recognition of his effort to communicate. Now it was his time to list accomplishments, or should I really say counter list. He used my listing in the exact order and proceeded to answer or again should I say tear apart what I had presented. Starting with astronomy the king said they studied the stars long before the Greeks and actually introduced them to the heavens. Even before the Greeks were known as Greeks.

Gunpowder, after having it explained to him, he said he would reserve that until last.

Third on my list was mathematics. He reminded me that they invented the zero and also how much more accurate their calender was. Other mathematical advancements were beyond my comprehension at this time. He then moved on to internal combustion which he said was unnecessary and would explain that further later on.

Flight and underwater travel he sort of laughed at and as before put it aside for a later demonstration.

"Now I've got him." I thought to myself. *"He cant keep up with our achievements. Their advanced scientific knowledge he was always spouting was just a lot of hooey, lip service so to speak."*

As for engineering he used his hand to span the structure we were in and the complex that surrounded it. He reminded us that no mortar of any kind was used and has survived what ever nature could throw at it.

I had to give him that one, what with all the sliding doors and passageways we found and all without cement.

Space travel and nuclear power was again, as before, put aside for future demonstration.

I still wanted to give him his equal time but I felt this was becoming absurd. He obviously could not explain away the more challenging ideas I had presented.

Communications was simply done with the power of the mind, no matter what the distance. The king felt this use of the brain must have slowly dwindled away over the course of time and non use.

I knew of ESP, but what the king was saying seemed very far fetched even for an enlightened one.

Computers, he stated were just advanced mathematics employed by functions of the brain, much too advanced for us to understand.

This I started to challenge and vehemently object to. I had enough of his holier than thou attitude and I let him know it. The king calmly smiled and held up his hand.

"Please Eric, let me finish my demonstrations and then if you still find fault with what I have said, further discussion can take place."

As incensed as I was I knew he was right. He did listen patiently to me, I should at least return the courtesy.

"All right." I answered. "But we are definitely going to further discuss this." I said authoritatively. I sat back on the bench and with a wave of my hand indicated he could continue.

Mario in the meantime was in a state of shock that I would talk to the king in this manner. While looking at me in a scolding glance he apologized to the king for my behavior.

With a wave of his hand the king dismissed this and smiling a placating smile he stood and retrieved his scepter as he did so.

"Follow me." He said softly walking to a wall. A gentle touch on a certain part of the painting and the wall moved back and angled slightly revealing a passageway. Indicating again that Mario and I follow him, he entered the darkness. After a few steps into the dark a small but extremely illuminating light appeared from the tip of the scepter. It grew in intensity till all seemed like daylight. The walls of the corridor were also painted. Scenes of unbelievable beauty and style with a combination of shades and color I had not witnessed before, even from some of the old masters. The scenes depicted were not just Mayan, but representations of ancient Greece, Rome, Babylon and who knows what else. It would take time to research all they resembled. Further on were detailed renditions of European sailing ships of the fourteenth, fifteenth and sixteenth centuries. Sprinkled among the European paintings were those of early Viking and Chinese vessels. What articularly caught my attention were representations including Chinese junks along with obvious European ships. There were harbor scenes with trading taking place. Another large painting showed what I guessed to be Phoenician sailing vessels sailing side by side with log and bark ocean going rafts of South American origin.

Mario and I were so taken by these paintings that we almost forgot what our mission was. A blunt reminder from the king brought us back to reality. A reality I definitely wanted to follow. I was anxious to show this king up for the charlatan he may be. Although seeing these paintings did add a dimension of doubt to my thinking the way I was.

Reluctantly we again followed the king with the corridor now descending and also becoming more narrow. The paintings stopped also and I assumed it was because of this narrowness. After what I judged to be about fifty feet the walkway was on the assent as the walls widened. Paintings appeared again. I lost track of exactly how many but it was obvious they would fill any big city gallery and then some. Unfortunately they could not be moved. What a loss to the world, particularly the art world. Perhaps a video documentary could be done in the future so the world could see this magnificent art.

Eventually we approached a set of stone steps going up. There were six steps that ended at a large flat stone slab not dissimilar from the last jungle entrance the king made me privy to. It seemed to magically open at the king's touch. We had to stand aside as dirt and debris rained down on us, evidencing it had not been opened for some time. When the dust settled the three of us exited to the jungle.

Mario was all smiles by now and remarked quietly.

"I have read about such things but did not know they really existed."

I nodded in agreement as we followed our host to a small clearing. There was even a break in the canopy showing us blue sky. Deciding this place would do the king turned his attention to us, mainly me. I was the one questioning his knowledge. The king spoke slowly and quietly, Mario translating word for word.

"As for your gun powder Eric." He smiled at saying my name again. "This is why we found it unnecessary."

Lifting his scepter and pointing it directly at a nearby stone of about two and a half feet in diameter, his hand moved almost unnoticeably, and with that a rose colored ray emanated from the tip and touched the stone. Instantly the stone disappeared.

"It is now part of the matter scrambled in the universe." the king explained.

Mario and I looked at each other in disbelief, both our mouth's hanging open. The king smiled smugly. Forgetting the king's smugness I tried to review in my mind what I just witnessed. There was no sound, no explosion, no flying shrapnel, the stone just vanished. It vanished while I watched it. I walked to where it once stood, saw the depression where it lay which was the only evidence of its previous existence. The grasses surrounding the area were brown and black tipped having been singed by something extremely hot, yet there was no heat felt by the observers. I turned to look at Mario who was still just staring. My gaze moved to the king who spoke quietly. I had to shake Mario from his trance to translate.

"**N**ow you know why we found your gun powder without use." he stated. "Before you ask any more questions, let me show you one more demonstration. I believe it will dispel any doubts you may still have as to my credibility. I acknowledged his request with a nod of my head and stood silent with Mario.

The king stepped away allowing more distance between us. Facing us again, still with that half smug smile, his hand moved to the center of the scepter, held it in front of him parallel to his body and slightly away and tightened his grip. There was a hesitation of a second or two then he lifted off the ground. Still there was no sound, no air movement, just a single body rising into the trees. Suddenly there was a drastic increase in speed as we watched the king grow smaller. I less than a minute he was just about out of sight.

Mario and I both started to say something but nothing passed our lips. Then as quickly as the king disappeared he reappeared descending slowly to touch the earth directly in front of us. It was then I felt the sensation of a disturbance. Exactly what, I couldn't say. It wasn't a breeze or wind but an unseen movement. My mind working overtime to analyze what I was experiencing. Paranormal thoughts were crowding me as if they were the answer. I told myself I was more rational than that. It dawned on me that I may be feeling a molecular disturbance caused by the scepter.

"You are correct Eric." I heard the king say.

I had been looking at him and his lips had not moved nor sound of any kind came from him, yet I heard him clearly in my own language.

"Do not doubt your thoughts Eric, your assessment is correct. I knew you would be the one to contact." The voice in my head continued.

I looked quickly at Mario, who still seemed to be in a state of shock and bewilderment. I could tell he had not heard anything. My eyes returned to the king observing an imperceptible smile.

"Only you can hear me." came the voice again. **_"Mario is not ready yet."_**

"Is he still reading my thoughts ?" I asked myself. _"Could we actually communicate this way ?"_

"Only if you allow it." the king answered.

I shook my head hoping for a return to reality. Anything to get away from this dream. Mario's voice helped pull me back.

"Are you alright Eric ?" he questioned. "You seem to be in a daze. I'm kind of in a fog myself. I guess it was the shock of what we just saw. We did just see the king fly, didn't we ?" he asked confused.

"No you're not crazy Mario. The king did leave the ground and with no apparent means." I answered.

Avoiding my eyes the king addressed Mario in his native tongue for him to translate.

"Does that answer your question my skeptical friend ? I can travel as well under water. There are no bounds to this power we have harnessed."

"I concede to you my doubts on the specific topics mentioned but this brings up a whole different set of questions even more relevant to what we just witnessed.." I answered.

"I thought it would." the king stated. "I would have been very disappointed if it had not. Before we go any further I must ask you both not to reveal anything that took place today. This was for your eyes only and I'm sure you understand why."

I looked at Mario and after a short hesitation he nodded in the affirmative. I agreed but with reservations. We must discuss this at great length. The king agreed enthusiastically. As we turned to go back to the pyramid I caught a glimpse of the king again squeezing the scepter around the middle. The grip[was less than a second. It was as if he was turning a flashlight off.

"I must learn more about that scepter." I thought.

"You will soon enough my friend." answered the king.

Of course, like before, was only in my mind.
Mario was still oblivious to these mental conversations.

Chapter 22

We entered the tomb from the hidden jungle entrance and slowly retraced our steps to the large chamber. The flight demonstration was temporarily forgotten as we viewed the wall art for a second time. The color, detail and style were incomparable. To me, the subject matter was the most eye catching. Their knowledge of contact between peoples of different parts of the world and of different era was mystifying. The intricate detail with which the ships were painted could only have been done with first hand knowledge. Perhaps the king has been right all along. Maybe they do possess a superior intellect and maybe they were the teachers of other civilizations. All of this, of course, led to other questions.

I soon found myself in shadows as the others had continued to the chamber along with the light from the scepter. I had to hurry to catch up and realized they had not even noticed I was delayed.

Back in the chamber with the passage door sealed again the king sat and reached for fruit. I declined this time, still standing where the door was. I could not detect any seams. This baffled me bringing in the question of the engineering. Here I was bragging how advanced we were then I see something like this, which defies logic. I guess I had been put in my place.

I rejoined Mario and the king settling myself on a bench. The king addressed both of us saying.

"I know you have many questions, as well you should but I ask your patience with me. I grow weary and wish to rest. I will enlighten you both as best I can at another time. With another sun perhaps I will be rejuvenated. I wish you to tale your leave now."

He spoke with a sincerity I had not heard before and he truly looked rather tired. Mario bowed and headed for the entranceway. I nodded my head and followed.

Once outside we took deep breaths, not necessarily for the

air, but to clear and settle our heads. The events we had witnessed were almost to much to believe. Had we not been there I would have doubted such a story from anyone else. We stood in silence for a while out of sight of the camp.

Mario spoke first, echoing my own thoughts.

"I haven't always agreed with you but this time we definitely should not tell the others what we just experienced. First of all they probably would not believe us. I'm not even sure I believe us. Secondly, there is too much going on in my mind to be sorted out to even discuss it further with you right now."

"Exactly my thoughts my friend." I replied. "We both need time to evaluate and consider. I think a few days separation from the king will fare us both well."

"I do not disagree with that but I don't know if that's a good idea either." Mario replied. "I get the feeling he's anxious to continue and for whatever reason he seems to want to continue with just you. The rest of us are only getting fragments of information, but with you he seems to bare his soul."

Mario said this without malice or jealousy. It was his own observation. I did not answer this but started to slowly walk back to camp. We both remained silent. We were met, as expected, with the usual questions from Frank to which I responded that we discussed more about the scrolls.

"I notice you don't have your cameras with you, have you finished copying them ?"

I laughed lightly and replied that I guessed only about ten percent had been photographed. Frank was disappointed with my answer but could see I was not in the mood for further questions.

"I just need some rest right now Frank. Let's review this after dinner, shall we ?"

It was more of an ending statement than a polite request but nevertheless he got my message and walked away. Mario turned away also saying.

"Catch you later, I need to think."

I went straight to my cot and sat with my back to the camp resting my head in my hands. Suddenly feeling sorry for myself I thought I would not be in this position if I just stayed home taking pictures. Who are you kidding Eric, you're enjoying every minute of this., I argued with myself. I lay back in my cot with both hands folded behind my head staring at the overhead canopy hoping for sleep to overwhelm me. I was trying to blank my mind but there was just too much attacking from too many directions.

"Okay." I said to myself out loud. "Let's try and make some sense of this. Perhaps if I put things in some sort of order then I can deal with them one at a time.."

As I was saying this, still talking out loud, another thought slipped its way into my conversation.

"I wonder if the king can still read my thoughts. He said only if I allow it. Well right now I don't allow it." I said determinedly. "I hope it's that simple. I'll have to do more research into this mind stuff. Now where was I ? Oh yeah, putting things in order. Geeze Eric you must be losing it, you're only having a conversation with yourself and you still can't keep up. Which leads me back to where I want to be. What do I do about the king. Situation."

I stopped talking aloud having convinced myself no one was eavesdropping. As fascinating as today's demonstrations were they were ultimately frightening. To have control of that kind of power source, unharnessed, could lead to the complete destruction of the world overnight. When you think about it, we're doing that to ourselves now anyway, just at a slower pace. I drifted to thinking about all the benefits such a power could yield. Heating and cooling with out the use of fossil fuels. That alone could make a difference in our planet. Lighting, agriculture, manufacturing would also be enhanced greatly.

Then there is the opposite side. War, weaponry, enslavement would increase exponentially. The evil of greed, at least in my mind, I'm afraid would win out in the long run. Apparently the king knows this or we would have already had such mechanisms in place for the good of all. Apparently the kings own era went through the same thing otherwise why would he still have the scepter and be trying to find a new keeper of the knowledge of the ages. That leads me to contemplate what happened thousands of years ago to have put this off.. Probably the same evil greed, I posited to myself. I had not even thought of the how and why this source of energy was discovered and why, after thousands of years it had not appeared again ? What was this special thing ? It appeared awfully simple, yet manifested itself in a manner that was unthinkable. The control of this unknown thing is what frightened me. Who ever controlled it would be the target of all sorts of unsavory people the world over. That brings me to my next question. If the king already controls this supposedly wonderful thing why has it been a secret for all these many years, and why now does he want to give it to me or whoever he feels is right.

Then like a flash bulb going off in my head my thoughts exploded. I had to see the king and **now** I thought. I jumped out of my cot, looked for Mario, who did not seem to be available and decided to head for the pyramid anyway. No one else appeared to notice or even care that I was going back alone.

I found the king resting on the bench, eyes closed and breathing slightly irregular Not really wanting to disturb him, yet I felt this was important. Important for both of us. I did not want to shock him awake so I avoided touching him. This is a good time to try this mental stuff I thought. Let's see if he is receptive to me. I concentrated my thoughts and directed them at the king. **"Please hear me."** I repeated a few times mentally. It only took about a half a minute when the king opened his eyes. He smiled softly and nodded in recognition. It was obvious he was in a weakened state although he tried to hide it. Again communicating only with my mind I stated;

"**I** had to see you. We must talk. I need to know some things.

"**I**t's okay." he answered. "I expected you would be back."

*"**W**hat a great way to communicate."* I thought.

"**Y**es it is." came a clear answer I didn't expect.

"**O**nce your mind is open, it is open until you chose it not to be."

By now the king was sitting upright looking some what refreshed but I could still detect an air of weakness about him.

"**Y**our assessment of me is correct my young friend and it is only you who knows this."

I read his meaning without him having to spell it out. My mind was racing again. I know I was fighting the clock. I decided the best way to get answers to my questions was to skip the formalities and just blurt it out.

"**T**his power source, the scepter, what will happen to it if you do not find anyone to pass it on to ?"

Hesitantly, and with a sadness in his expression the king answered.

"**I** guess it will just have to be destroyed. It can not be left without the knowledge of its use."

"**C**an it be destroyed ?" I asked curiously.

"**O**h yes, quite easily and safely." he answered calmly.

Now came the important question.

"**Y**ou're dying aren't you ? Your time is limited here on earth. That's why you are in such a rush to pass on your secret. That's why you singled me out from the others. But why me ? I'm no scientist or a world leader. I'm sure there are thousands of others eminently more qualified to be the caretaker of this knowledge."

"**I**'m sure you are right about that Eric but I am not looking for a world leader, or scientist or even a statesman. You are correct, I am dying and a successor must be found. You are that man Eric. It is true you are not Mayan, but you possess all that is Mayan, the Mayan of old. I can read it in your heart, in your eyes. You care Eric. You care greatly. You possess fairness and reason. Your whole being is compassion. I believe in fate Eric, and it was fate that brought us together. As much as I respect the others for what they represent, Mayan or not, they do not collectively have what you have in your heart. A little history if you will."

I sat before him, humbled and still confused, yet I nodded in agreement to listen to more.

"**E**ons ago." the king continued, "Our race of people, as advanced as we were, also succumbed to the evils of greed. The true ways were being thrown aside and replaced with a thirst for material possessions. It slowly advanced to taking what wasn't theirs to take. They found it easy to conquer other peoples and eventually turned on their own for the sake of control and power. It was then that a group of The Chosen Ones, as we were called, decided to put to sleep this beneficial knowledge. We would wait for a better time when acceptance would be forthcoming. There were originally five of us. Each went to different lands through out the world, the thought being, as people grew in maturity, the handling of this discovery and its benefits for all mankind would be more easily welcomed. Each of us five had our loyal followers who administered the life suspension gasses. The fate of the other four is obviously unknown. The period of time of our ultimate death after reawakening was never established. There was no way to know or test it. It was hoped to be lengthy to allow a proper time to find the appropriate caretaker. On this point we greatly misjudged."

The king paused as if out of breath even though he was not physically talking. He slowly drank of the water I provided. He thanked me and proceeded further.

"**I** would like to fulfill my mission Eric, and you can help me do that. From what you tell me of your advancements I'm sure the peoples of the world are ready for this knowledge,"

The king paused again to rest. I started reviewing in my mind the world's history as I knew them forgetting he could and did read my every thought. The positive highlights were easily overshadowed as I recalled wars, enslavement, and genocide that was still going on to this day. I portrayed to the king that as much as we have learned over the thousands of years we still have learned nothing. Greed and power existed now as it did then. The king became extremely saddened as he listened to my thoughts.

"My choice is clear then." he answered sadly. "This power source must be destroyed. I have waited all these years with high hopes for mankind only to find nothing has changed.."

I could tell he was deeply distraught in having to make this decision but I had to agree with him. The world was still not ready for such advancements.

"The scrolls ?" I asked. "Must they also be destroyed ?"

"No, they are yours to study. They tell only of our history and contact with other nations. The formula of our discovery was never recorded for obvious reasons. Once the scepter is destroyed it will never be found out again. Of that I am confident. It will truly be a loss for all time to come. Will you help me Eric ? I feel my time is growing near. Come, we must go outside to the wind."

I helped The Chosen One up, he grabbed his scepter and we made our way to the wall. He opened the wall and with his lighted scepter we slowly walked the passageway past the magnificent paintings of the past. Outside he instructed me to hold his free hand. He then squeezed the scepter and we rose in the air. I was startled at first, but realized there was no sensation of flight. We traveled through the canopy overhead and in no time at all were standing on the beach of the gulf.

The head of the scepter was removed and a powder like sand was thrown to the wind and was carried out over the water. Sudden panic overcame me and was answered by the king.

"No need to worry my friend, there is enough of the original source to return us to my home. The scepter was closed and once again the king reached for my hand as we lifted off the beach.

In no time at all we were back at the outside entrance to the pyramid. As soon as we touched the jungle floor the king squeezed my hand even harder and reached his other arm to steady himself against me. I put his arm around my shoulder and assisted him down the steps to the painted corridor. Once back in the great room I made him as comfortable as I could on his bench.

I heard Mario's voice behind me.

"Is he all right ?" he asked.

"For the moment." I answered.

The glance between us told the whole story. He had come to the same conclusion I had when he could not find me in camp and rushed to the tomb. The king himself confirmed Mario's suspicion and suggested he get the others for a last talk. Mario turned as he was bid and left us alone.

"Quickly my friend get me that small earthen jar. The one with the cover."

I retrieved the small vessel and set it beside him on the bench. The king then proceeded to open the scepter again and emptied the remaining sand mixture into it. Covering the jar he handed it to me.

"This is yours my friend and yours alone. Put it out of sight before the others return. Do not attempt to analyze this, it will do you no good. The elements that make up this mixture no longer exist, or shall we say will be impossible to locate. You will know what to do when it is time."

I secreted the jar away knowing there was only minutes before the others returned.

"I am sorry I could not help the world with our knowledge. It saddens me greatly but I do understand your reluctance to accept the responsibility as caretaker. Our decision was for the best for all. Perhaps some day people will learn to coexist without greed and hatred. Your efforts should always be toward that goal. I hope you see that day Eric and when you do, remember me. I feel we could have been true friends and wish we had more time together."

Not knowing what to say at this point I took his hand with a gentle pressure. Our eyes met and words or thoughts were no longer necessary.

The king slowly smiled as Frank and the others entered the room.

"Come sit and let me answer your questions." The Chosen One commanded through Mario.

Diego was the first to speak inquiring about the mural.

"Can I add you to this event drawing ?"

Touched by his sincerity the king answered.

"Paint me as I once was, not as I appear before you now. The world is not ready for such contradiction."

We all knew his meaning. Frank jumped in on the king's last word.

"Can we still have access to the scrolls ?"

Sensing the discomfort and annoyance in his Mayan descendants at this question being asked the king slowly smiled. Looked directly at Frank and said.

"I'm sure Eric can arrange that for you when you are ready."

Frank's anger was obvious at this answer as he snapped his head around and glared at me. Our four Mayan friends were extremely attentive to the king discussing his final time and burial wishes. They assured him all would be done according to tradition. Frank again made an inquiry about the ancient history. Before the king could answer, Mateo being unusually stern, turned and answered.

"Now is not the time Frank."

He continued his stern look for a few seconds before returning his attention to the king's needs. Words were now being mumbled in their native language that neither Frank or I understood.

"I will miss our discussions." I thought to myself.

"As will I my friend." came an answer in my mind.

I turned my attention to the king and realized those were his last words. The serenity of peaceful sleep overtook the king's face. I shed no tears but felt a sudden loss.

The room remained silent for the next five minutes or so. The quiet was only broken when Frank turned to go not seeming to care what happened next.

The four native Mayans, after an appropriate period of tome automatically went about the task of the king's burial according to what they knew of tradition. The body was stripped and washed then redressed with the finery befitting a Chosen One. The feathered cloak and headdress along with bracelets and necklaces were the perfect finale to salute this king.

I stood respectfully aside watching the four administer to their ancient king. I thought about asking if I could be of help in any way but decided against it and remained silent.

Carlos was studying the stone pure where we first discovered the king and after a few misplaced touches found the key stone that slipped aside and the cover was moved away length wise. It was the king's already prepared coffin, lined with finely woven cloths of many colors. Precious gemstones, although mostly jade, were strewn about along with gold and silver jewelry pieces. A most curious trinket that captured everyone's eye was that of a horse made of gold mounted on a stand with wheels, with a finely woven gold chain attached like a child's pull toy. I always thought horses were unknown to the Mayan culture. This would make the perfect picture I thought but again out of reverence of the occasion I restrained myself.

When all was ready and preparations completed the four friends most gently lifted the body of their ancestor and carefully placed it in the stone casket. The only thing left now was the scepter. Mario picked it up from the bench and carried it forward to the pyre. Here he hesitated and looked at the others as if for approval. The three nodded affirmatively. Mario walked to me and held out his arms offering me the ritualistic scepter.

"The honor is yours." he said quietly.

Without thinking I reached and accepted the symbol, overcome with one last feeling of a connection to the king.

I walked to the king's now eternal home and lay it across his chest and joined the hands around its base and stood back reverently. All was silent once again as final farewells were silently spoken.

Frank reappeared and joined us at the pyre and with proper humility bowed his head. Mateo uttered a few words in his native tongue and the phrase was repeated by the others. The stone lid was then slid back in place and Carlos re-locked the small key stone.

We lingered a few more minutes, then one by one left the pyramid. As Frank left he gave me a look that showed he was not happy. I equated it to a child who did not get his way and chose not to let it bother me. Mario and I were now alone. He searched my eyes inquisitively.

"The Scepter." he said quietly. "What about the scepter ?"

Since he and I were the only ones privy to its amazing power I made sure no one was within ear shot. I related what happened between the king and I and his decision to destroy the advanced knowledge of the centuries past rather than let it be used for domination. He looked relieved when I told him this. As good as it could have been he feared this power for obvious reasons.

"How do you feel about its destruction ?" he asked.

"I was in favor." I replied "Like you, I could see the many benefits but what I feared most was its control by the wrong people. I know that would happen no matter what you and I personally thought. I truly believe mankind is better off without it, at least for right now. Perhaps some day such a thing will come to pass and be justified but I doubt it will be in our lifetime. The world is just not ready for peace and harmony."

Mario was actually delighted right now that this decision was made. We both pledged our secrecy that this matter would never be revealed.

We paid our final respects to this wondrous man and left the tomb which it truly was now.

Chapter 23

Walking back to camp we agreed to tell Diego of the corridor of paintings. All would know after that and arrangements could be made by Frank for its video recording for all the world to see. This, we thought, would satisfy his ego and give him the world recognition he seemed to be yearning for.

The camp that night was somber. Only absolutely necessary conversation took place. Frank stayed pretty much to himself which I think pleased everyone. He definitely avoided me. There was no real dinner, everyone fended for themselves if they even ate at all. I know I welcomed being alone. It started to rain again which added to the heavy mood.

Rather than be accused of staling a precious artifact I emptied the contents of the earthen jar into an empty film box I had. Tomorrow I would return the jar to the tomb. I viewed the strange silky sand for a while wondering what gave it its unique character. No matter I thought, at least it would not be used for any evil purpose. I resolved then not even to tell Mario of this gift from the king. I closed the box, sealed it with some tape and tucked it away deep in my personal pack.

I lay down, relaxed by the rain, thinking of my encounter with this man from another world.

Chapter 24

I was startled awake, as was everyone, when Carlos dropped the empty coffee pot.

"Sorry guys." he mumbled.

It was still raining only now it was more like a heavy mist. We all automatically went through our morning ritual before breakfast. Frank acted as if nothing happened yesterday, planning for the day's activities. He spoke to me like an old friend asking if I could continue recording the scrolls. I said I could as long as my film held out. This satisfied him. He then went on to assign tasks for the others. Mario took me aside and suggested we discover the painting passageway today. That way it would eliminate any curiosity as to why only we two were shown this hidden treasure. I agreed and relayed to him about where I thought the king touched the wall to open it. He said he would try to do it in the presence of Diego. Pleased with our plan we attended to our other chores before going to the pyramid.

Mateo was the only one to stay at camp. He was working on Glyph translations Diego could include in his mural. The remaining five of us entered the great room to continue our research. The missing presence of the king lent a air of emptiness to the room, at least for me it did. I went about my recording work with the scrolls almost without interest, thinking about the king's dedication to a world of peace. Wouldn't that be something.

I heard the excitement of raised voices. I smiled to myself knowing they just discovered the paintings.

Carlos shouted to me.

"Eric, you have to come and see this and bring your camera."

I took advantage of this distraction and returned the small

earthen jar to its place. I then joined the others and was surprised to see the beauty of the wall art. Even though I had seen them before I was still genuinely captivated by them. Mario was as excited as I was now that we could study them in a more relaxed manner. He winked at me acknowledging our little secret. The excitement of our find overcame even Frank. I took this opportunity to suggest to him the video idea. Mario and the others supported this thought which Frank then took and made it his own. The rest of the day was routine for me. Eventually, Mateo joined us and was also amazed by the paintings. Diego was acting like a child at Christmas as he studied the art work. I never saw anyone so completely involved in art before.

The next few days followed routine almost to the point of becoming boring. Without the king's unique presence things became predictable. I personally missed him more than I thought I would.

The rain became more frequent and at times was getting heavier. It was decided to end this particular expedition. It had been a success beyond ones wildest dreams. Further excavation and research of this new city would have to wait for next years dry season. Frank was already discussing plans for the next venture, wanting to have more crews at more sights.

We carefully packed our gear and sadly resealed the tomb and pyramid. It was like leaving an old friend. Speaking of old friends, my favorite camera was returned to me by Mateo. It was like another connection with the king for me.

Chapter 25

       Our trek back to civilization was totally uneventful and anti- climatic though I still found the jungle fascinating and mysterious.

       We held a celebratory parting dinner in Mexico City and relived our adventures. It was at this dinner I presented Frank with two of the jade stones the king had given me. I offered them to help finance next years expedition. For once Frank actually appeared humbled, and I was glad he accepted my offer. Whether or not I would be asked to go along again, or even if I wanted to go again, I did not know yet. I kept the third piece of jade as a memento of this wonderful but strange journey.

       We all parted reluctantly but had to go back to what would now seem our mundane lives. I promised Frank I would follow up with all the photography as soon as I finished the processing and logging.

       My return flight to Vermont was tiring and thoughtful. I relived the whole experience in my mind and was not unhappy with it. Once back home I took my time unpacking and caught up on some much needed sleep. I transferred the king's gift of the silky sand to a clear glass container and placed it on the mantle. It would always be a reminder of exciting times.

       For reasons unknown to me the glass jar constantly drew me to it whenever I passed. Once, just before going to bed, I stopped to study it for the umteenth time. Holding it in my hand I remembered the king's actions. I was quite tired and was thinking that I should be going upstairs to bed. Unconsciously I squeezed the small jar and instantly lifted off the floor and floated up the stairs without touching a single step.

~ ~ ~ ~ ~ ~

And so began my next journey. !!!

~ ~ ~ ~ ~ ~

The Dead Living Mummy

Part II

Chapter 26

Floating up the stairs was startling, yet not uncomfortable. A feeling came over me though, that this was a natural thing. I instantly recalled my flight over the jungle with the king. Mixed emotions flared up again regarding the scepter. I was sad and disappointed in the destruction of it's power, yet deep inside I knew it was the right decision.

Recollections of the entire expedition started flooding my head. As tired as I was. I suddenly became too excited to sleep now. I sat on the edge of the bed contemplating the glass container of mystical sand. Questions raced through my brain.

"What was it ? How did it work ? Why did it work ? How long will it work ?"

Questions, but no answers. Why did the king have to die ? I was just learning from him. I know it sounds silly but I was angry with the king for dying. I had so many unanswered questions for him. So much more I wanted to learn.

Listen to yourself Eric. It is so out of character to throw yourself a pity party. Be thankful for what you were witness to and for the trust this stranger put in you.

My self counseling, surprisingly enough, worked. I was truly thankful for what the king shared with me. The power of his presence yet the gentleness of his manner was a unique combination that few possess. I wanted to be with him again.

A strong urge to repeat the experience came over me. I wanted to contact Frank and make immediate plans to return.

"Whoa, slow down boy." I thought to myself. *"Come back to earth and think about what you are saying."*

I laughed aloud to myself.

"Of course you can't go back now stupid. You wouldn't be able to get through the jungle now." I explained.

I was calm once again and could feel the sleepy's creeping in again. I put aside the magic sand and as I lay down on a proper bed I thought about my hammock and mosquito netting. Smiling, I closed my eyes and allowed myself to drift off, only this time without my jungle serenade.

Chapter 27

    The clock read ten forty five and the sun was pouring in my window. I stretched for the mosquito netting which of course was not there. When my feet touched the hard floor I realized I was no longer in the jungle and believe it or not was saddened by this. I wondered whether or not I could make coffee thick and syrupy as I headed for the kitchen. I looked at my living room disaster of the half unpacked luggage spread over the furniture as I passed through. Oh well, no one is here but me. Waiting for the coffee to brew I turned my attention to the many boxes of film I had collected It was almost depressing knowing the size of the job that lay ahead.

    The week passed faster than expected with positive results. The boring film processing was now behind me, I had even completed the categorizing and logging. A call to Frank was in order.

    Much to my surprise Frank sounded genuinely pleased to hear from me. The plan was for me to send a sample of the preliminary results for his perusal, then we would finalize who gets what for study. I would also include my diary notes for him to compile with the others to produce a multi- sided final report for the college "Big Whigs".

    Before we hung up Frank asked if I would be interested in returning with him next season. I immediately answered yes. Frank then admitted the others knew my answer would be yes. He added that he also was pleased with my affirmative answer. A few more niceties were exchanged and finally we hung up. I was a bit surprised with Frank's attitude. I honestly didn't expect such a changed outlook on his part.

    I felt myself becoming anxious once again. I just couldn't wait to get back to the jungle, which was pretty funny since I hate the heat so much. I missed everything about it. To wait six months would seem like forever.

~ ~ ~ ~ ~ ~ ~

There was plenty of time before anything had to be prepared for the next expedition. In the meantime there was the present which meant a ton of work ahead. The site pictures were pretty much self explanatory and just needed identification names. The biggest challenge, of course, was the historical scrolls. I worked diligently on them to obtain the best quality possible. I was amazed at how well they turned out considering the lighting challenge in the pyramid library. I truly hope they are in proper date sequence.

I wish I could read "Yucatecan" or whatever the heck he called it. For right now I have to wait along with the rest of the world to have it translated. I made up a sample set of prints for Mario to work on and shipped them special delivery. He was now teaching at a small college in Arizona specializing in pre-contact American studies. I figured I would give that a few days, perhaps a week and then call him. I wanted his feedback before proceeding.

Diego was next on my list and much to my surprise I learned he was also at the same Arizona college teaching early American art. I made up some proofs of the wall murals for him to study and remembered and found the shots I took of his portrait of the king marveling at his rendition of the king for its lifelike qualities. I paid special attention to the copy I made for myself. I placed this on the mantle with the container of mystical sand.

Having become so obsessed with this Mayan theme I let my regular work slide. So much so that I actually stopped taking on new assignments. I fact, after two months, I actually closed my business. For right now my first and foremost consideration was my commitment to the Mayan King and learning his history.

Chapter 28

Weeks turned into months before I realized it. I was totally consumed by these Mayan studies.

I kept in constant communication with all five members of the team. Again I was surprised to learn Carlos and Mateo also moved their studies to Arizona so all could continue to work together. It seems Frank was the only one to go back East to Pennsylvania which was only natural since they funded his research and expedition. Mateo and I spoke frequently of the Glyph translations. Apparently the stereo optic photography I sent him was of great value to him. It enabled him to more accurately study the fine detail of the carvings at length. He and Diego shared their talents which naturally produced magnificently detailed artistic renderings.

"What an asset this would be for the world." I thought.

Carlos, with whom I spoke often was working with Mario on the scroll interpretations. His Mayan oral history knowledge was constantly put into play. We all professed our excitement of the return trip to our jungle. Each of us in his own way was making preparations for the return to the as yet unnamed city. It was the reference to the unnamed city that brought to mind the fact that we never did ascertain the name of our "Chosen One". Perhaps the scrolls interpretation will enlighten us.

Chapter 29

With less than five weeks to go I came to the conclusion there was nothing else of interest I could do here in Vermont. I started packing what I thought I would need for the expedition. I did some shopping for the jungle living necessities, the best I could find of course. I was like a child looking forward to sleeping in a hammock again, listening to nature's symphonic serenade.

I even went so far as to rent my house out through a friend who promised to look after it for me. My valued papers, drawings and Mayan photos that I was not taking went to a bank vault for safe keeping.

At the three and a half week point before the start of our sojourn to South America I boarded the plane for Arizona. I knew Frank would be headed there about the same time.

The flight cross country was uninspiring as usual, so I just put my head back and let my imagination take over. Some imagination, I slept straight through. The hostess had to wake me to put my seat upright for landing.

I had made reservations at a housekeeping motel since I would be here for a few weeks. I rented a car, drove to my temporary housing and called Frank. He too was making early preparations.

Preliminary plans were discussed over drinks that night. It was good to see Frank was as enthusiastic as I was. We parted after dinner with the understanding I would see him and the others at the college tomorrow. That was one meeting I was looking forward to.

Only seven months had passed, but you would have thought it was a highschool twenty five year reunion the way we all acted. We had to take our exuberance behind closed doors. We were acting worse than the college kids at a party. We were finally able to curb our excitement and discuss our research up till now.

Late that afternoon Mario and I managed some alone time.

What we had shared with the king sort of gave us that extra bond. We reminisced about our times with the "Chosen One". It appeared that he missed the king as much as I did. We spoke positively of him hoping our relationship with him would grow through the scrolls.

Back at my temporary housing I started reviewing last years notes for the umpteenth time to make sure I did not overlook anything, and possibly even get new ideas for the upcoming expedition. It was good that we could all be working together for a time before we set out for the jungle. This familiarity would make our work easier.

Putting aside my notes I turned to prints I made of the hidden wall murals. I was still astounded at their color and artistic accuracy. Their artistic value aside they were just plain pleasing to look at. Feeling a little sleepy from the excitement of the day I decided to turn in. I nursed a small snifter of cognac while sitting in bed and reviewing the mural pictures. The detail of the ships of many nations, present history had at being unknown to each other, was mind boggling. An actual date had not been pinpointed yet but most likely we are looking at one or two thousand years ago.

I could feel the cognac doing its job so I put the pictures aside, killed the light and buried myself in the pillow. A lat note to myself, pick up a bottle for the trip in case wants to get even this year.

I awoke at four in the morning tearing at my brain. I could not put my finger on it. I couldn't even say if it was a dream or not. Something just did not fit. Fit in what I didn't know. I refreshed myself with a glass of water and went back to bed. I still had four hours before I had to get up.

I was plagued by my four o'clock awakening as I drove to the college. It was not till mid morning when I had an epiphany. I immediately sought out Diego, my young artist friend.

"Diego, do you have prints of the murals with you ?" I asked hurriedly.

"Of course." was his friendly answer. "I study them whenever I can."

"Could you get them please and if you have time, help me look for something."

"What are you looking for." Diego inquired.

"That's just it, I don't know." I answered.

He looked at me confused but proceeded to get the pictures and lay them out on a display table.

"The closest hint I can give you is to look for something that does not fit." I volunteered.

Question marks filling his eyes, he answered with a smile;

"Yeah, right. That males it clear. Should be simple now."

We both had a chuckle over his answer but started looking closely at the photo's.

"I never tire of viewing these works of art." he commented.

"I know what you mean." I mumbled, concentrating on what I don't know.

A half hour passed without another word between us. Diego broke the silence.

"I have a meeting to go to, but you can stay here as long as you like." he offered.

"No, perhaps we both need a break." I said as I started to gather the photo's together. "You go ahead and I'll put these away for you."

"See ya later." he yelled and disappeared through the door.

The rest of the day was productive. I worked with Carlos on his history studies and felt honored to be privy to such sacred information.

The day felt rewarding and accomplished so I headed home. I stopped at a local shop and picked up some dinner makings, not wanting to go out again. I had changed to more comfortable duds and just sat down to eat when the phone rang.

"I think I just found something that doesn't fit. Something you didn't know you were looking for." Diego screamed at me. "Get back here as soon as you can."

"But..." was all I could say when he interrupted.

"I'll leave the back door open for you." And then hung up.

Stuffing a few fork fulls into my mouth while putting on my shoes put me totally off balance. I'm glad the couch was there to catch me. Forty seconds later I was in my rented car aimed back to the college.

The lab door was unlocked as Diego promised. I saw him slumped over a table, large magnifier in hand.

"I'm glad you're here." he said without looking up. "I think I found what doesn't fit."

Eventually he looked at me smiling.

"Here, take this." handing me the magnifying glass.

There on the table was a print of one of the murals that was hidden in the secret passage way. This particular mural combined ships of all Naval era's. Early Phoenician, tall ships of the fifteenth and sixteenth century, Viking dragon ships, and even African bark boats. Detail was painted to perfection. This truly was *"ART"* at its ultimate.

Shaking my head from fine art back to reality I used the glass to scan the print. Moving rather quickly I browsed the photo both horizontally and vertically. I stood back turning to Diego with an obvious blank look on my face.

"Try again." he said, "But slower."

I did as he suggested moving more slowly. Approximately a third of the way down, between a tall ship and the dock, A dark object caught my eye. I studied it for a few seconds then looked up at Diego who was now smiling.

"It doesn't fit does it ?" he commented.

Not believing what I saw, I took another look changing the light angle slightly. It was there and there was no mistaking it. The center control tower of a submarine. But how ? A longer and closer inspection showed its design similar to a nuclear submarine of today. A thought flashed through my confused brain and looking up I said.

"Jules Verne."

My words were echoed by Diego at the same time. Why that name came to mind I have no idea. That's not true I guess. His submarine "Nautilus" was a totally out of place idea in its day. Diego and I were both smiling.

"Could it be." I suggested, "That our mural artist got the idea from Jules Verne ?"

"I would say it was the other way around." countered Diego.

"What do you mean ?" I asked, my mind open to any plausible idea.

"Well, we don't know how long the "Chosen One" actually lived. Chances are it was many hundreds of years. Since he appeared to have a never ending source of knowledge, perhaps he or one of the other Chosen one's taught this to us."

I reflected on this for a bit and conceded that Diego was

more than likely correct.

Carlos entered the lab.

"I was working late and just leaving when I noticed the lights on here. What are you two up to." he inquired casually.

Diego jumped in and related our discovery and what we were positing. You could see the keen interest developing just by the look in his eyes.

"When did Jules Verne write the story ?" he asked.

"I believe it was sometime in the late eighteen hundreds." I answered.

While I was answering, Diego went to his desk sorting through some papers. Finding what he was looking for he turned to us, reading:

"Eighteen sixty nine."

Carlos instantly engaged his "library brain" and within seconds he was smiling.

"That corresponds with some of our history." he stated. "There is a story of our people introducing the non- enlightened people to such things as underwater travel. Of course we were laughed at and our words were disregarded as ridiculous. The lore, in spite of this fact, goes back a lot further though, that it is many hundreds of years the Chosen Ones have practiced this technique."

My mind went to the night Mario and I were on the beach when the king spoke of this to us. That part remained the secret to only Mario and I.

"This mural was painted long before Jules Verne's day." reminded Diego.

"True." answered Carlos. "But that doesn't mean he did not hear about it from our people. Don't forget, the king said there were five Chosen Ones through out our planet. One of those could have been in France, which is where Verne was born, I believe. Jules Verne obviously was one of the few who had an advanced imagination and acceptance of things beyond the immediate world around him."

"Let's just accept the fact that it's there." I interrupted. "Let's face it, all these murals are a point of serious credibility when you consider the probable time period of their creation."

This sort of capped the discussion and just left our unquestionable acceptance.

We knew Frank, Mario and Mateo would also be interested in this discovery, but that could wait till morning.

It was one in the morning when I returned to my now cold dinner.

"Oh well, all for the cause." I thought and I ate it anyway, my mind still going in circles about submarines hundreds of years ago. This certainly is no longer a mundane world. Of course no one is going to believe this and it's going to be next to impossible to prove.

I finally crawled into bed thinking tomorrow is another day.

~ ~ ~ ~ ~ ~

The next morning the others were filled in about Diego's discovery. Frank was thrilled and actually smiled. We all took turns with the large magnifier each making his own comments and suppositions. Collectively we agreed this truly fit with what the king had been suggesting.

Our combined plans for our revisit to the Mayan city were coming together faultlessly. Our shared passion could not be dampened.

Chapter 30

We were actually ready to go a week before our scheduled flight. It felt a little awkward not having anything to do. Except for some paper work accompanying us, all files were secured for our absence. We agreed to keep ourselves from boredom we would visit some of the areas early Native American archeological sites which proved to be quite enlightening. Our Mayan friends were able to point out some similarities in structures and drawing and even language. This was something I never connected before. Again, it seems the king was correct. Their dissemination of knowledge was worldwide. This would, as a matter of fact, change a lot of history as we know it. Unfortunately I most likely will not see any significant changes in my lifetime. Nevertheless this change will come.

Visiting these local sites filled two days for us which was extremely welcome. The day before our actual departure we had a pre-celebratory dinner. This solidified our bond of friendship and gave us high hopes of another successful expedition. Our mood when we parted that night could not have been more relaxed.

Our departure flight was scheduled for nine AM. Because of all the gear we were taking, Frank had commissioned a private plane, approved by the University of Pennsylvania. Our enthusiasm that morning was running high and we were loaded and in the air twenty minutes ahead of schedule. By early afternoon we were checked in at the Juarez Hotel. We would be there two nights to give us time to get all our papers and permits in order.

The heat was the same as last year with daytime highs bordering one hundred and six degrees. As much as I did not like heat of this nature, I did not seem to mind knowing of the discoveries that lay ahead of us.

D-Day finally was upon us and we headed for the boat landing. Not a thing had changed since last year. The same flat bottomed boat was there waiting for us, and, if I'm not mistaken it was the very same boatman. We managed our gear on board and immediately shoved off. It was a duplicate eight hour river voyage into the dense jungle to spend another night in the broken down wooden building which had apparently suffered some additional storm damage last rainy season. No matter it was still home for the night.

All was unloaded and as our transport moved away the silence of the jungle slowly recaptured the atmosphere. Oh how I missed my jungle. My orchestrated symphony of natural sound that I found so mentally and physically relaxing. I was momentarily hypnotized by my surroundings. I could pick out each individual sound though they blended as one major chorus. I knew I would sleep well tonight with the music I had learned to love. Mario gently nudged me back to reality.

"**T**hinking about the king ?" he softly whispered.

I just smiled not wanting to destroy the mood.

We routinely set up an overnight camp, had an MRE meal and turned in for the night.

I was the last to go to bed wanting to savor the evening serenade just a bit longer. My thoughts drifted to the king and I found myself, as wrong as it was, still angry with him for dying. I wondered if any of the other "CHOSEN ONES" were still alive and if so would we ever meet them. Probably not, I told myself. Who knows where on this planet they are or were. My thoughts still on the kings gentleness, I took to my cot and peacefully entered the dream world.

~ ~ ~ ~ ~ ~

Unlike last year I was the first one up and finished making the coffee before anyone stirred. We enjoyed a good breakfast and had everything ready as the two large dugout's pulled ashore. I can't be positive but I believe the same people were manning the paddles as last year.

I found our trek upriver even more enjoyable this time.

Now, knowing what to expect, I guess I was more relaxed and being that way I noticed more of the beauty of the surroundings.

It was three in the afternoon when we spotted last years clearing. The last box of supplies barely touched the muddy ground when both canoes shoved off disappearing down river. Carlos, making light of the matter yelled after them;

"Was it something I said ?"

Even Frank got a chuckle out of it.

We loaded up and were on our way. You could barely pick out the path we took last year. It really is amazing to see how quickly the jungle heals itself from our machete slashing invasion of last year. I had envisioned our trek inland to be easier and faster than previous. That certainly was not the case. Thank goodness I kept myself fit in anticipation of this. We stopped for the night not recognizing a thing from our last visit. The others jeered at me somewhat because I was the first one to have my hammock up. I felt like an expert and was quite proud of myself. They applauded as IU finished with the mosquito netting. I politely bowed in return.

Although tired from our slashing exploits of the afternoon the group was in great spirits. We had a good meal and pleasant conversation. Just like last year I did not want to know what I ate even though I found it quite tasty. Each having his own private thought of the evening we drifted to our respective sleeping area. That's when we heard it. The screaming cry of a large cat. Not that close, yet not that far either. We looked towards each other, still not a word was uttered. Not a sign of discomfort showed even as we heard it a second time, definitely closer. Whether anyone actually closed their eyes right away we'll never know. Some things are very personal. I know I for one turned my attention to other sounds of the night orchestrations. Perhaps I should have been scared but I longed for my symphony much more. Either the night became silent or I fell asleep because the next thing I knew it was daylight. I had coffee brewed and fruit on the table before anybody stirred. I took a little harassment from the others for being so "Gung Ho", but I know it was all in good fun.

Once we hit the trail again I found myself with renewed energy, unlike the prior year of always following last. I knew we were close to the same trail as before yet the jungle was just as unforgiving. The day was long and hard yet somehow appeared rewarding knowing what our destination was. We made camp mid afternoon, mainly because our muscles dictated it. I swear the jungle thicket got tougher over the last year. The rest was welcomed by all. Today our hammocks were the first part of camp setup, everybody choosing a quick siesta before any other work commenced.

That hour's nap brought us back to normal, well sort of, and spirits were high. A better cooperative group did not exist. Our camp routine was just that, routine; yet it was anything but boring.

Just before dark we heard the cat again. It was closer than last nights second cry. We kind of admitted it was probably tracking us, so to be on the safe side we scheduled a watch rotation and made sure the gun was loaded. A second cry sounded from the opposite direction. "Were there two large cats ?" we wondered. Diego assured us it was the same one. He could tell by the voice. We looked at him questioning. Apparently he was holding out on us. He went on to explain his younger training was understanding the life of the jungle, and big cats were his speciality. As long as we can hear the cry we'll be alright. He or she is just disturbed by the presence of something that doesn't belong in his world. As long as we stay alert we should be okay. Thankfully the night passed without incident.

The next morning, maintaining our enthusiasm, we struck out for the lost city. I sometimes wonder how the early explorers got from here to there without GPS. The jungle being so unforgiving and covering it's manmade wounds so quickly, how did they ever return to the original discoveries. The route was extremely difficult this day just like yesterday. I don't believe this is the same trail as the year before, although the GPS confirms we are going in the right direction.

A cry like a women's scream about mid-day alerted us that our local neighborhood cat was still with us. No one showed any emotion one way or the other. I guess that was a good thing. The balance of the day was again routine. Our stalker made his presence known just after dark, which prompted the repeat of the nights watch.

Day dawned to a cool ninety eight degrees. The sky, what we could see of it, appeared clear. Looking forward to the last dat of hacking with our machete's we were about to step off when there before us was our night visitor not more than ten yards away. This was one of the biggest Jaguars I have ever seen. It would have been useless to run knowing their speed and agility. O quiet whisper from Diego not to move while he took a few very slow steps towards the curious cat, who in turn gave out a warning cry. I felt myself stiffen, as I'm sure the others did, then I noticed Carlos slowly raise the gun to a half ready position. Diego took another small step all the time holding eye contact with our visitor. The cat made another growl, this time the volume was down about half. Diego continued this creeping procedure until he was within ten feet of the animal never breaking eye contact. The growls became softer and less frequent and less threatening. Finally there was total silence. Even the jungle was suddenly silent. It was a contest of minds. The natural resident and the intruder. I dared not move to check my watch but I bet a good eight or nine minutes passed ever so slowly, neither pair of eyes being averted. I'm sure the whole team was as tense as I was. Tense but for whatever reason not frightened. Without warning this magnificent creature turned away from Diego and not looking back walked away, not a sound being heard.

Taking our clues from Diego no moved till he did, which was a good two minutes. He faced us smiling softly and said;

"We can go now, he won't bother us."

Leisurely he picked up his burden and moved into the jungle. The five of us stood there dumb founded still not moving. With the renewed sound of Diego's working machete the jungle also came alive. We all chuckled in our own way and without any words being uttered we picked up our packs and followed the sound of Diego into the dense green growth.

~ ~ ~ ~ ~ ~

Late afternoon found us in familiar surroundings. It was like coming home, for me any way. My mind instantly flooded again with my moments with the king. I stall felt his presence. We chose to set up base camp in the plaza where the pyramid of the king's tomb resided. Here is where most of our research will continue.

By dark we were pretty much settled and enjoyed a leisurely dinner. No one pushed Diego for an explanation of the morning's deed. We respected his communion with nature. I for one was thankful he was there for us.

After dinner I was the one to break out the cognac to every ones surprise, for a toast to our success. This we all enjoyed thoroughly.

Chapter 31

We were pleased to see nothing was disturbed. Of course nature was trying to reclaim what was originally hers, but all in all it wasn't in too bad a shape. With more ceremony than usual Carlos opened the sealed door, and each in turn paid his own homage to the kings burial pyre. Mateo checked to make sure it was still secure. I made my way back to the scroll library, hesitating before going inside.

I didn't plan on doing any photography today, I just felt drawn to these bits of history. Locating the hidden lock mechanism I entered and stood there in awe as I did a year ago. With my hand in my pocket I became aware of the treasured glass tube housing the discovery of all ages. Unconsciously squeezing it softly I detected a glow. That had not happened before. Recalling the king's use of the scepter as a lighting instrument, it then dawned on me it may be that perhaps the way it was touched controlled its different functions. Prior to this I had only used it to lift me up the stairs. I would have to further research its varied uses, but not now. I will wait till I am totally alone, since no one knows of this special gift from the king.

Frank interrupted my thoughts entering the library.

"This has got to be one of the greatest finds of archeology." he remarked. I'm glad the king took a liking to you or we may not have ever known about these scrolls. Do you think you'll be able to finish copying them on this trip ?" He was warm in his remarks with his hand resting on my shoulder.

"That is my hope Frank. I know I have enough film this time." I answered smiling.

Diego poked his head into the vault room stating he would be in the mural hallway to continue work on this discovery event the king commissioned him to do.

"Okay" Frank answered, but stay in contact every now and

then."

"Gotcha." Diego called back as he left.

Frank turned back to me asking if he could touch and look at one of the scrolls. It was good to see this new respect he acquired.

"Of course Frank." I returned. "Pick which ever one you want."

He gave me a half smile of thanks and nervously reached for one almost not knowing which to pick. Settling on as choice he carefully, almost reverently, unrolled it.

"Wow" he whispered. "I wish I could read this."

"That makes two of us." I responded softly.

"Three of us." said a voice from behind.

Carlos had joined us.

"It would finally be nice to connect dates to some of this oral history I have stored in my head. I'm sure glad we have Mario. There are not too many like him."

Laughingly Frank added; "With this many scrolls his career is now set for life."

"By the way, where is Mario." I asked.

"He and Mateo are doing some Glyph work by the king's burial pyre." Carlos answered.

"I have some questions for Mateo." Frank said carefully re-rolling the scroll and handing it to me.

He left Carlos and I entranced by this vault of knowledge.

Our preliminary inspection over, which was most of the day, we, one by one managed our way back to the work area. After the usual journal entries we got together for a dinner meeting. We made plans for the weeks ahead, which were a bit ambitious, but we felt up to the task. The evening passed quickly. Without realizing it we were pushing close to eleven. Feeling calm and relaxed we meandered to our chosen sleeping areas. I was glad to be alone at last.

It was not asked for but I felt a bout of melancholy coming on. Being back here the kings presence took control of me once more. Not just missing the king, but the Mayan jungle world engulfing me. I felt completely part of my surroundings. I was more than just being relaxed, it was as if my very soul had become part of the jungle. I found this rather odd, considering my life up to now was metropolitan and suburban. I'd had photo assignments in the wild before but never was I consumed mind, body and soul as I am now since entering this new world.

Forcing myself to move I climbed into my hammock adjusting the netting. I lay back, my hand s behind my head, planning how to orchestrate my symphony of the night, as If I could control it. I felt as if for the first time in my life I was in total harmony with myself and the world. I was truly content. I slowly allowed my mind to bring in the instruments of the night. The birds, the bugs, next the frogs, the infrequent monkey chatter in the background and other creatures yet to be identified, filling in the complete orchestra and chorus. My symphony now complete, I let myself be captured by the music and entered the world of dreams.

Chapter 32

The next four days were productive and fulfilling for us all. Frank was the happiest. The culmination of his dreams was happening right now before his eyes. Forgetting the press and fame; he was working for the sake of knowledge as were we all.

Mario and I shared warm moments with our memories of the king. I still had not revealed information of the king's gift.

We took turns in pairs following up leads of additional outlying settlements. Two or more were discovered and many more yet to be researched. This would turn out to be the largest city state discovered to date and possibly be the oldest. I chose not to speculate on that considering I'm not an archeologist or anthropologist.

This morning it was my turn to stay in camp and prepare lunch and dinner, in between recording data gathered the day before, and journal updates. I looked toward the quiet time to also study my magic sand properties. Could I possibly do more then rise off the ground.

The morning went by quickly and lunch was relaxing and fun, proving even scientists know how to have fun. With lunch over I planned to disappear for a while to see what power, if any, the scepter formula still had. With mixed emotions over doing the testing, I did not want to obsess over it, nor did I want to be taken over by its potential power. The king and I often discussed what man's greed could do to his mind. I am pleased the scepter's total power is no more, but I do admit to a strong curiosity about the small amount of sand I now possess.

I walked the short distance to the river where we fish for additional privacy. I hesitated, but my curiosity won out.

Squeezing it the way I had grown accustomed to, I rose into the air. A repeat of this brought me back to the ground. Trying to remember exactly how I touched the glass container the other day I watched closely as I probed with my fingers. Eventually, results showed themselves as a soft glow started. It slowly grew in intensity as my fingers increased their pressure. It was not an uncomfortable pressure to maintain a wonderful daylight balanced illumination. I held this for a while, then wondered what would happen if I increased the pressure. Looking around to make sure no one was there, just for safety reasons, I took a deep breath and slowly tightened my grip. The light kept the same intensity, so I squeezed even harder. Unprepared for what happened next I almost dropped the glass container. Startled, I watched as a thin, rose hued beam leave the tube in my hand, hit a nearby tree which vanished before me. Instantly I released the pressure and gazed down at the innocent looking glass tube in my hand. I was frightened a bit.

"What have I done ?" I thought. I remembered the king and a similar demonstration he put on for Mario and myself. It too was a rose colored beam but more controlled than what I had just performed accidently.

I sat down, back against a tree and witnessed my hand trembling slightly. I returned the tube of sand to my pocket, took a deep breath, and exhaled slowly while looking at the sky, what little I could through the canopy overhead. I thought about what had just happened. Now I truly understood what the king meant about this power in the wrong hands. He destroyed it to save us from total annihilation. I would keep my souvenir a while longer but promised myself to destroy it also.

I went back to the work area to reestablish reality and lost myself in preparing dinner, my emotions going every which way. It felt like the weight of the world was upon me. I mentally reached out to the king. Of course there was no answer, the king was dead. The thought of reaching out to him though, did make me feel better. Perhaps that was the answer.

The team drifted back one by one asking about dinner. Carlos and Mateo brought news of another small flat topped pyramid approximately one mile south of our present position. As expected, this piqued Frank's interest and he immediately moved to the plotting map to record the find.

Conversation was lively at dinner that night and the good humor was contagious. I topped off the evening by serving a fresh baked cake to everyone's surprise. It was nothing special, only a box mix I managed to squeeze in my personal luggage, icing mix also. The confectionary delight was the hit of the day. It even turned the night time talk to non business topics. All in all it was a much needed escape.

As every evening I looked forward to my nightly lullaby

and promised myself not to dwell on the scepter. Sleep came quickly.

~ ~ ~ ~ ~ ~

Adhering to schedule, four of us were assigned to work in the tomb while Mario and Diego went searching for additional sites. One in particular which was north of our present location, and looked very promising on the air photos.

Research study in the tomb was quiet but constant. We were learning more every dat. Mid-day it was agreed we break for a little lunch and a breath of fresh air. We barely reached the work area when we heard rustling from the jungle outside the entrance portal followed by indistinguishable voices. Thinking Mario and Diego were returning early we paid little attention. Suddenly we heard a voice loud and clear.

"Hey Gringo! What are you doing in my jungle ?"

The accent was heavy and definitely Spanish. Startled, we all looked to the arched portal entrance. Several men dressed in camo garb and carrying what I guessed to be AK-47's stood there, each with menacing looks though each was smiling. The speaker, with a snide laugh continued:

"Oh, I see you have cleared away the vines for my men so they can have a place to rest. That was very nice of you, but you did not ask my permission. That part is not very nice."

The men with him were laughing. They moved further into the compound only to be replaced by several more men similarly attired. They also moved to the cleared area and in turn were replaced by others. They kept coming, group after group, until finally there were about fifty or sixty men filling the plaza. A quick scan of the small army showed a variety of weaponry including small rocket launchers. We were now totally surrounded by this out of nowhere jungle army.

"What is the matter Gringo? You do not know how to talk? I asked you a question."

Frank took a step forward, trying to sound professional and assertive, answered.

"We are a scientific Archeological team doing research on these ancient pyramids. We have all the necessary permits from your government."

Laughter was repeated.

"That may be so sen`or, but you still did not ask my

permission. I am the government here."

Raising his voice slightly, Frank retorted firmly.

"I don't need your permission."

"I see you are very brave sen`or, but also very stupido.  I will forgive you this time because you are just an ignorant American.  I see you have working slaves with you.  Very good sen`or, maybe you are not so stupido."

Protesting voices could be heard at the plaza entrance. Mario and Diego, their hands tied behind them were being prodded forward at gun point.

"Here are two more of your work slaves Gringo."

Our Mayan friends were forced forward to where we stood and with a final push fell to their knees next to us.

Frank instantly stated, almost yelling,

"They are colleagues and scientists, not slaves."

"Sen`or, again you are not being nice to me. You should remember your place." stated the leader in an annoyed tone accompanied by a harsh look.

Carlos stepped forward speaking respectfully and quiet.

"He is right sir. We are scientists studying our history in these ancient ruins."

Hearing this the leader turned his head and nodded to his men. Before any of us could react, a rifle butt slammed into the side of Carlos's head. Down he went with blood seeping from the open gash. I rushed to Carlos and was pushed back.

"Do not waste your time on these inferior beings, sen`or. Ity seems they do not know their place. We conquered them once. I guess we will have to do it again to teach them their place under our rule."

Returning his attention to Frank, the self appointed leader addressed him saying.

"Now, Sen`or Gringo, I will ask you again, what are you doing in my jungle without permission ?  Perhaps you are one of those Yankee spies looking for my gardens.  We do not like that sen`or. You are not welcome here."

You could see Frank was irritated. Knowing how hot his temper could be, I tried to intercede.

"Calm down Frank." I urged.

He waved me away with his hand. Red faced he shouted;

"Listen you ignorant bastard, you are intruding on a government backed research project. Now get your stupid ass out of here and return to the jungle that bore you."

The leaders expression changed to one of instant hate. His eyes remained locked on Frank as he spoke.

"Esteban, this Yankee scum is being disrespectful. Show him the results of his rude attitude."

A figure that entered with and was standing behind the "El Jefe" moved forward approaching Frank. With an action both quick and unexpected by us , he withdrew his machete from his belt and with one uninterrupted motion slashed Frank from the joint of his neck and shoulder down to his belly, leaving the collapsed body at his feet. It was obvious no life remained in the fallen form.

Mario and Mateo attempted to go to the body but I held them back.

"A wise decision, Sen'or. You show good control of your slaves."

At this point I was glad I had closed the scroll library wall.

"We will allow you to be our guest a while longer while we decide whether to kill you now or wait until later."

Other members of the small makeshift army moved to tie our hands behind our backs and herded us under one of the canopy's. We were told to sit on the ground. We remained silent waiting for a chance not to be heard. Carlos was dragged by two men to where we were. He was conscious again and still lightly bleeding. Mario and Mateo managed to scoot over to him and get a bandana against the wound.

"Thank goodness I have a hard head." he quipped. "Don't worry, I will survive this."

The guards kind of let us be while standing about twenty five or thirty feet away. I don't think many of them spoke English anyway. It suddenly dawned on me if I could get hold of my glass tube of magic sand I could get out of here, but in retrospect I could not leave the others. Especially with the disdain in which they were treated.

"Any ideas on how to get out of this mess." I asked.

All eyes locked on mine as if I had the answer. Carlos contributed his two cents.

"We could pile into my car and drive away."

He was smiling through the pain.

"The mural hallway." Diego said aloud.

"What about it ?" we asked.

"If we could get to it we could hide there until they leave." he said enthusiastically.

"Nice try." remarked Mateo, but how do we get there ? The pyramid is still sixty yards away."

Mario looked at me. I knew what he was thinking. If we could get there we could escape to the jungle. He and I were still the only two to know about the secret doorway to the outside. It emptied out far enough away from the structure to possibly negotiate an escape. Speaking to all, yet Mario knew I meant him, I said;

"Let's give that some thought and see if we can create any other ideas, such as how do we cross that sixty yards in the open with numerous soldiers between us and the pyramid."

There was some commotion by the portal. Looking up we could see a few men dragging Franks body out to the jungle. They returned rather quickly which means they just dumped it somewhere in the undergrowth. After witnessing that we were silent again. I'm sure we were all paying homage to Frank in our own way.

Hours passed slowly. Carlos, in spire of the blood loss was regaining strength. He reminded us in a whisper that his hands were not tied. It's funny it had not hit upon us that this was a fact. Over the next half hour we, on by one, maneuvered over to him to untie us. We kept our hands behind us holding the ropes in place. At least that was one step toward freedom. I must admit though, the chances of escape looked pretty slim, what with fifty odd gunman about.

"What if we can make up a story of some kind to get them to lead us to the tomb." suggested Diego.

"That sounds good." answered Mateo, "Except that it is literally the tomb of the "Chosen One". I, for one, don't want to think about what they may do to the kings coffin."

"I'm glad we resealed the main door." added Carlos.

"Let us hope that it will be enough of a deterrent to keep them out." I speculated

"Okay, let's work on this." said Mario "If we do get to the tomb it takes two of us to open it. That's kind of like advertising what we're doing. Any other suggestions.

There was a few minutes of silence. Smiling slightly, he followed with;

"Don't all talk at once." trying to keep their situation light.

Nothing was forthcoming. Silence prevailed.

Mateo spoke softly;

"Do you think there would be a chance after dark ?"

That gave me an idea. Without explaining my whole plan I volunteered to go after dark, but then it hit me. To what end. If one of us does get to the tomb, then only one of us gets to hopefully escape. That's just not right I told myself. I explained my reasoning to the others. Back to square one.

Dusk settled over the plaza and small fires started throughout the compound. The men gathered in small groups around the many fires. Our food supply was raided and literally stripped bare. Diego noticed a dropped piece of fruit. Ay great personal risk he managed to retrieve it. It was slowly fed to Carlos to hopefully further rejuvenate his strength.

Full darkness was now upon us and gave me a further sense of aloneness. My active mind took over again.

"The sand." I thought. "It does have the power to destroy, only I don't know how to control it yet. If I was to try to use it, not really knowing how, I could wind up getting us killed earlier then El Jefe planned and to what gain. Think Eric, Think. Do I dare use a potential power I know nothing about ? What if I blow my chance and the sand falls into the hands of these wacko's ? Talk about scary. Having a conscience can be frustrating sometimes and this is one of those times."

I gazed through the dark at the others and you could tell, like me , their minds were working. Stay positive I told myself.

It was already after nine o'clock so it seemed to me they had nothing more planned for us tonight. That gave me until daylight to come up with some sort of escape plan. But what? Carlos needs some serious medical attention. I'm surprised he's holding up as well as he is. If there could only be some sort of diversion, then perhaps we could make it to the tomb for safety.

I tried to think of how we could create the necessary

diversion. My thoughts were giving me no answer. I could feel myself getting discouraged. My mood changed just as abruptly. The lights finally came on in my brain. We could not create a diversion, but I could...

Chapter 33

    I waited patiently for another hour to pass. The major part of our captors were asleep. There were now only three men watching us and frankly they weren't doing a very good job. I asked myself if I should take this opportunity, I might not get another. Trying not to disturb my four colleagues I quietly reached into my pocket to retrieve my scepter sand. A fast look around and gauging the right moment from my sitting position, I gently increased my hand pressure on the glass container and ascended slowly to about twenty feet, then took up a course over the wall into the jungle.

    Once out of sight of the compound I could feel myself relax and breathe easier. Eventually I found my way to the river where I touched down to the jungle floor. I figured I had approximately seven hours before daylight. Do I really want to do what I'm thinking of doing ?   I really wasn't sure. I tried to reason that it was to help my friends, but I'm not sure I even believed in myself.

    I did do some practicing of aiming the beam and seeing how much power I could generate. I was able to vaporize a few small rocks. Perhaps I could use it on the weapons they carried. I decided that was not a good idea either. Maybe if they put the weapons down ?

    I rested a while my head still swirling. The angel and the devil in me fighting it out. My final decision was made just before dawn when I returned to the compound. Nothing was stirring, even the guards were half asleep. I floated down slowly to the very same spot I left from, and returned my special container to my pocket.

    Mario whispered , "I'm glad you're back." He smiled and rested his head back on his arm.

    He knew, I realized. I smiled to myself and vowed to share the whole secret with him when I got the chance.

Chapter 34

Daylight was showing through the trees and soon a few sunbeams were touching the open compound. Our unwanted guests began to stir. They really were a lazy bunch. They were laughing and eating the rest of our stores. During the night my Mayan friends managed to tend to Carlos's injury as best they could. No one even seemed to notice. It appeared they did not care we no longer had our hands tied.

El Jefe and his few close confidants lazily crawled out of our hammocks. From the looks and smell of them, they had not bathed in weeks. Apparently it didn't bother them in the least. The morning ritual out of the way the head man shouted a few garbled commands in Spanish. The men formed into a few groups, except the ones guarding us. We had no choice but to watch though our minds were on escape. One of the men with a rocket launcher knelt down on one knee and took aim at the pyramid.

Diego saw this and panicked.

"The murals." he shouted. That's the side with the murals."

He took off in a run for the rocket launcher screaming.

"Stop ! No ! Wait ! You can't do that. Stop !" he screamed even louder.

That was the last word he spoke. As feared by the rest of us, many shots rang out and Diego fell to the ground motionless. A few overly exuberant soldiers moved closer to the fallen body and fired many more shots into our already dead companion.

Mario inched closer to me whispering;

"Go now, my friend while you have the chance. I know you can. I saw you last night, so go."

"I can't leave you guys while there's still hope." I whispered back.

"Hope ! What hope ?" Mario said as if giving up. "There is no hope. You saw what just happened. They even enjoyed it."

We looked toward Diego once more as two men, each holding a leg dragged the limp body into the jungle.

Only now, for whatever reason, did our guards realize we no longer had our hands tied. Mumbling phrases in Spanish they ran to us and with their feet pushed us down to a prone position. El Jefe saw this and started toward us but stopped when he heard the firing of the rocket launcher. It hit the side of the pyramid that had Diego so upset. The explosion was loud and destructive. This was apparently exhilarating to the jungle army. They shouted, cheered and laughed. Another soldier repeated this, if soldier is the right word to use for these maniacs, and the tomb took a second hit just as destructive. The mob cheered again as a third man prepared to fire.

"Mateo." shouted Mario, "When I say go, run to the east as fast as you can. I'm going to the west."

I looked at Mario with shocked and pleading eyes.

"Do your thing my friend." smiled Mario. "God speed and tell our story to the world. Now Mateo, run."

I directed my eyes to Carlos. He had passed out. Turning back to Mario to plead with him not to do this, it was too late. Both he and Mateo were gone. I thought for a second they were going to make it, but that was just wishful thinking. In less than ten seconds you could hear the gunfire.

This was my distraction and up I went. Anxiously waiting for the bullets to catch up with me I observed the collapse of the kings tomb as rocket after rocket found it's mark to the cheers of the ignorant. One half of the tomb was now in rubble. The side not yet hit by rocket fire was where the scroll library was. T^he fact that it was still standing and solid was a testament to the Mayan engineering and construction methods.

Luckily for me no one looked up. I moved to the undamaged part of the structure and let myself down to the jungle floor. There was enough commotion in the plaza to cover my absence.

I was truly disturbed by the brutal slaying of my friends yet there was nothing I could have done.

I knew what I had to do and there was not much time. The group partaking in target practice were re-supplying themselves with rockets to continue their destruction of the kings place.

At a distance of about thirty feet and guessing approximately where the library was I aimed the magic sand vial and squeezed and kept increasing pressure until I saw the rose hued beam. Seconds later there was nothing there. I knew the scrolls were now lost forever. I felt terrible, but I also felt good. They would never be in the wrong hands. Who knows what knowledge they contained and how it would be used.

The vanishing act made quite an impression on the gang in the plaza. They stood there, eyes wide and mouths open. A few dared to advanced to the ruins trying to figure out what just happened as they watched. I took this as my cue to get away as fast as I could. I went farther into the jungle as fast as I could. Either they had not discovered I was missing or they didn't care or possibly didn't remember how many of us there were. I would rest for a while and check the camp later.

Because of lack of sleep I dozed off against my wishes. It was mid-afternoon when I awoke. Still groggy, I set off for the plaza and camp. Of course I took to the air again. I figured it would be safer.

Approaching as high as I dared I surveyed the plaza and a significant area around. Not a soul was to be seen, but to be on the safe side of caution I lowered down behind the rubble that once was the kings tomb. Seeing the wanton destruction made my heart heavy. That on top of witnessing my friends brutally cut down brought on emotions I never knew I had. I could feel my chest heaving and my eyes begin to tear. I made no attempt to control them and just let it happen.

With no tears left in me I composed myself and set about a job I really had no stomach for. It took close to three hours but I finally located the bodies of my dear friends. Carlos was still where I saw him last only this time with several bullets in his head. It wasn't much and I did the best I could with their burials.

I collected what I could of their personal things but it was obvious even the bodies had been plundered. My emotions of loss and love had now turned to anger and hate.

I salvaged what little I could for my trek out of here. There wasn't much to save for one machete and two MRE's that were overlooked. The plotting table and all the maps were totally destroyed. There was not a record left of the year and a half's work and devotion all of us put onto this expedition except for some papers locked up at the small Arizona college, and the photocopies of the scrolls I did on our first trip. With a last look and a small prayer, I said goodbye to my five colleagues and the "Chosen One".

Going strictly by the sun I set out, on foot, for civilization.

-138-

Chapter 35

     Thank goodness for the machete or who knows how long it would have taken me to find my way back. I did take to the air a few times though just to ascertain that I was going in the right direction. I perhaps could have used my little glass tube more, but I did not know how long it would last, in spite of the kings assurance that it would be forever. I recalled it only took three and a half days to come into the jungle but we also had GPS to guide us. Who knows how or what the GPS was being used for now. I'm glad I learned so much from my Mayan friends. Not knowing certain things could be disastrous in the jungle. I knew I would not starve and I felt certain I was headed in the right direction.

     The river and the broken down cabin by the landing was a welcome sight. It gave me renewed confidence and at least a roadway to follow to safety. Because of the Caman population along the river banks it was much too dangerous to travel by land, therefore I would need some sort of water transportation. At least I had a real roof over my head tonight. That little bit extra was also most welcome. I knew this might be the last time to be an audience to the symphony of the jungle which I tried to enjoy regardless of what had transpired over the last week or so. My night time music, combined wit exhaustion allowed me a nights rest.

     I awoke at sunup, had some fruit to eat and reflected on breakfasts past with my friends. Struggling to pull out of this self imposed funk, I at last was able to face my next challenge, boat building. Well, not actually a boat, solely something to keep me afloat. Surveying my nights lodgings I decided no one would miss a few boards off the sides that could be made into a raft. It would be a bit much for one man to handle, especially if a Caman became too curious. Then again, what other choice did I have.

     I don't know what drew me to it, providence perhaps, but I stumbled on to a sort of gate type door that gave access to a storage space under the already falling apart cabin. It was dark and almost scarey because of some very ugly, hairy looking spider things. My mystical sand saved the day yet another time.

"How lucky can you be Eric." I said aloud.

There before me was a ten or twelve foot canoe. A dugout canoe. It seemed in pretty good shape but I really would not know till I got it out into the daylight.

"Oh lucky me, another challenge." I muttered out loud again.

A struggling forty minutes later it was in the sunlight in all its glory. On close inspection I decided it would do. It would have to, I didn't have much of a choice. Lack of choices seem to be routine with me lately.

I made a makeshift paddle and as afterthought designed and built a type of outrigger to help me keep from turning over. What I did not need now was a swim with the Camons. Before I knew it the sun had begun to set. Oh well, one more night in this so called shelter. I finished the last MRE and lay down thinking of home.

~ ~ ~ ~ ~ ~

Startled awake, I opened my eyes yet did not stir. I definitely could hear movement outside. The cat was the first thing that came to mind, but this was much too noisy for a large cat. Then I thought of the camo-clad thugs who so freely shot people. Now I was frightened. I was afraid to even blink. Then I heard some clattering sounds like a wooden drum.

"The canoe." I panicked.

Dawn's light was creeping across the river as I ever so slowly moved to the glass- less window. Not wanting to be seen I noticed a crack between two wall boards, enough for a quick peek. I identified the noise and breathed a sigh of relief. Two curious monkeys were about the canoe and banging the makeshift paddle. I quickly moved to the door, the noise of which alerted them as they ran screeching for the trees. I surveyed the canoe for damage and found none. I breathed even more easily.

Surprisingly I received very few mosquito bites over night considering I had no netting, Then again they probably stayed away from me because I smelled so bad not having washed for days.

There was nothing to eat so I launched my vessel. I let it

soak up what ever water it would drink for an hour before getting in myself. So far so good. I reached for the paddle, stroked the water and was on my way. I can't tell you how good I felt knowing I was returning to a more hospitable place. I loved the jungle and the symphonies it played for me but right now I just wanted to go home.

I was only in a canoe once in my life at boy scout camp. The canoe then was designed to cut through the water easily. All I was in now was a dead tree with a hollowed out space in the middle. It didn't cut or glide through the water, it sort of pushed it like a bull dozer. Controlling it was not an easy job. At least I was heading in the right direction. I paddled till my arms hurt and I grew tired, then I would let it drift a while. That's what the plan was anyway. When I stopped the paddle motion the canoe all but stopped. I was thankful there were no rapids in this river, none that I remembered anyway.

Time dragged on. Maybe I should have stayed in the air. Recalling it was an eight hour trip up river with a motor, I figured this should take me three days. The air route was tempting but I did not want to risk being seen. I'll just have to take my chances resting at night. A rain, however, would be welcome about now. It would help keep the mosquitos away and I'd be able to wash up a bit. Then maybe I could stand being next to myself.

The next two days went by without a hitch. It was slow going but I was going.

Memories of the king and my friends were constantly plaguing me. Soon I would be at a place where I could report this whole experience to the authorities. Perhaps some proper justice could be extolled.

At last, there it was, the boat landing. What a sight. I don't know why but some sort of second sense took hold of me. I decided to hide the king's present in my shorts, making sure it was undetectable and secure. The last thing I wanted was to lose that or worse yet, have it discovered by someone else. Someone who may be the wrong type of person.

I managed, with some difficulty to get my log transportation to shore. I was hot, tired, hungry and just plain worn out. Resting for a few minutes let mt catch my breath before I walked the short distance to town. When I arrived at the main street, actually the only street, I recognized what would pass for the local constable.

"Take me to the authorities, please." I asked. "I want to report a brutal slaying and multi murders."

I guess he understood enough English because he answered;

"Si Sen'or, come this way." In very broken English.

I followed him down an ally to the rear of what passed for the general store. Above the back door the sign read, "Policia" The office was considerably bare, housing a crudely built cell, iron bars and all. Behind the corner desk was a thin mustached, lean man sporting a sly scowl. He was dressed in a wrinkled khaki uniform wearing captains bars, a silver star on his left pocket.

I spoke right up;

"I want to report a murder, several murders, brutal murders."

I could feel myself getting tense. The captain stood, smiled and in perfect English, said,

"We have been waiting for you Sen'or. You are under arrest. I'm glad you are confessing to these crimes so willingly. We like to keep law and order in our country."

As the captain was speaking, he nodded to the constable, who instantly grabbed my arms and had cuffs on me before I knew what was happening.

"What do you mean, under arrest. I'm here to report these murders, not confess. I saw who committed them." I shouted in answer.

"Ah, but Sen'or we have an eye witness. A very reliable witness." the captain replied.

"What witness ? I'm the witness. I'm the one reporting the crime. Now let me go and I'll show you where this took place."

"Nice try Sen'or, but do you really think I'm that stupid."

I hesitated for a second but finally said exactly what I was thinking.

"Yes, you are stupid if you're arresting me while the real murderer gets away."

The captains face quickly changed expression from the sly smile to a look of contempt, at the same time his arm swung up and dealt a stinging slap across my face..

"That was not very nice Sen'or." he added. "Show him to his room, Ramon."

I was roughly pushed to a cell. I ended up on my knees next to the wooden plank that served as both seat and bed. Ramon smiled a happy smile as he slammed the iron door shut.

As he was exiting the office a camo uniformed man came in. It was him. The El Jefe of the cut throat band that destroyed the tomb and my friends.

"**T**hat's him." I yelled from the floor. "That's the murderous bastard who killed my five friends."

By now I was standing close to the bars of the cell. Back to the sly smile, the captain replied.

"**Y**ou must be mistaken Sen`or. This is the esteemed Colonel Mendez of our militia. He is our witness ti the dastardly slaying you perpetrated on your colleagues. He is here to sign his sworn statement."

"**B**ut I'm telling you, he's the one who killed them. He destroyed our whole Archeological study." I screamed repeatedly.

"**A**h, there again Sen`or, you did not have permission to be there." the captain replied softly.

"**W**e had all the proper permits from your government." I returned.

"**Y**ou are not listening Sen`or, you did not have our permission to be there." was the repeated answer.

"**W**hy am I arguing with you. You are the one who does not understand. I feel sorry for you in your ignorance." I said more softly.

"**W**e shall see soon enough Sen`or, who is the ignorant one.

The captain smiled and turned away. He returned to the colonel by the door holding out his hand. He blatantly received a pile of dollars or pesos or what ever they use for money down here. Both looked at me laughing lightly until the colonel left. Moments later the captain left.

~ ~ ~ ~ ~ ~

Here I was hungry, tired, dirty and sitting alone in a jail cell. I calmed down somewhat so I could think. It was only a few days ago that everything was looking so rosy.

"**N**o pity party, Eric." I said aloud. "You have got to think of what your next move will be."

I spent the rest of the day totally alone. Not even Ramon returned to check on me and of course no food. That certainly did not help my attitude. I made the decision to wait for dark.

"Might as well get some rest."

There I go again, talking to myself.

Laying down presented a problem with my hands cuffed behind my back. With very little effort I was able to pull my wrists apart. On closer inspection the cuffs appeared to be children's toy hand cuffs constructed of cheap plastic. One easy step towards freedom I thought.

I must have dozed off from exhaustion because the next thing I knew it was dark. I sat up to get my bearings. No one had returned. I tried the cell door, unfortunately it was not made of plastic. It was ten o'clock and nothing appeared to be moving out side, but to err on safety's side I waited until after midnight.

At twelve twenty I retrieved my glass tube. After one last look around, I aimed at the back wall and squeezed. Moments later the familiar rose beam shot out and a section of the wall quietly disappeared. I waited in a corner for a few minutes to see if there was any reaction from outside. I heard and saw nothing. Moving ever so slowly I made my way to the missing wall. Still hearing nothing I finished my exit. My friendly jungle music was all there was to be heard in the distance calling to me. It was amazing, the calming effect it had on me. Rather than risk running into anyone I chose to take to the air.

I let myself down at the rivers edge. Here I could stay until there was enough light to navigate properly.

Chapter 36

It was good to be on the move at last. I followed the river curves staying just inside the wood line. Low enough to clear the trees. When I felt a comfortable enough distance from the town I set down to find something to eat.

My stomach now satisfied along with a short rest, I continued my journey to safety and hopefully justice.

It was a long two days when I finally sighted Candelaria. I set down and walked the last two hours. Exiting the jungle I was almost unnoticed. After a few different inquires I located the office of some local authority. I told my story but could tell it was not believed.   Notes were not even being taken. After many frustrating hours I was politely ushered out. I believe they thought I was a bit touched in the head.

I found a clothing store and purchased some new clothes and shoes. Not exactly my style but they would do. Thank goodness my wallet was not confiscated. I still retained my credit cards and passport.

Satisfied with my new attire I found a hotel to check into. A shower and shave made me feel totally renewed. I donned my new dids and made for the closest restaurant.

While eating, my thoughts were flowing like water, confusing though they were. Why could I not get anyone to believe me ? Was this a commonplace story around here ? Am I the one that's losing my mind ?

My thoughts then turned to transportation. The first thing tomorrow I would make arrangements to get to the nearest city with an airport. I was told there was a train to Campeche. It was a slow, boring ride but it did giver me some much needed rest time. I even managed a few hours of sleep.

Campeche was my next destination. The authorities there

treated me pretty much the same. Perhaps I am losing my mind. No matter, I felt so much safer now even with the sorrow I carried for my friends. I also thought about the great historical loss of the new Mayan city. That piece of history will never be recovered now. I am the only one witness to it and who is going to believe me, a non Archeologist. What a shameful loss to all mankind.

~ ~ ~ ~ ~ ~

My return flight to the states was anti-climatic. Checking in with customs at the Tucson airport in Arizona, I inquired about who to talk to about my frightful experience. I wanted to report this heinous crime and seek justice. I was directed to the embassy of Belize at Washington, D.C. There was, however, a local office and an undersecretary at Tucson.

A day later I was repeating my tale. I received the usual boiler plate answer. "They will look into it."

"Doesn't anybody care." I said out loud as I left that office.

Out of frustration I headed home to Vermont. I would write my experiences down and see what mu local Senator and State Department could accomplish. All I knew was that I would forever have this sadness deep inside me.

~ ~ ~ ~ ~ ~

The remainder of my trip home was trance like. I was operating on auto pilot, not caring about anything.

Lucky for me the one who rented my house terminated the lease early and moved out of state.

It was almost dusk when I entered the house. I went right to the liquor cabinet and poured a double Cognac. I sat down at the kitchen table and stared out the window into the darkness waiting for my jungle serenade to start. Another disappointment.

I sat there in my dazed state for a couple of hours. I don't even know if I was thinking or not.

Chapter 37

The phone ringing shook me awake. I was at a loss as to where I was. I finally grabbed the receiver on the fifth ring.

"I thought you were never going to answer." said a familiar voice.

"Frank ?" I quizzed. "Frank, is that you ? But you're." I stopped myself.

"Are you alright Eric ?" Frank asked. "I've been calling all day. Are you sure you're alright."

"Uh, Oh. Sure. I'm fine. I must have been asleep." I answered still groggy.

"Good for you. I wish I could grab a nap during the day." he joked. "I'll get right to the point of why I called. We're planning our second trip to the lost city and were hoping you would join us again. The others are counting on you. I have to admit you were of great value to us last year."

I was silent, thinking about what apparently was a dream, or more like a nightmare, I just experienced.

"Eric, you still there ?"

"Yes Frank, I'm still here. Sorry Frank, I'm going to have to beg off on this one. My schedule just won't permit the time. I wish all the guys good luck and success."

Frank was of course disappointed but seemed to understand. Another minute or so of general gossip and we hung up.

My mind instantly went to the vial of sand. I went to the mantle only to find it not there. I reached into my pocket and closed my hand around it, walked straight to the bathroom and flushed the magic sand down the toilet.

"Good bye, Old Friend."

The Dead Living Mummy

Part III

Chapter 38

I stood there in a dazed state for a while staring at the bowl, spellbound by the ripples in the water. When the tank filled and the sound of the rushing water stopped, I was jolted awake.

"Eric." I scolded. "What have you just done ?"

I stared at the empty vial. Upon closer inspection there was not a grain of sand to be seen. Without thinking I returned the urn to my pocket and went back to the kitchen. I repeated my earlier question aloud.

"What have you just done ? What stupid thing have you just done ? "Do you really want to throw away the second chance of a lifetime ?"

I suddenly felt fully recovered and reached for the phone. I punched in the appropriate numbers and listened to the ring.

"Frank? Eric here. I don't know what I was thinking before, I guess I was still asleep. Of course I'll join you. At this point you couldn't keep me away."

Frank was genuinely pleased with my answer and repeated how happy the others were going to be. We spoke briefly of some preliminary plans but since we had many months to go we agreed to fine tune things at a later date.

After I hung up the phone I couldn't believe how good I felt. The dreams hold on me, or more like the nightmare's hold on me, finally released its grip. Happy with myself I proceeded to make a new pot of coffee.

Reaching into my pocket I retrieved the vial, took one last look at it and threw it into the garbage pail with no regrets. Oh yes, I would miss the few conveniences it afforded me but I absolutely believed I did the right thing just as I had agreed with the king. I was not the one to hold the power of the world, let alone be its caretaker. No matter how hard I tried I still did not understand why the king chose me to be his confidant. I was neither Mayan nor qualified as were the others. My thoughts led me right back to the magic sand I just disposed of.

My emotions played angel and devil with me again. Should I have done what I just did ? Why get rid of something that was one of a kind in the world ? I answered my own question as reality took over. There was not a darn thing I could do about it now. My gift from the king was gone forever. Obviously there was no need to mention it to anyone, not even Mario. I laughed at my self as I walked to the bathroom and flushed the toilet again for pure satisfaction.

I forcibly cleared my mind deciding I should return to the real world and try to accomplish some work. I still had to pay bills. My day was extremely busy after my morning's little interlude and I felt no qualms about returning to my research work later in the afternoon.

Hints of my dream crept back into my mind as I started reviewing the copies of the wall paintings. I even caught myself looking for the submarine. In a way I was glad no such thing appeared.

Enough wishful thinking, tomorrow I would continue more serious work on the scrolls. The thought that they might hold the answer to the world's questions was truly intriguing.

Chapter 39

I was up early, skipped breakfast and engaged my profession as diligently as I could to take care of the paying jobs first. I was all fired up about my return to the kings lost city and knew that a lot more research would be necessary in preparation and I wanted to give myself as much time as possible to complete it.

My mind was fighting a battle with itself all day between keeping on the job at hand and thinking of the king and his teachings.

~ ~ ~ ~ ~ ~

The next few weeks turned into months, while I worked non stop to fulfill my two priorities; first to build up enough capital to outfit myself for the next expedition, secondly, and just as important, to continue study and research in order to prepare for whatever we may encounter at the lost city.

I no longer considered myself a neophyte. I knew I had a long way to go to be any kind of professional archeologist or anthropologist but I proudly felt I was beyond the neophyte stage. I patted myself on the back for having successfully come as far as I have. So much for self praise.

I thought of the king often. I was still angry with his passing because there was so much more I wanted to learn from him. The most intriguing, I guess, was who he really was and where did he originate from ? Was he always a "Chosen One"

~ ~ ~ ~ ~ ~

All in all the work went well. So well in fact I was ahead of the time schedule I set for myself. By maintaining frequent contact with the others I learned they also were further along than they expected.

Apparently our multi discipline team was performing beyond our mutual expectations.

~ ~ ~ ~ ~ ~

The scrolls turned out far better than I anticipated considering the lighting conditions I was working with. I truly hoped Mario would be successful interpreting the symbols they contained. I don't know why, but I just had a feeling that whatever revelations came out of this effort would be earth shattering and forever change history as we now know it.

A sudden protective feeling flushed through my being. I knew the original scrolls were safe, at least for now, in the kings tomb. Right now these negative copies that I was shooting took on a new importance that I had not felt before.

I spent the next day and a half duplicating all the negatives. These duplicates would now be my working copies. Upon completion I secured the originals in a safety deposit box in the bank vault. I then proceeded to write an explanation of their value, sealed the envelope, only to be opened by my expedition colleagues if something were to ever happen to me.

~ ~ ~ ~ ~ ~

With my latest call to Mario it was agreed that I spend a few weeks with the team in Arizona. Together we could better finalize the plans with all present. A change of climate and scenery wouldn't hurt either. The warmer weather would help me prepare for the upcoming heat of the jungle.

I smiled to myself as an after thought because of my anticipation of the return to my jungle serenades.

"You will have all you want my friend."

These words suddenly filled my head. The voice was so clear that I looked around the room for its owner. My body followed with a shudder.

"That's him." I said aloud. "The king is alive. He must

-151-

be."

I waited for more. There was no more. The echoes in the room were silenced as fast as they had occurred. Sheepishly I looked around almost embarrassed at my actions.

"I'm glad I'm alone." I thought. *"I'm really losing it. I must get a hold of myself. I'm a grown man and I should not let myself get carried away with these mental wanderings."*

A cold glass of water helped me regain a sense of normalcy, but I still wondered about the king's voice in my head.

Packed and ready to go, I ran through a mental check list to assure nothing was left undone. At last satisfied, my taxi arrived and off I went to the airport with the excitement of a child.

Chapter 40

After checking in at the motel, I hastily headed for the college. It took a few inquiries, but eventually I located the right building.

Our reunion was as exciting as I anticipated, it did not have the furor of the one in my dream, nevertheless we did have to tone our noise level down a notch. It really was great to see these guys again. I found it amazing that a project like this could cement a relationship such as ours. A half hour of catch up stories and we finally settled down and began to act like adults again. Frank amazed all of us by his willing participation in our exuberance of the moment.

Not too much actual work was accomplished the rest of the day, only sharing and updating each other on achievements to date.

Before we quit for the day, Diego pulled me aside and mentioned he had something special to show me; something that did not seem to fit with the wall murals. My mind was quick to panic although I had no reason to do so.

"Why is this dream plaguing me?" I asked myself trying not to look alarmed. I agreed to meet with him alone a little later.

I waited in the car till I was sure everyone else left for the evening, then returned to Diego's work room. Not knowing what to expect, I let him take the lead. Making sure no one else was around Diego closed the door and directed me to the back table where he uncovered one of the enlargements of the tomb paintings. I could feel myself getting tense as he pointed to the area of the submarine of my dream. Handing me a magnifier he said;

"Look, this just doesn't seem to fit."

The area indicated surely did not fit with the rest of the painting. It did not take me long to realize the problem and I breathed a sigh of relief, it was not my dream taking shape again.

Apparently a drop of black ink fell onto the finished print

and dried in such a way as to make an unidentifiable distinctive shape. I explained this to Diego and even he was relieved. His reasoning in pointing it out to me privately was not to have Frank think I was doing a shoddy job. I thanked him and appreciated his concern but mentioned it wasn't necessary. I didn't think Frank was that petty. A replacement print could easily be made.

As he relaxed he said;

"As much as I like viewing the photo copies I sure do miss being with the originals."

"I know what you mean." I answered. "Not just their beauty but for their historical significance."

We parted company for the evening, both much relaxed and worry free.

On the drive back to the motel my thoughts drifted to the jungle and the soothing evening music of nature. I was so caught up in my memories, I passed the motel by about six or so miles. I reversed direction, stopped for some Chinese take away and at last found my lodgings. TV was the usual wasteland, so radio music filled the void while I ate. It was nine PM yet I was alert as ever and decided to review last year's notes.

It's funny how the least little thing can trigger a memory, even though it wasn't an old one. As I read my journal remarks of the king, the room once again filled with his voice.

"There is much to learn, Eric, even though I will not be there with you physically."

Unconsciously I looked around as before, and of course there was no one there.

"Am I imagining this voice or is the king actually communicating with me. Perhaps I am more tired than I thought." I quizzed myself.

"Do not lose faith in me my friend. With you I can yet accomplish many things. Let us not fail to move the people forward. Do not give up hope in me, in yourself or on this planet."

This time the voice appeared to be more distinct. Again I

looked around the room. There was only me. I put down my notes, sat back and cleared my eyes. The kings image came into view sitting on the special bench in the tomb, the same questioning smile accompanied the all knowing eyes.

"Accept my voice Eric, and yes, ask what you must. When the time is right you will have your answer."

Slowly my eyes opened, I felt groggy and that was even before I had a drink. I felt like an external power had taken over my mind and body. As an after thought I guess that's exactly what it was. If the king can contact me this far away, what is it going to be like when we get to the tomb.

A sudden feeling overcame me as if my body demanded rest. I did not fight it.

~ ~ ~ ~ ~ ~

I rose early the next morning without a trace of the tired's. There was however, a vague trace of last night's events which I chose to ignore successfully. A substantial breakfast and a second cup of coffee and I felt ready to face the world.

It was great to be working with the team again. We were no longer just study companions but shared in the association of true friendship. Our departure date would soon be upon us and our excitement was building. We again decided on a departure celebration dinner two days before leaving. The mood was pleasant with not too much business being discussed. Frank graciously toasted me for the gift of the jade pieces I gave him. Their value actually made this second trip possible. The university's budget was a bit lacking this year.

Our final day was spent checking and double checking each others lists so nothing was left out. All was delivered to our chartered plane and we were finally on our way.

Before we knew it, we were checking into the Juarez Hotel where nothing had changed including the temperature. With a light supper and a quiet night we slept anticipating the next days trip up the river.

Haunted by my dream yet again, as we walked down to the

boat ramp we passed the local constable. Ignoring the others he gave me a sly smile of recognition, while nodding his head. The name on his ID badge was Ramon and from his belt hung the same plastic handcuffs that adorned my wrists in the dream.

"This can't be happening." I told myself. *"I never saw this man before today except in my dream."*

I hid the fact I was a bit upset as best I could as we loaded our equipment on board the slow moving motorized boat, and yes the boatmen were the same as last year.

It was a lazy ride up river to the same landing as last year. My dream proved true again as we observed the broken down wooden building even more decrepit than the previous year.

Even though we were up early, the two canoes were already waiting to take us further up river on a slow but enjoyable ride. Most of us managed to catch a few winks. The quiet sound of the jungle and the slow rhythmic paddle strokes was very conducive to the hypnosis of sleep.

We reached our second landing, and once unloaded, the canoes disappeared as quickly as they appeared.

A relaxing night with minimum effort and we were all in our hammocks early. I felt totally at home with my jungle nighttime sonata.

~ ~ ~ ~ ~ ~

We departed early for the tomb and surprisingly there was no big cat incident. I casually brought it up in conversation and received a classic reaction from Diego, who admitted he hated the big cats and was terrified of them. Well, so much for the dream.

The trail was somewhat over grown since last year yet identifiable enough so no time was wasted. As usual I drifted to the sound of this magnificent green beauty.

"Oh, how I missed this music." I thought to myself.

"It is peaceful, is it not Eric, especially in today's upsetting world."

I was no longer disturbed by the kings interruptions.
I hoped it would continue when we got to the tomb. I did remember,

however, what the king had said about me allowing his thoughts to be received, and right now I wanted my music. Without much effort I closed my mind to the king and let the jungle sooth my whole being.

Enthusiasm was high knowing this was our last day of slashing through the jungle. The thought of being at the lost city and tomb spurred us on like excited children. Not much could have stopped us this day.

Soon we reached the plaza archway, its splendor still held us captive. The surrounding jungle had started it's reclamation but not enough to hide its beauty. Quietly and slowly we passed through its portal to the same plaza we set up camp a year ago. Carlos without hesitation continued on to the tomb followed by Diego. Carefully they climbed the pyramid and opened the hidden doorway. One by one the four Mayans entered the sacred tomb and silently paid homage to their ancient king. Frank and I stood aside quietly and I believe each in his own way paid our respects.

"It is good to have you close again Eric, we have much to discuss."

The king's voice sounded as an echo throughout the chamber yet no one heard but me. I answered mentally as I was taught.

"Not now my friend, I have much to achieve with the others first."

"As you wish Eric."

The voice seemed to fade away.
"I hope I did not insult him." I thought.

The rest of the afternoon and evening we were all engaged in setting up our working camp and sleeping areas. Each man finding his own special niche away from the working area. It was well into late evening when we felt satisfied all was in working order.

A snack appeased our hunger. I think we were all more exhausted than hungry. With out much prodding we crawled into our hammocks and let nature tale its course. I chose not to contact the king tonight but closed my eyes to the music of the night.

-158-

Chapter 41

The jungle voices changed shifts as the dawn declared morning. It was our alarm clock. You could almost feel the enthusiasm in the air as we shared breakfast coffee. We excitedly made plans for the day with all favoring the day at the tomb. Carlos worked his magic on the pyramid's door once more and we entered a lost age willingly. Diego instantly made for the hall of paintings while I, of course, headed to the scroll library followed by Frank.

I was amazed at his genuine interest and respect for the scrolls. Asking my permission first, he handled them even more gently than I.

"Do you think you can finish copying them on this trip ?" he asked.

"I gave you my word Frank, I know I have enough film and based on last years experience the job should go quite smoothly.

My answer pleased him, which pleased me. I left Frank in the library and joined Diego at the murals. He was putting some finishing touches on his own commission. I was mesmerized by his work. After careful study I could not tell the difference between the ones that were thousands of years old and his modern day work. His masterpiece had the allure of the murals of ages ago. You could not tell the difference. I remained there, without moving for ten minutes or more until the trance was broken by Diego's touch on my shoulder.

"Wake up pal, I've been talking to you for minutes, didn't you hear me ?" he said smiling.

"I guess not." I heard myself say. "I was lost in your painting. I wish I had your talent. What were you saying ?"

"I honestly don't remember now, I guess it wasn't that important."

We both smiled at that and Diego went back to his artwork.

I figured I had disturbed him enough, so I returned to the library. Frank was no longer there. I was glad of that because I really wanted to get some real work accomplished. Doing a mental inventory to refresh myself as to where I left off I started rearranging some shelves. After moving scrolls I knew I copied last year, a nice surprise awaited me; I uncovered a niche in the wall. It was well covered by a stone cut and worked to fit as a cover. Under a quick perusal it appeared undetectable. Clearing some space to make the area more workable, I carefully started to pull out the stone. It was slow and tedious but it was moving. When I realized how deep the stone was I knew I would not be able to handle it alone. I returned to the main chamber for help. Mateo was the only one there. He said the others went back to the plotting table to discuss new sites.

I relayed what I had discovered and he reacted with more excitement than I did, so much so that he was back at the library before I was.

It took some doing but we managed to pull the secured stone out. It was not just a niche or shelf but the entrance way to another small room.

Another twenty minutes was exhausted, to no avail, trying to find the opening mechanism to gain entry. We then guessed it was not meant to open as a door. Part of their fantastic Maya engineering I guess.

It was a very tight squeeze but I managed to gain entrance by slithering like a snake on my belly through the opening. Mateo passed a lantern through and there before me were more scrolls. These, however, were different. The material was of better quality, and each was carefully secured with a cloth ribbon. It was more like a fabric, soft and supple.

Mateo, questioning my hesitation prodded;

"**O**pen it, open it."

I slowly slid the binding off and unrolled the cloth. Staring at me was a writing of sorts mixed with Glyph's. Half way down my eyes stopped. I was looking at a different kind of symbol. From my own minimal research I recognized them as numbers. Calendar numbers.

"**W**ell ? Well ?" Mateo urged repeatedly.

"**S**orry." I answered. "There's a writing I've never seen before. It's not like the other scrolls, but I do recognize some number Glyph's. I don't know enough to read them though.

"**L**et me see." Mateo said as he reached in his arm, hand open. The scroll was passed. The next thing I heard was a slow whistle from Mateo.

"You're right. I never saw the writing either. The Glyph's, though are definitely a calendar date. We have to get this to Mario."

"Wait !" I exclaimed. "Do you really want to take them out of here ? This place has been their sacred home for who knows how long."

Mateo looked at me and smiled.

"Are you sure you are not part Mayan ? You're right of course. We'll bring Mario here. After you copy these then perhaps we can safely study these dates."

Holding the lantern higher it was now my turn to whistle. In the corner was a highly polished bust in Jade standing about eighteen inches high. Moving closer I saw the face of the king staring back at me. There was no mistake about it.

"Yes Eric, that was done in my honor right after my arrival."

I guess I forgot to turn my mind off to the king. I wasn't trying to be rude, I just found it difficult to share my thoughts with other people around. I chose to ignore him for now.

I pulled Mateo away from the scroll saying,

"Can you see in here ?"

I moved away from the jade sculpture as he managed to push his head and shoulders through the narrow opening. His immediate comment was;

"Wait till Diego sees this."

He returned the scroll to me and backed out. I followed as quickly as I could.

We returned to camp to get the others and at the same time I retrieved my camera gear. By the time I collected the appropriate items the others were already running for the tomb. I arrived at the library to a multitude of calls.

"Hurry up, What took you so long ? Show us what you found."

I was almost annoyed until I saw the smiles. They were politely waiting for me to slither into the secret room again extending that courtesy since I was the one who discovered the treasure scrolls. In I went head first. It was a little easier this time. Having remembered what not to do. Once regaining my balance I handed the scroll in question out to the others. I could hear the excitement in their voices as it was unrolled. Mario's voice was easy to distinguish.

"The writing is unfamiliar to me but this is definitely a calendar date. Let's see, this is...ah..." He hesitated silently for what seemed like an eternity. "No, this can't be !!!"

"What can't it be." asked Frank a little impatiently.

"I'll have to check my records back at camp, but I think this is..." His pause repeated.

"What Mario ? What is it ?" Frank continued urging.

"This is the beginning. The beginning date of their long count of the Mayan current Great Era. The one that ended in 2012. December twenty second to be exact. That long count that covers over one million eight thousand plus days. This puts it back to the year 3114 BCE. (Before current era)

Not a sound was heard from the others outside the hidden room. Obviously we were all stunned by Mario's statements.

"I told you together we can accomplish great things, Eric."

The king's voice rang out like an echo in my head. I chose to answer him this time.

"You have done a great thing by showing us this. Perhaps now the world can end it's speculation of Mayan greatness."

"Do not act too hastily my son, there is still a whole world of doubt to overcome. We will discuss this and more later."

I did not know what else to say so I chose to remain silent. With some difficulty I brought my mind back to Mario and his reading of the scroll as I heard Frank say;

"Are you sure Mario ?"

"I'm quite positive Frank, but let me check my research first to confirm my thoughts.

"Do you have it with you ?" Frank enquired anxiously.

"It's in my backpack, at least enough that I can verify what we are looking at.'

"Do you know what this means gentlemen ?" Frank continued. 'This could..."

I interrupted him with,

"There's more Frank."

"Oh!" was his annoyed answer.

"Can you look in here ?"

With a sort of struggle he gained a partial entrance, just enough to see inside. I directed his gaze to the carved Jade. He was speechless for a short period and then finding his voice muttered.

"That looks like...."

I interrupted a second time.

"It is."

Frank continued to stare. I could feel in the air the fever pitch rising in everybody.

Frank finally returned to reality and eventually pulled himself out of the opening to this hidden room only to be replaced instantly by Diego, who also became speechless. Each in turn slithered into the opening to be awed by the Jade masterpiece.

The excitement surrounding the scroll was overpowering so all six of us returned to the work tables for Mario's verification. The original scroll we left in the tomb and sealed the doors for the night not planning to go back this day.

While walking to the campsite I was becoming uncomfortable. Something was tugging at my mind. I fell back a few steps to supposedly tie my shoe. I opened my mind to the king.

"There will be more to come, my young friend. Do not rush to conclusions but be prepared for a great enlightenment."

I asked in turn what he meant by this, but received no answer... It was the king's turn to be silent. I ran to catch up, attempting a sense of normalcy.

At the plotting tables Mario asked for some alone time so he could concentrate. He wanted no mistakes or suppositions on what and how he interpreted the Glyphs. Though disappointed in having to wait, Frank conceded knowing he was right in his request.

I was conferring with Diego on the beauty of the sculpture when Carlos interrupted us.

"Eric, do you think you can get the bust out through the wall space as it is now ?"

My immediate answer was "NO" I didn't think so. Carlos then added.

"Then tomorrow or whenever we go back there, let me have a closer look at the room. There may yet be a release lever. We possibly just overlooked it."

"Wouldn't that be nice ?" I replied.

"I know." said Carlos. And smiling added, "And it would make Diego extremely happy."

It was more than an hour of Mario's pondering over his notebooks, and Frank pacing in circles, before we had any news. Then out of nowhere Mario shouted.

"I was right. This is the beginning. The first recording of the start of the current ERA."

"Are you absolutely positive ?" replied Frank, now a nervous wreck.

"Yes sir, I would stake my life on it."

"Let's hope it doesn't get to that." quipped Frank. He was all smiles now. Patting everyone on the back and as he approached me said,

"Looks like you've done it again, Eric and I'm supposed to be the pro here."

He grasped my hand firmly and I could actually feel his sincerity.

"Gentlemen, wait here one moment." I answered as I turned toward my sleeping area. Secreted away in the bottom of my pack was a bottle of Frank's favorite Cognac. I felt it was my turn to treat. I held the bottle high for all to see as I returned to the work area.

"Gentlemen, a celebratory toast to success."

"I am honored, and we have only just started." added Mateo. There were no refusals for a mid-afternoon party.

A much relaxed attitude lingered for the rest of the day. Oh, a little work was done, but no one was in a rush. Eventually Mateo joined Mario for more study of the calendar date, while Frank buried himself in his recording journals. Diego, Carlos and I returned to the tomb and the now not so secret room. Within minutes Carlos found a hidden lock mechanism to swing a small section of the wall open that allowed walking entrance. Diego was in like a flash hovering over the sculpture. He was taking in every detail with his eyes and fingers. He persuaded Carlos and I to help him remove it to the main chamber where there was a more efficient light under which he could study. Diego became so involved with the bust that Carlos and I did not seem to exist.

Laughing, we just left him to his art with Carlos returning to the work area while I revisited the hidden room.

I stood there not really seeing anything in particular but contemplating the advanced engineering these so called "Primitives" had.

"Look closely, Eric and you will learn much."

The king's voice released me from my dream state. He sort of startled me, yet again I chose not to answer him. I believe by now he understood my reasons.

I quickly looked over the additional scrolls in the small room and decided we had enough excitement for one day, besides for whatever reason, I was feeling tired, almost physically worn out. The sad part was that I had no idea why.

The scrolls would just have to wait. I re-secured the small room and left the library, sealing that also.

The fresh air felt good despite its high temperature. Darkness would soon be on us and I was already hungry, so perhaps an early dinner and hit my hammock to let my jungle symphony work its magic on both body and brain.

I lay in my out of the way spot listening and thinking. I missed my small vial of magic sand, though I knew I made the right decision in destroying it. The others left me alone this night. I figured they sensed I was in a tired funky mood. It felt good to be alone. I mentally laid out my work schedule for tomorrow and the next thing I knew I could smell the coffee. I swung out of my hammock feeling like a new man. I guess the rush of excitement and the travel preparations took their toll on me. No matter now, I felt great and just had a feeling this was going to be a perfect day.

$\mathbf{B}$reakfast appeared to be extra special today, at least to me anyway. No mention was made of yesterday's mood which I was grateful for. My camera gear spent the night in the scroll library, so I knew I had a full morning's work ahead of me.

I was scheduled with Carlos for the afternoon outside the compound to check another possible out building. I always looked forward to these jungle treks.

While nursing my second cup of coffee I reviewed the aerial photos for the direction we were heading. Something did catch my eye. An odd tree pattern. It would be extremely unique if it was produced by nature. I picked up the compass heading from the map and figured it could not be more than three quarters of a mile away from our present location. I shared this information with Carlos then walked to the tomb and my photo work.

Chapter   42

     Copying the scrolls was pretty much routine by now and I was seriously regarding this afternoons sojourn through the jungle.

     "What you seek, you will find today Eric."

     The kings voice was soft this morning.

     "Remember yesterday's scroll."

     "Is there a connection between the two ?" I asked in return.

     I received no answer. I was not too upset by this though. The king had his way of teaching me.

     The photo work went splendidly and before I knew it Carlos was here with some water and fruit. I closed the library and we were on our way.

     It took us about an hour and a half to travel the three quarter mile distance with quite a bit of hacking at the undergrowth. It was as if the jungle was refusing to give up anything further. The birds and monkeys did not like our intrusion either, and made it known with their chatter and screeching. At times the noise was so great I thought I was in Manhattan at rush hour.

     We both could tell we were nearing something of interest because of the way the jungle density changed. Another fifty yards and we were facing a wall of trees planted so closely they were impenetrable. On closer inspection it appeared that only every other one was real. Cut trees had been attached between the growing trees and with the natural growth of the jungle a solid wall was formed.

     Our interest was revitalized at seeing this, knowing man

was at work here. Usual pictures and GPS readings were taken, then we proceeded parallel to the wall to find an entrance. We must have traveled sixty feet or more before coming to a corner, not a ninety degree corner though. It was more like one hundred and thirty degrees. We took another GPS sighting and continued following this formidable structure. The jungle canopy was so thick and low, there was no way of telling how high it was. Another sixty feet and we met another corner. Again it was not a ninety degree angle, more like sixty degrees. A GPS reading and we continued our walk. We knew we were parallel to the original side where we started but walking the exact opposite direction. The third corner was like the first. We marked it with a reading and resumed walking back to where we started.

An impressive wall but no gateway. This, of course, triggered Carlos' mind of folklore tidbits and he accepted the challenge of locating an entranceway. His first motion was to go to the east side, the rising sun being important to Maya history.

Twenty five minutes of hands and knees work in the underbrush finally paid off in both positive results and many bug bites. I never imagined there were so many bugs and crawly critters in the world.

Carlos located a stone lever to open a narrow portal. Even with all the undergrowth cleared away I could not tell that the stone placements meant a portal. It was great to have someone like Carlos on this multi disciplined team.

It required many attempts with the lever to open the doorway because of the extreme overgrowth of the jungle vines. Without our machete's it never would have happened. We at last managed to open the gate enough to squeeze through. It seems that's all I've been doing of late.

Once inside we were astonished. We were looking at a flat topped, parallelogram, constructed of blocks of granite, but even that I'm not quite sure of. These blocks were massive and if I had to guess, each weighed tens of tons. Precise and careful workmanship showed in how they were fitted together. The ten or twelve feet above ground with each side measuring approximately fifty feet.

Carlos spent more time on hands and knees and at last determined the major part of the structure was buried, intentionally buried, not just debris covered.

The tree palisade was only ten foot away from the stone outline. This obviously accounted for the strange shape I saw in the aerial photo's, but being high altitude photography I was not able to discern too much detail.

While we both rested a while Carlos said he was convinced this structure went deep underground. I asked how could he tell.

"By reading the trees." was his answer.

I looked at him totally confused, which I'm sure showed on my face. He laughed at me saying;

"I'll try to explain on the way back."

We finished with pictures and GPS readings and exited the complex re-closing and scattering jungle debris over the stone lever area. Not that we were expecting anybody, but protection of archaeological sites is of the utmost importance.

Just before closing Carlos brought my attention to the trees, roots and vines inside the gate. After closing the gate we looked at the same things immediately outside the area. Then, walking away from the wall about one hundred feet on the trail home we stopped to review the same growth of underbrush and trees.

"Do you notice any difference ?" he asked.

It took me a while but once he pointed certain things out I could see differences. Shades of color, texture of bark, thickness of roots, shape of leaves and other things he drew my attention to.

"Some are very much older then others." he added.

"You mean to tell me that this structure could be two hundred feet across, most of it buried ?" I asked.

"That's exactly what I mean. Chances are it goes down some fifty feet. Also from looking at the stone work it was made by another people even before the Maya. Another thing I find amazing is that even though this many years have passed, the difference in the tree and underbrush growth can still be detected. Difficult yes but doable.

I stood there with my mouth open, contemplating the history we were viewing. History that could possibly go back just as far as the eastern hemisphere, or even further for that matter. There was no way of telling, at least right now.

Frank was really going to be excited. He will be writing papers or even a book about this for the rest of his career.

"How do we tell Frank and hold him down in his seat at the same time ?" I mumbled out loud.

Both of us laughed and started for camp.

~ ~ ~ ~ ~ ~

Dinner was almost ready when we arrived through the arch. Frank was seated at the work table and without looking up inquired,

"Any luck finding anything ?" he said in a matter of fact way expecting nothing for an answer.

Carlos who was known to tease once in a while answered,

"We're really hungry, lets eat first. We can talk after and walked towards Mateo who was tonight's designated cook.

Frank considering this a "NO" answer continued whatever he was working on. I walked away smiling and headed for a washup before dinner.

About halfway through another dinner of mystery ingredients, Carlos slowly laid out our day's events. You could see Frank getting more on edge, nervous and excited until finally jumping up and yelling;

"Why did you wait so long to tell me ? Where is it ? Let's go! I've got to see this."

As expected, it took all of us to calm him down and convince him it was too late in the day. The sun was already setting and it would be at least an hours travel time. You could see he was already making plans to go tomorrow.

He actually was in a good mood which we made even better when the Cognac appeared to toast our good luck. The evening's mood was light and jovial. Frank kept on about this being the biggest find of not only the century but of the millennium. Established academia would npw have to sit up and listen. He was already envisioning visits by the worlds top archeologists and anthropologists. We, as a team would be doing a world lecture tour with proof of our findings. This yet to be named city would now become the largest Maya capital. The teacher of all Maya.

Yes, Frank was getting carried away, which hopefully would pass. The excitement of discovery, aided by Cognac was now talking. We let Frank have his moment planning on his return to normal tomorrow. My own thoughts were not that much out of line with Frank. If this really was the beginning of the "Present ERA", perhaps additional light would be shed on who, and or what, was before the Maya. The king may yet honor me with some of that insight. At least I could hope.

The excitement soon faded as each of us drifted to his own

area, for privacy and rest. It had been an amazing two days.

$$\sim\ \sim\ \sim\ \sim\ \sim\ \sim$$

As expected Frank was up early and raring to go. He just could not wait to see this new underground pyramid. Carlos volunteered to guide Frank and the others. I chose to stay behind and continue to copy the scrolls. Along with Diego, who had further work to do on the mural the king had commissioned.

It was wonderfully quiet when the four team members left. Diego and I finished a quiet breakfast, cleaned up, then headed for the tomb.

We all, by this time had become proficient at opening the outer door of the tomb and once inside Diego and I went our separate ways.

The copy work reached the point of almost being boring, therefore I gave myself a break about mid day, had some fruit and reentered the secret scroll room. There were sixteen other special scrolls. I say special only because they were on fabric, not paper. In moving them so I had a place to sit I noticed one of them was longer than the rest. A little more than twice as long. Of course this tested my curiosity, so I opened it. At first I was confused; it was just a bunch of squiggly lines. Then as the squiggles took shape in my head things became familiar.

"Keep looking Eric and you will learn many things."

My mentor was still with me and still leading me. Not answering him I continued to look at the newly opened scroll. I saw need for more light and more room to stretch out the complete rolled fabric. I moved to the main chamber where there was adequate light and some loose stones to hold the open roll. Once secured I stood back to gaze at the overall. At first I did not believe my own eyes yet the more I looked the more things I saw. Familiar things that started to clarify themselves.
There was writing; I guess you could call it that, here and there at certain points on the squiggly lines. The writing I recognized as the same on the scroll with the calendar dates, though still unreadable, for me anyway. I scanned the entire surface, then, like a mist clearing, I saw it. It was a map

of the east coast of North and South America along with the West coast of Europe and Africa. There was no doubt in my mind. There was Florida and Cape Cod, the gulf of Mexico, and the Yucatan. My heart was thumping, I broke into a sweat, my hands were trembling. I purposely turned away, took a deep breath and slowly counted to ten. Thinking of the king I thanked him in my mind.

"Remember Eric, between the two of us we can advance many things."

On the word things, the echo of the kings voice appeared to fade away. Thinking back now I realized the king predicted this for me.

"I really should pay more attention to his riddles." I thought to myself.

Bringing my pulse back to normal again I turned to the scroll once more. Attempting to be professional about it all I viewed the map carefully and more slowly.

There was a less dense line just off but following the east coast of the America's, also following the west coast of Africa. Observing even more closely, these two separate dashed lines both originated at the same place. A rather small and very northern land mass, which I do not ever remember seeing on a map of the North Atlantic. I kept staring at the drawing when some markings at the bottom caught my eye. They were comparatively small and when I looked closer they were Glyphs similar to the ones on the scroll Mario was interpreting that was found yesterday. Perhaps these also were dates. One could only hope anyway.

The Glyphs themselves were slightly different; they were not of the same ink or print. Obviously added at a later date. This would definitely have to go to Mario for translation.

"Time is the secret to unfold my friend. Knowledge awaits you."

I stood quietly for a moment thinking of the king's words. I guess he really meant it when he said together we can accomplish much. Frank and then others think I have brought them some sort of special luck. If they only knew.

I answered the king with "Thank you my friend." and

let it go at that.

I wandered over to the mural hallway to let Diego in on my latest find. He was mixing some color from local materials. I find his knowledge of the ancient arts amazing. In my opinion he surpasses our modern world in the art category, yet he is relatively unknown and most likely would have a hard time being recognized as a true artist that ranks with the best, no matter what ere.

By now I'm sure Frank has already dug down to the bottom of the newly discovered structure with his bare hands, I laughed to myself. I truly hope they are gaining insight to this new city. Just on what was discovered to date will take many years of dedicated study to document and share with the archeological field and history buffs.

Diego willingly accompanied me to the map. He was as taken with it as I was. He confirmed that they were date Glyphs but their meaning was beyond his scope of knowledge. He agreed with me that it was definitely a map and quite accurate at that. He also guessed it was very old considering some coastline changes. He briefly mentioned the floods eons ago and how they changed land masses. That along with volcanic activity reshaped a lot of the world. I sad I had heard of the flood from the bible of Nosh's time but not the others before that.

"The flood of Noah's time was the most recent." he answered. "There were others before that."

"How many others." I pursued.

"I'm not sure, you'll have to ask Carlos or Mateo. Perhaps they had come across something in their Glyph translations."

"What do you make of this writing ? It looks like the same as that of the scroll you found in the hidden room."

"I thought so also." I replied. "But I'm far from being a writing expert."

"We definitely must get the others involved." Diego shared.

"We obviously have to wait until tonight though. Do you think Frank can take another surprise so soon ? This would make three days in a row."

"Probably not." he replied. :He's going to want to see it right away, but it will be dark then. Tell you what, I have Mateo's Polaroid camera with me. We'll take a few shots with that to show him. It won't be the quality you get but at least he can see something. I would rather not risk removing the scroll from its proper place."

I affirmed his feelings and we proceeded taking a few Polaroid's. I returned the scroll to its chamber and we both went about our original work.

~ ~ ~ ~ ~ ~

"This will definitely need a total excavation." said Frank. "I have no idea where we can get that kind of financing. We're talking a lot more than the university can come up with. We obviously can't do it this season either. There just isn't enough time."

"Why dig at all ?" Carlos inquired.

Frank quickly spun his head around towards Carlos with a look of total disbelief at his statement. Startled at Frank's reaction, Carlos put up his hand saying;

"Hold on Frank, hear me out."

Just as fast, Frank did back down and changed his expression. Carlos went on to explain.

"This structure was meant to be buried. This is not just jungle growth and dirt accumulation over time, although God knows there was enough time. This was built to be underground."

"How do you know that ?" asked Frank in a much calmer tone.

"Mostly from folklore." he replied. "Also from the jungle signs, tree growth and the like."

Now it was Franks turn to look confused.

"This top platform." Carlos continued, "Was for ceremonial practices. Exactly what I don't know, but there must be an entrance to the interior someplace. This protecting wall signifies a place of importance. The answer lies below us."

"Can you open it?" was Franks next logical question.

"I don't know." was the disappointing answer. "I have never come across this before."

Frank took on a look of disheartening rejection.

"All we can do is try Frank, though I suspect it will take some tome." Carlos offered, not too convincingly.

It was apparent Frank was not happy with the answer but

he knew he had to accept it.

The rest of the day they were occupied with measurements and some Shallow digging. The digging did net them some artifacts, a few of which were of totally unknown items. Carlos dedicated himself to the tedious job of searching for any kind of entrance to the massive structure.

With the waning sun they headed home to the campsite with mixed emotions about the success of their day.

~ ~ ~ ~ ~ ~

Diego and I had supper prepared when the site searches returned. Frank appeared to be okay but you could tell not everything went his way today. Diego hinted that maybe our news would cheer him up. It was a shame Frank took so much so seriously. We have to find a way for him to relax more and not carry the weight of the world on his shoulders. We all respected his position, professionalism and knowledge but he truly needed to lighten up a bit. The city is still going to be here tomorrow.

During dinner Frank spoke of the numerous things they couldn't get done today, the information they could not collect because of this, that or the other. The fact was he was at a new find of unknown origin seemed to have slipped his mind. He completely overlooked the main theme that this was an unprecedented discovery.

Diego waited for the right opportunity and took the lead to tell of our day. Frank still in a slight hyper mood, was reanimated with excitement on hearing us tell our story. We chose not to wait too long before showing the Polaroids. We hoped this would keep him from charging to the tomb in the dark. Luckily it worked. A more positive mood took possession of Frank, and the rest of the evening was relaxing and enjoyable.

Both Carlos and Mateo were fascinated by the map story and couldn't wait to see the real thing. There just was not enough detail in the pictures to read accurately the date Glyphs on the map, but having ever so much more patience than Frank, were willing to wait until tomorrow.

Finally our plans were set for the next day and I made my way to my hammock looking forward to my nighttime symphony.

I lay there thinking how well everything was going. This archeology thing could be habit forming. I could not understand why Frank was so disturbed by what established academia would think about our work.

Things are what they are. This is definitely a new city, and a very large one, with a lot of new finds, so what is there to question. I vowed to myself to help Frank in whatever way I could, both here and back in the States.

"There is yet more to discover Eric. Things that will be questioned and doubted by others, perhaps even by you. Keep faith my friend, the truth will out. A change in history is long overdue."

As usual the king's words were succinct and right on the money. My interest keyed, I decided to pursue some questions.

"Do you have a name other than king ?"

"I have been known by many names by many different peoples, but my given name from my original home is ATAL."

"Thank you for that, Atal, where is your original home ?"

"That will be yours to learn at another time."

I can respect that for now." I answered. "What else is there to be discovered. It already has been overwhelming."

"Time is long overdue, Eric. Your world should know of its beginnings. Acceptance of these new things can make this a better place. It has always been difficult but perseverance must be practiced by a few such as you for the betterment of the many. Reflect on my words and we can talk yet again another time."

It was obvious I was being dismissed. I accepted this, settled back and let the night take over.

Chapter 43

With the initial excitement over, we settled down to try and keep to a routine which still included away from the tomb site visits. Who knows how big this city really is or even how old. I concentrated on the scrolls knowing I could finish in a day or so. That would leave me adequate time to pursue other discoveries with the king or Atal now that I have a name.

At mid-day I was feeling a bit hungry and rather than go back to the camp site I remembered the hidden entrance the king showed me where he always got his fruit. I found the passageway and opened it and followed the dark hallway, using my pocket flashlight, I found the outer hatchway. Pushing it open allowed the sunshine to flood the tunnel. I found the fruit trees in short order and enjoyed the sun and fruit together. Returning to the tunnel I ran into Mario. *"Might as well tell about* the *tunnel."* I thought. Mario of course knew, but now with the king gone the others should know. Mario suspects a little more than I'm telling although he has not confronted me yet. How do I explain my relationship with Atal or why he chose me out of the six. I let it go for now knowing it would come up again.

Mario and I spoke of memories of the king as we slowly ate the fruit. I could tell he wanted to ask questions of me but I guess the time was not right yet. He finally changed expressions and the subject. He possibly was waiting for me to broach the subject first.

"I have double and triple checked the calendar Glyphs on that scroll you found and I am absolutely certain they are the AGE beginning. The one that just ended in twenty twelve. Have you checked the other scrolls from the hidden room yet ?"

"Just one." I answered.

"Just one! What have you been doing all morning ?" Mario smiled in reply.

"Wandering around out here eating fruit." I quipped in return. "I found a map." I then said quietly.

"A map of what ?" he questioned seriously.

I hesitated trying to find the correct way to explain it.

"The coastline of the America's and Africa."

Mario's eyes widened and he was momentarily struck dumb. Finding his voice he stuttered;

"You, you're pulling my leg, right ?" You're just joking with me. Please tell me you're joking."

"I'm afraid not." I replied quietly. "This is real and looks completely authentic and accurate. Not only that but there are, I guess you would say, annotations on it in the same script as the calendar scroll, totally unreadable to Diego and me."

Mario continued looking at me but now he was smiling.

"Frank is going to have an absolute coronary if we keep having this kind of luck or shall we say, if you keep having this kind of luck."

I had no reason to be, but I suddenly felt embarrassed. Mario must have sensed this because he added,

"Come, show me. This has really got my attention."

Back at the main chamber Mario hypnotically stared at the outstretched map. Moments later Diego joined us.

"What do you think of that ?" he quizzed. "Quite a find, Eh?

Mario was so taken with the map I don't think he even heard Diego. Recognition finally came but not with an answer. Diego took the lead saying,

"Do you remember that strange writing on the scroll with the number Glyphs that you found ?"

We both answered yes.

"Well, I think I found a little more on the mural of the kings portrait. No reason but I was studying it some more and I think I see more of that same type of lettering. Somebody signed the portrait.

Both Mario and I looked at Diego, then at each other then back to Diego. This was becoming too much to believe. What was writing, or script or language, however you wanted to identify it. What ever it was it appeared to be pre-Maya. Perhaps we really have stumbled upon a history change. I thought to myself, *"I must pursue this further with the king."*

The three of us moved to the mural passageway where Diego pointed out the artist mark. He was correct in his judgement. It was the same script. Mario was ecstatic.

"We can possibly use this as a base line for translation. Diego, do you still have the Polaroid with you ?"

"Yes, it's in my backpack." he replied already walking to it.

"Good, get as close to it as you can and get some shots, from forty five degree angles also, not just straight on."

I volunteered to take some shots also. It would be a while before we can see any results, but at least we'll have it recorded. I walked towards the library.

"Why shots at angles ?" inquired Diego.

"Because the shadow of lighting can sometimes bring out areas of depth you don't ordinarily see. We do that for rock carvings or recording Glyphs. That shadow delineation can sometimes change interpretation."

"Gotcha." answered Diego as he moved about shooting the different angles.

I returned and took my turn at getting some exposures while Diego and Mario started to study the other murals for similar markings.

An hour or so later our detailed study netted a marking on each mural. Pictures were made of all. In addition Diego was able to sketch, quite accurately I might add, each one of them. Mario mentioned that he and Mateo could start working at these tonight.

The three of us decided we had enough discoveries for one day as we methodically put everything in order and secured the tomb for the night.

Arriving back at camp we surprisingly found Frank in a rare spirit. He had been at the base site all day journal writing and some necessary ground work for a formal presentation paper. Carlos and Mateo had also returned from an off site trek. They also were upbeat.

Dinner that night was a mix of everything with everybody pitching in. Frank did his fair share at the grill cooking the fish Mateo returned with. As in my dream, I quietly made a cake, icing and all, that I had secreted with me in my pack. It appeared to be the perfect night fot it, and it was a big hit. Dinner conversation was productive and we toasted our good fortune with cake. It was a fine and restful evening with laughs well into the night till one by one we drifted to our beds for a relaxing sleep. I was the last one up, listening to my natural music, trying to drift into the past.

I awoke at first light still sitting in my camp chair, a little stiff here and there but fully relaxed. While making coffee, thinking of my day ahead, I heard the king.

"Danger lies ahead Eric, be on your guard."

That was the only message. I tried many times, unsuccessfully to reconnect with Atal, to no avail. Troubled by the kings words, yet I chose not to alarm the others. I would play it by ear.

The morning humor was a continuation of last night with all anticipating another great day. The aura of the day was soon interrupted.

Halfway through breakfast a group of men of very questionable character invaded the quiet of our plaza. There appeared at the archway a group of seven men armed with what looked like AK-47's. This unkempt group advanced uninvited with weapons at the ready.

"**V**ery good Sen`or, you have breakfast ready for us."

Frank was already on his feet protesting rather vehemently against the armed intrusion. I moved to Frank's side quickly, my hand on his shoulder.

"**E**asy Frank, let's not do anything hasty." All I could think of was my dream.

"**V**ery good advice Sen`or, I appreciate extreme cooperation. I see you Gringo's and your slaves are here to dig up and ruin our history. These are not your temples, they are mine to do with what I want."

With that he fired off a dozen rounds of ammunition in the direction of the tomb.

Not really panic but horror showed on the faces of our Maya colleagues. The next words were directed at me.

"**A**re you in charge here Sen`or ?"

Before I could answer Frank knocked my hand from his

shoulder and hastily answered.

"No, I am."

"That is too bad Sen`or, I see you have no patience. I will have to shoot you for that."

He let three rounds go at the feet of Frank who never moved.

"Now we will try again Sen`or. Since you say you are in charge, then I will talk to you nicely. You will kindly pack up all your supplies for us, including your money, cause Gringos always have money, and you will happily give everything to us, Si ?"

"No." was Franks loud and firm answer.

"What did you say Sen`or ?"

"I said no." Frank repeated loud enough for all to hear.

"Oh, that is too bad Sen`or, now I will have to shoot you because you are not being nice to me."

Something was said in Spanish by the leader to one of the other men who in turn grabbed Mateo and pushed him at gunpoint out of the compound. A few moments after disappearing through the archway a single shot was heard. A short time elapsed and the gunman could be seen at the plaza entrance. The leader repeated his command and a second man grabbed Carlos pushing him towards the gateway. Frank moved to interfere and was struck down by a rifle butt. When Carlos vanished through the portal a second shot was heard.

"Okay, Okay." shouted Frank. "Take what you want, just leave us be."

"I knew you would see it my way Sen`or, but it is too late for that now. Oh we will take all that you have but we will kill you anyway. You have seen us do a very bad thing and we would not want you to tell anyone."

A movement by the archway caught my eye. The two men who left were returning followed by many more similarly dressed. The two lead men were without their AK-47's.

"That's odd." I thought.

The group advanced quietly and with one quick movement surrounded our unwanted guests. A short conversation in Spanish took place and our captors dropped their weapons. Additional movement at the archway manifested in Mateo and Carlos entering accompanied by a man obviously in charge. He was dressed in partial military attire with prominent eagles showing on his collar. Then it hit me. It was the colonel from my dream who caused all the wanton destruction tom the tomb. I could feel myself get tense. When he drew near enough to speak, he asked in near perfect English, with only a hint of an accent;

"Who is in charge here ?"

Frank still showing anger answered louder than necessary.

"I am."

"No need to be upset Sen`or. I assume you are Mr. Frank Thurber then ?"

"Yes." Frank replied hesitantly.

"Good, my government gave me instructions about seeing to your safety. I think the work you and your team are doing will be of great benefit to my country and its history. I am Colonel Juan Ramirez of the local militia at your service."

He extended his hand to Frank which was warmly received. He then extended the gesture to the rest of us. We all started to relax, all that is, except our original captors, who appeared to be nervous. Mateo and Carlos were all smiles. The Colonel, upon shaking my hand gazed at my face with a smile asking,

"Have we met before Sen`or, your face looks very familiar. I feel I have seen you elsewhere, possibly Juarez ?"

"I have been at Juarez, though I do not recall actually meeting you." I answered although I was thinking *I did meet you in my dream and you were not the good guy.*

"Perhaps I am mistaken." uttered the Colonel.

The Colonel returned to Frank.

"You will have no more worries now Sen`or Thurber. These men are drug cartel renegades that we have been tracking for some time. They will be dealt with by my government, and for your further safety my patrols should never be more than a mile or two away."

"Thank you Colonel, for your consideration, now we can continue our study in a more relaxed atmosphere."

The Colonel and his troops rounded up the cartel baddies and left us to our silence.

We all had questions for Mateo and Carlos referring to the gunshots. It seems that was the Colonel's idea to keep his presence unknown. It was one of his own men who appeared at the gate signaling for Carlos to be taken. This way it did not raise any suspicion that would hinder their silent approach. Mateo mentioned the Colonel had another forty men outside the walls. Their approach certainly was silent.

My dream had become apparent yet again with different results. Thank goodness for that. The Colonel recognized me but I know we never met. My life sure has come across many strange things since I joined this expedition last year. I still have no idea why. These experiences have not harmed me in any way, they have just been out of the ordinary considering my life up to now.

An extended breakfast and more coffee appeared to be in order as nerves began to calm and we reestablished a normal atmosphere. There remained a weird feeling in the back of my head about the Colonel. He was the exact same man from my dream who seemed to know me. Yet another possible question for Atal.

Mario and Mateo were already at work on the possible description of the unknown script found on the scrolls while Frank and Carlos buried themselves in the map. Diego and I quietly took our leave and returned to the tomb to our rather mundane repetitive tasks. I purposely chose to finish the copy work of the scrolls in the large library before opening any more from the hidden room. It took me into the evening, but that boring task was now behind me. I'm sure Frank will be pleased. Diego had returned to the work area a few hours earlier leaving me alone at the tomb. I did not mind at all though, I felt perfectly at home here. So much so that I remained a while longer in the main chamber. I relaxed myself across from the kings stone pyre admiring the art work of the Glyphs on the base.

"I feel you have many questions my young friend. Perhaps I can help."

That certainly picked up my spirits. I figured I would dive right in about our newer discoveries.

"**W**hat can you tell me about the unknown writing we found on some scrolls ?" I inquired.

"That writing, Eric, is my native tongue. It is

millennial old. It is what we chosen ones were trying to bring to the world."

"**Y**ou were trying to bring writing to the world ? I thought you mentioned bringing new science and invention to the uninitiated." I questioned confusingly.

"Of course you are right Eric, that is what we spoke of last year. In order to do that we had to develop a common data base and a universal language used by the world. This appeared to be the ideal way."

I decided to go for the big question.
"**W**here are you from ?"

"I knew you would get ti that my friend and I guess the time is now."

I could not believe my good fortune. This could be the key to many things.

"Many thousands of years ago, long before the land masses became what they are today, there was another rather large island. It was located in what you now call the North Atlantic. Originally know by others as the White island because of the polar ice and snow. We were an extremely advanced people compared to those populating this planet at the time. Due to planetary axis shifts there was much melting of the northern polar cap which caused cataclysmic floods."

"**H**ow long ago was that." I interrupted.

"By your present calendar it was thirteen thousand years ago. Please do not interrupt again."
I knew I had been scolded by the tone of his voice. He continued as if there had been no interrupted.

"These floods resulted in the total demise of my home land. It was torn apart and taken to the depths of the ocean in a very short time period. Very few of us escaped this annihilation. Others of our kind were already settled elsewhere throughout the Atlantic both North and South. We, who were the last to leave, were eventually known as the Chosen ones. We had vowed to take our knowledge to the rest of the world not expecting an ill reception. At that time we were masters of engineering, mathematics, astronomy, physics and the art, medicine and sundry other things necessary to world growth. Our original outreach representatives were already throughout the world as evidenced by some of your archaeological excavations. Most of those places of residence were also destroyed by the big flood and other succeeding floods. You are now finding evidence of these structures throughout the oceans. My homeland was given the name Atlantis, thus my name Atal. Now Eric, if you have questions, this is the time."

I momentarily paused trying to phrase my questions appropriately without being insulting.

"If you were that advanced in your technology, why did it take this long for us to get where we are, which is still not equal to your advanced state."

"You are a wise one, my friend. I'm sure you already know the answer, yet I will give you a brief synopsis. At first contact we were welcomed but feared. In the beginning you learned well, and then the most wicked of human traits took hold: Greed and Control. These two things led to power over others. That is when serious learning ceased. Our teachings of using this knowledge for the benefit of all were ignored. We held back further instruction, hoping for a more accepting generation. This never occurred. Oh,

there were several individuals over the many thousands of years who tried to take up our message. Their words too, fell on deaf ears. Eventually our people passed on or were purposely eliminated. You have come a long way but are still governed by Greed and Power. Not until you learn to coexist peacefully will you earn true advancement. Some things presently exist but until you cooperate within yourselves, true progress and contentment will not be found. Does that answer your question, my young friend ?"

I was silent for a long time digesting these heavy words, so simply spoken.

"I sincerely thank you for your wisdom, Atal."

He quickly answered;

"I gave you nothing you did not already believe yourself. Now continue on with your work. You have much to uncover that will benefit all historical knowledge. Continue with the special scrolls for enlightenment. Forget not what lies beneath your feet."

"There he goes again with his riddles." I said aloud.

I have other questions about past history, can you further explain some of these puzzles ?"

I waited in silence. There was no answer, I had been dismissed.

I stayed seated contemplating all that transpired over the last year or so. Who would have thought that so little could change my life so much ? I was still honored by the kings attention and had yet to understand why.

I could see the light was fast fading therefore I collected all my gear and closed the tomb for the night.

Camp tonight was not as joyful as the night before, though good humor prevailed. Each of us busied themselves with personal journals and the like. I detected a melancholy air about the place that night, possibly the results of this mornings surprise. I kept to myself mulling over the kings words.

How do I explain to others my talks with the king without them hauling me off to the loony bin or losing my credibility ? Who could blame them if they did.

Chapter 44

$\mathbf{I}$t never ceases to amaze me how soothing the jungle sounds can be. I really consider it my personal symphony because I believe all things have a musical makeup about them, just more pronounced here in nature's pristine world. Any natural habitat that has minimal human intervention allows this music to be heard. All we have to do is listen.

$\mathbf{P}$art of me is looking forward to today because of what new things I may uncover, the other part of me is not looking forward to today because of what new things I may uncover. I know it's silly, but due to the king's influence I'm the one who is coming up with all the new finds. As if I haven't annoyed Frank enough. Now I feel like I'm pouring salt on an open wound.

$\mathbf{M}$ario filled his mug with our dark syrupy coffee and joined me at my hammock.

"$\mathbf{Y}$ou look a bit confused and upset, and I bet I know why."

$\mathbf{I}$ looked at him not surprised by his insight.

"$\mathbf{L}$ook Pal, I know you had a special connection with the king, and perhaps still do, but there is no reason to feel guilty about it. You are being overly sensitive. Our mission here, and I mean all of us, is to further explore our history, both for our personal satisfaction, and even more importantly to benefit the world of the missing Maya culture that has proved to be more influential to the world's history than others want to accept. If it takes whatever connection you personally have with our ancient king to reveal these truths, than so be it. You can not let Frank's sensitive feelings influence you one way or the other. If you can help us find our past, no matter how you do it, then you should accept this responsibility, knowing you are furthering knowledge of all humanity. Do not fight yourself Eric, contribute what ever you can."

$\mathbf{M}$ario smiled warmly at me as he extended his hand in friendship saying,

"The how you do it you can explain to me at another time."

He turned and walked away, still smiling. I just knew he had me pegged for something and he knew it too. I also smiled as he strode away. I have to admit though, I did feel better. He was exactly right, my concern should be for the success of the overall mission, not just Frank's feelings.

By the time the days plans were finished I was a new man. I even told Frank I wished to pursue the new scrolls today and asked if he would join me. I could tell he was excited by my offer. He revised his day's plans and after a few changes we were on our way to the tomb.

Mario and Diego went off site for new finds connected with the city while Carlos and Mateo were assigned camp duty and dinner this day.

Frank was like an excited child as we approached the hidden scroll room. Once inside his excitement changed to quiet reverence. I let him pick the first scroll. He appeared nervous as he unrolled it and stared at it motionless when he finished.

"What is it Frank ?" I asked not receiving an answer.

I stepped towards him to gaze over his shoulder. As I moved into position to observe what froze him, I saw Glyphs. Two lines of them as he mumbled.

"This is not possible."

"What's wrong Frank ?" I asked. "What's not possible ?"

Frank, suddenly aware of my close presence turned to me,

"I remember these number Glyphs from Mario's work on the calendars." He volunteered. "If I'm not mistaken in my reading of these, it is saying these scrolls are from the Era before the one that just ended. This is telling us there was intelligent civilization around in the thirty one hundred BCE or even earlier, not just rock throwing cave men."

Even I couldn't believe my ears. But then again, why shouldn't I Atal predicted I would find things that could change history.

"Are you sure Frank ? Could you be mistaken ?"

"I suppose the possibility exists, but since the other discoveries, I have purposely been studying as much as I could. I don't believe I'm mistaken."

Knowing Frank as I did, I believed also that he was correct in his readings.

While he continued musing over the date Glyph, I picked another scroll. My hands were shaking a bit as I unrolled it. It was my turn to be spellbound. I was viewing a translation dictionary. I could feel myself becoming weak kneed so I slowly sank to the floor resting my back against the wall.

This document was the missing key we needed to decipher the strange script that was discovered earlier. In my mind I was yelling for Frank to come and look yet no sound escaped my lips. With a difficult and concentrated effort I managed to mumble something. Frank turned only to find me on the floor still mumbling incoherently.

"Did you say something ?" he asked followed with a surprise, "What are you doing on the floor ?"

All I could do was hold up the scroll and point. He took the half unrolled scroll and within minutes joined me on the floor. I found my voice and asked Frank,

"Do you know what this means ?"

Still stunned he rushed through his answer.

"I know one thing it means. It means we have to do an awful lot of explaining and convincing to an awful lot of people if we expect them to believe this."

He looked at me admiringly and added,

"You must have been born under a bed of four leaf clovers. I should have had you join me on expeditions a long time ago and I apologize, my friend for ever doubting your interest and sincerity. This is not only a great discovery, it is the find of the century, for that matter the find of the last few centuries.

Both reclaiming a sense of calm yet not taking our eyes from the scroll, Frank started to rise from the floor.

"I've got to get this to the others right away so we can start work on the translation."

"I can't let you do that just yet Frank." I commented.

Turning to glare at me, anger on his face,

"And why not ?" he questioned curtly.

Smiling gently I replied quietly.

"I think we should photograph them first. We wouldn't want anything to happen to them and lose them forever."

Frank eased his tension, now also smiling, replied;

"**R**ight again my friend. I guess I'm getting overanxious."

I quickly went about setting up my camera equipment and started the copy process. Frank was a most willing and cooperative assistant.

An hour later I was alone again. Frank had taken the translation scroll to the work area, handling it like a new born baby. Preferring ti be alone at this point I used the secret entrance to gain access to the jungle and let the daily serenade envelope me. I walked to the small lake where the king demonstrated the scepter's power, sat by a tree and just let my body relax.

"**T**hank you Atal." I tried. This time my message was received.

"You are most welcome Eric. There is more yet to come. You remarked the other day about riddles."

I suddenly felt embarrassed.

"I want you to reflect seriously on what I said."

I knew I was alone again. Even the jungle was soundless. It became a surreal atmosphere. My mind accepted this without fear. While I sat there my eyes were hungrily devouring the scene around me. I have no recollection of how long I remained like that, and then quite abruptly I sensed a presence. The dream like scene before me slowly faded, regaining once again the deep lushness of the jungle. The presence I felt was real as a beautiful sleek jaguar silently emerged from the underbrush establishing eye contact with me. For some unknown reason I was not afraid although I made no attempt to move. Remembering my dream and Diego's action in that dream I maintained eye contact, trying to mentally communicate with this beautiful creature of nature. We were only separated by a distance of eight feet which would have been a mere single leap by such a creature. For some time we silently and motionless gauged each other. I honestly think our minds were trying to meld. I felt a strength run through my body like I never felt before. My heartbeat became one with the cat in a slow rhythmic movement. Then as abruptly as she appeared she turned to the waters edge, satisfied her thirst and vanished into the thicket from whence she came. I sat there continuing to look at her faded image marveling at her muscled grace, beauty and majesty. I was doing a mental comparison with the king. I was totally at peace with my jungle.

Reality returned when I heard Mario's voice.

"I thought I would find you here. It is quite peaceful isn't it ? Don't worry I'm alone, I came out the same way you did." he said referring to the hidden passage. "Not now, but someday I would like to hear the story of you and the king. Carlos also might like to add it to his folklore repertoire.

Again I was slightly embarrassed but smiled through it.

"Yes, my friend, someday I will tell you of the king. And I will do it willingly. Just promise not to laugh."

"I don't think I will do that." he answered softly but seriously.

"Not to change the subject but did you need me for anything ?"

"Oh, yes, I almost forgot what I came for. Frank would like you back at camp for a big dinner meeting. We have already started on translations."

"I figured as much, he was kind of hyper when he left the tomb."

I followed Mario to the pyramid and it's back entrance. Assuring the tomb was sealed for the night we headed for camp.

~ ~ ~ ~ ~ ~

The mood at dinner was highly charged with talk of changed history. Our plan was now settled for many month's to come, years for that matter. We would continue with our normal search and find additional sites and artifacts, but a major part of our time was now being allocated to translation work.

I stole away as early as I could to my hammock, there was a lot I had to review. I was speculating on where all this would lead. I was hoping Atal could help along those lines.

I dug out my journal for today's update, and as I started my entry the king intercepted my thoughts.

"Do not forget my last words with you Eric. You know the reason for your slow advancement. You have a lot of

growth to accomplish just to get where we were more than three thousand years ago. Beware, however, the greed of those who would control. The dangers will increase before they can be subdued. "

"**I** still have further questions Atal." I pushed but silence prevailed. I had been cut short.

"*Why does he do that to me ?*" I questioned myself. The only answer I can come up with is that he wants me to answer them myself. I was becoming lightly frustrated.

Back to my journal I slowly forgot about the king. Writing about the Jaguar made me drift, yet again, to the peacefulness of the jungle and my special music.

I awoke with the sun, book and pencil still in hand. While feasting on my breakfast of fruit and coffee I planned my day at the tomb, the king's riddle still nagging my mind of what lies beneath. The clue, I guessed was the obvious, but how and where to access the "underneath" would be my challenge. Perhaps Carlos can remember an old folk tale of such a thing. As luck would have it he was up before the others. After pouring his coffee he joined me at the mao table.

"This new city certainly is an impressive sight."

I started running my hand across the map encompassing all we had found to date. Carlos answered with these words;

"**I**t is definitely the largest and probably will turn out to be the greatest Maya discovery. My people can once again be proud of their heritage."

It was a perfect lead in for me.

"**N**ow that you mentioned the Maya heritage, in your historical folk tales, have you come across monumental structures being built on top of others ?"

He paused, his coffee cup halfway to his lips, half squinting his eyes, a sly smile grew on his face.

"**Y**ou're still in touch with the king aren't you ?" he quizzed.

Taken by surprise, I slowly smiled.

"**D**oes it show that much ?" I asked.

"**A**ll of us have guessed as much, except for Frank perhaps.

We absolutely respect your attachment and would never interfere. I think we know you well enough that whatever you learn you will share eventually. Now to answer your question, if I recall correctly, there is a story from long ago about a king living under the earth. There were many kings. Each city or state had its own king. Their cities were spread across what is now known as the Yucatan Peninsula. From the pacific to the Gulf of Mexico, to the Caribbean Sea. It was told that the king who lived under the earth came from this area. You must remember, translations and interpretations sometimes change over millennium. Not much was handed down from this present era we are now in. It was as if it was sacred and should not be spoken of, especially with the uninitiated, in other words someone who is not Mayan. All that being said, yes, there is the possible existence of structures that were built over others because it was considered a sacred place.

Carlos paused, smiled a suspecting grin and asked.

"You think this is that place ?"

I smiled in return.

"Let's just say I have reason to believe so. The king was fond of talking in riddles which of course lead me to think that. You seem to have a great knowledge of hidden locks and doorways so I thought we may be able to find such an entrance."

He hesitated for a moment then answered.

"I know Frank has special plans for all of us today but it is still early and no one else is up yet. Why don't we take advantage of this time and go have a preliminary look."

I was excited and pleased with his answer. I quickly grabbed my camera and lantern and off we went. Carlos refilled his coffee and took it with him.

"Where were you when you had this revelation ?" he asked half jokingly.

"I was standing in the main chamber at the time I had this revelation." I joked back.

"Okay, then that's where we will start."

As Carlos worked his magic to open the tomb's main door, the king chose this time to speak to me again.

"*Your perseverance will pay off Eric.*"

Atal's voice faded at the pronunciation of my name and I knew it would be useless to answer him but his message was encouraging.

Once inside Carlos and I went direct to the main chamber.

"I have to hand it to you." Carlos remarked. "I never thought to consider a structure beneath this one. It was such a rare thing in our oral history, it has almost been forgotten. If this was built by the king you have become so attached to, it's going to be tricky to find the opening, if there is one."

"Let's just say I have it on good authority that there is something beneath this structure."

Carlos smiled his quiet smile.

Atal made his presence known again. His words echoed in my head.

"Beneath the sky above is the earth below."

I turned away from Carlos hoping to further contact Atal, but as I suspected there was nothing. I quietly mumbled to myself. *"Beneath the sky above is the earth below."* I repeated it a second time forgetting Carlos was nearby.

"That's it." he said aloud.

"What's it." I questioned.

"What you mumbled. It's like a line of a riddle. All we have to do is figure it out."

"He sure had the riddle right." I thought.

He stood quietly, slowly scanning the whole interior.

"And I think we just found it."

I saw a big grin and of course joined him and inquired.

"Where ?"

"Look around, what do you see ?" was his teasing reply.

"I see engravings, Glyphs, abstract designs and...."

Then it hit me. Part of the overhead ceiling was adorned with various scenic paintings. One particular section near a corner was a facsimile of a sky dotted with constellations, Orion, being the apparent center. I unconsciously repeated Atal's riddle. *"Beneath the sky above is the earth below"* I now broke into a very excited smile. I felt as if my whole body was smiling.

We both moved directly under the painted false sky. Here is where Carlos applied his expertise searching for seams of hidden keystones while he was talking aloud to no one in particular.

"I remember how important the star Venus is to the ancient ones along with it's alignment with Orion. Following this imaginary alignment to Venus at the end of the painted sky he stopped about six feet from the wall. There he stayed, slowly staring at nothing. I was tempted to say something but thought better of it, not wanting to disturb his concentration. I sat myself on the king's favorite bench and watched Carlos. Eventually he did move stepping closer to the wall. With out stretched arms his hands worked like a safe cracker, feeling every minuscule portion of the wall. His precise and practiced movements amazed me. It was watching an artist at work.

Almost ten minutes elapsed when I heard quiet words.

"There you are, you little devil."

I stared as his fingers traced an imaginary horizontal line until;

"Ah ha !"

The air was then disturbed by a deep rumble as a section of wall pivoted from a central point allowing an opening of about thirty inches on both sides. Carlos turned and started to run.

"Come follow me." he yelled and went straight for the main entrance. I quickly followed remembering last year when we first opened this tomb that had been sealed for hundreds of years. The smell wasn't half as bad as the first time but we both agreed this precaution was necessary and the fresh air was welcomed. We knew we had at least an hour to kill so we relaxed against the outer wall of the pyramid.

Carlos, being curious, as I guess they all were, shyly asked,

"How did you know ? You know, how did you know about another structure below this one. For that matter, how did you know about all of our discoveries really ?"

I could feel myself getting flushed with embarrassment though I know he didn't say that on purpose.

"Would you believe me if I said the king told me." I blurted out.

"Yes." he answered frankly.

I was not surprised by his answer. He added nothing more

at the time. I knew he was waiting further clarification from me. I paused looking for the words of explanation. Rather than phony something up I decided straight talk would be best, after all, these were my friends.

"Why the king singled me out, I have no idea. I do know, as you all have seen, his help has been invaluable. I realize it's long overdue, however a full explanation is now due to all of you. I'm not trying to be evasive but if you can wait until tonight I will fully reveal what I have been going through."

Showing no annoyance or disappointment at all Carlos smiled saying, "You got it Pal." and dropped the subject.

We continued to enjoy the rest and early sunshine.

"Before I fall completely to sleep perhaps we should check out our new find." Carlos smiled.

~ ~ ~ ~ ~ ~

"Just to be on the safe side we should put our bandannas over our nose and mouth." Carlos ordered.

"These are your people Carlos, I think you should be the one to first see your history." I suggested.

"Thank you my friend, I am honored." he answered humbly.

We switched on our lanterns and passed through the door and entered a narrow hallway. We proceeded further noticing a torch hung high on the wall. AS we approached its light emanated from the top bright enough to be natural daylight. Carlos was startled and stopped to look at it. You could tell by the expression on his face he was puzzled about its workings.

"I'll explain that to you tonight also." I said.

He gave me a double take look and shrugged his shoulders, looking confused and continued on. A second torch lit as we neared illuminating stone steps leading down. He looked up at this also still confused. We slowly descended to another series of torch lights self lit as we approached. The steps spiraled somewhat, I judged to be about thirty degrees. The angle was rather steep and for some reason I can't account for I was counting each step. When we reached the bottom we had traversed sixty two steps, the height of each step varying slightly. Doing some quick mental calculations, I put us down about fifty feet plus or minus. Once we were both off and away from the steps, a series of touches turned on. Instantly captivated we stood there mesmerized.

We were in an extremely large room or chamber if you will. Everything was a dazzling white. The walls, floor and ceiling were all massive blocks of stone precisely cut and polished smooth. Each individual block was about four by six feet. Who knows how deep they went.

The room had to be eighty feet square with entrance portals on all four sides. We counted three to a side. At one end, we later determined was East, was a raised platform approximately twenty by thirty feet of the same white stone. This stage stood five feet off the floor and stationary on top of that were tables and benches also of stone. There were three of them, we guessed to be eight feet long. We figured it to be some sort of meeting chamber. Lesser stone benches lined the other three sides between the portals.

As brilliant as the white was it had an intriguing quality about it that did not offend the eyes. We talked while walking around and to our surprise it was apparent that the acoustics were perfect. You could easily hear from one end to the other without raising your voice. This must have been one of the engineering feats Atal referred to.

An hour passed by as minutes and we were still marveling at this gigantic hall. We had yet to check out the portals to see what lay behind.

After glancing at his watch, Carlos commented on the time. He suggested we go back to tell the others. We agreed on the move, considering Frank had the day preplanned. He would not be very happy if we weren't there and would be even less happy if we didn't inform him of this discovery.

It took us a while longer before we left because the wonderment of the place held us captive. My mind was ablaze, as I'm syre Carlos' was also, with thoughts of science and engineering behind this obvious functional masterpiece. What a true musical artist wouldn't give to perform in these perfect acoustics.

With great regret we finally pulled ourselves away from the white magnificence.

~ ~ ~ ~ ~ ~

Once we exited the tomb and were walking back to camp

Carlos asked;

"What did you mean when you said you would explain the torch light to me tonight ?"

"Just that." I answered. "I'm not holding any secrets, I just thought it best if everyone hears all at once. I believe I can shed light on a lot of things."

"Okay Eric, I won't push any further."

"How do you think Frank is going to react ?" I asked to change the subject.

"First he's not going to believe it, then he's going to want to see it instantly. The others are like me. Right now we believe anything you say."

I repeated my embarrassed feelings.

As we approached the map table we could tell Frank was annoyed, and he did not hide his feelings.

"Out for an early stroll." he said sarcastically. "We went over plans last night, and we agreed on a schedule, and look at the time, we're already an hour and a half behind. You know we have limited time before the rainy season starts and you two are out lollygagging in the jungle."

While he was taking a breath to continue his tirade Carlos quietly put forth;

"Frank, we found another hidden chamber."

Frank instantly turned and stared at Carlos annoyed at being interrupted. Carlos went on slowly and quietly.

"An underground chamber."

"That's ridiculous, there were no underground chambers way back then."

"We found one anyway Frank." Carlos continued softly.

Frank, finally was stumped, he whipped his head to me.

"Is this true Eric ?"

I answered as calmly as Carlos,

"Yes it is Frank."

You could see the excitement in the faces of the other three though they chose to stay silent during this word exchange. Carlos spoke up yet remaining placid.

"The engineering of this chamber makes us look like beginners Frank."

Frank was suddenly quiet. The rest of us stared at him waiting for another outburst. He returned his book and papers to the table and in a defeated voice, almost sarcastically, exclaimed, let's go see this so called wonderment, And took off in the direction of the tomb. The rest of us quickly moved to catch up.

Carlos volunteered to lead the way with Frank close behind. As he neared the torch he turned and said.

"Watch this."

When the lights came on by itself, all were mystified as Carlos was. I repeated my words that I told Carlos.

"I'll explain that to you all tonight." And of course received many confused glances. Frank looked at me with almost an expression of disgust. The lighting of the stair as we descended fascinated all.

Arriving at the white chamber was the epitome of surprises. Frank was literally stunned to silence. He remained in one spot moving only his head and eyes.

Returning from his original shock he managed the words;

"*This* is absolutely incredible. This is not possible. Don't anyone wake me from this dream."

With the initial surprise waning we collectively met in the center for an initial discussion. Frank as usual, wanted to set up a plan and assignments for studies of this amazing structure.

"And you, Eric, I understand will be explaining things tonight, whatever that means.

I smiled and shrugged my shoulders.

Frank chose to stay in the main room along with Diego. I was paired with Mario and chose a portal to explore. Carlos and Mateo chose another.

Slowly we passed through the rounded archway and as expected a torch illuminated a narrowed hallway that led to another set of descending steps. These were extremely narrow allowing only a one person passage. Mario chose to go first still being intrigued by the self illuminated lights. The steps spiraled round and round, straight down, what seemed like forever. We judged to be down at least another fifty feet or so. Running out of steps found us in a circular hallway about eight feet wide and a most pleasant color of green, imitating a light shade of Emerald.

Choosing a direction we followed the curved walkway seeing nothing but the remarkable engineering of stonework. It, at first, appeared to be sanded wood or modern day wallboard of its smoothness, but it was definitely stone. What kind we had not ascertained yet, further testing was still needed. We resumed our walk and met Carlos and Mateo. This chance meeting let us realize there remained another half a hallway to be explored and that lead to the same place. This design did not exactly make sense to us. There must be more to this maze.

The four of us stayed together following the other direction. We passed our starting point and turned our concentrated attention to the walls again. Another thirty feet brought us to a definite seam. All eyes turned to Carlos awaiting his magic touch. As he neared the seam the wall parted on its own taking us by surprise. It was obvious we were facing a massive room but it remained darkened. Not until we crossed the threshold did lighting come on. What we faced was almost beyond description. This truly was a treasure trove that would make any museum jealous. From floor to ceiling were gold, silver, copper, gemstones, statuary and paintings. This was an "El Dorado" unto itself.

There were pathways between stacks of treasures. It wasn't really stacks either. Everything was neatly organized and properly supported. There was no danger of falling objects. This round cavernous space was approximately fifty feet in diameter. There was no way to give a quick estimate to the contents of this safe, if you will.

"Why, with this amount of treasure, is there such easy access ?" I asked aloud.

I was just thinking the same thing myself." replied Mateo. "Frank is going to go wild again with this, he's so intense sometimes. I hope he doesn't have a heart attack." he added.

I think I just found the answer to the easy access." Carlos exclaimed.

We followed his voice around one of the pathways. There he stood over two bodies, clothed in armor and helmets of the Conquistadors. This had been their burial vault for over four hundred and fifty years. Carlos then cautioned, rather loudly,

"Don't go near the doorway."

His stern remark froze us in place. Carlos anxiously looked

around the treasure piles, finally settling his gaze on something, a rectangular wood carving about four feet long with inlaid gold designs. Carefully lifting it . He carried it to within eight feet of the door where he placed it on the floor. He then got on his hands and knees behind the board eyeing it as if to aim. Judging the amount of push needed he heaved the wood towards the opening. Within four feet the door started closing and rather fast at that. The board and door reached the threshold at the same time and lucky for us his timing was perfect. The carved board blocked the door from closing all the way and sealing our fate as our two companions in armor.

Carlos, looking up at us:

"Those Conquistadors could have been us. Once the vault closes, it cannot be opened from the inside."

That definitely was a scary thought.

"These two men probably broke away from the main body of their party and discovered this on their own. Otherwise this heritage would have been lost forever." Carlos filled in.

The three of us had not moved yet, thinking of ourselves along with the two soldiers.

I don't know why but something struck me odd about this.

"How did they get in ?" They sure as hell didn't come in the way we did. So how did they get in ?"

"Very good question." answered Mario smiling. "Why don't you ask the king. ?"

I smiled in return thinking it was not a bad idea, but not now.

"There must be another outside access to the round hallway." I suggested.

"You're probably right." Carlos chimed in. "First things first though. Since you have your camera with you why not start documenting what we've seen so far. Mateo, go back and notify Frank as slowly as possible, Mario and I can start looking for that other entrance."

No one challenged Carlos' take over bid. We, as a group just did not function that way. We all respected each others authority whenever it was exercised.

I started photographing for the record, though I wondered if even this evidence would be enough to convince some of the sceptic academics and nay sayers.

This treasure was beyond imagination. This is what the Spaniards were looking for. I believe the exploration and discovery of land was the excuse to be here. At least the Mayans of old were able to secret their heritage. Their cavitation however was destroyed by the greedy European white man.

I was photographing the mass piles as they were stacked. It is going to take a dedicated team to inventory this lot and attempt to put a value on it. I find it ironic the Maya did not value it for its worth but for its beauty. They could not, understand the Spanish greed for wealth. The Maya value was ceremonial. I caught myself getting taken in by its beauty and design. To me this was truly art in its greatest form.

I thought of Atal. I hoped I could contact him. I was sort of hidden at the moment.

"I am here Eric. It seems you have a question my young friend."

I was more than thankful he answered.

"Atal, you can rest assured your treasure will not be abused. Your heritage will be safe."

"I'm sure you are right Eric. I have complete trust in you and your Mayan companions, otherwise I would not have shown you this room. I also sense you are looking for an outside entrance, and you are right in doing so. It has not been used in over four hundred years. Beware of its dangers."

"Where do we find this entrance and what are the dangers ?"

"Poisonous gasses abound from thermal columns and you must ascend the western staircase."

"What do you mean by the western staircase ?" I further asked, but as usual I was apparently dismissed again.

I heard voices entering the treasure room. Carlos and Mario had returned exclaiming no luck. I sheepishly looked at them saying;

"**I** know I just spoke to the king. The other entranceway is located in the western stairway."

They both smiled and left. I quickly followed calling after them. Thank goodness I caught up with them before I forgot to mention the poison gas. At this they stopped. It was agreed we did not need to know of this entrance just yet. We three returned to the treasure room to await Frank.

Carlos, with a small smile quietly asked;

"**S**o you really did talk to the king ?"

Returning his smile and not embarrassed this time, I answered straight forward,

"**Y**es I did while you and Mario were searching the hallway."

"**H**ow do you do that ? BY ESP ?"

"**I** guess you could call it that or something like that. IT's more like a mental telepathy thing."

Mario, also with a sly smile joined in.

"**Y**ou've been doing this all along, haven't you ?"

With a gentle smile I answered.

"**T**he king and I sort of developed a bond. Why me I have no idea. It should have been one of you, which would have made more sense. He's the one who taught me this mental telepathy thing. I thought with his passing that would be the end of it. As you can well understand I was a bit shocked when he connected with me after his death."

Carlos was about to say something when Mateo returned with Frank and Diego. I was glad of this, that way I could explain all to everybody tonight as planned.

The look on Frank's face was priceless as he stopped dead in his tracks, mouth open but not uttering a sound. We let him have his time. Leave it to Frank to make the statement he did when he finally spoke.

"**M**y God, this could pay off the national debt."

He looked at me directly

"**Y**ou have a lot of explaining to do tonight." He did say it with a smile though. "There's no way in hell we can inventory this before the rainy season." Again looking at me he followed with, "You are going to record all of this, are you not ? Of course you are." He answered

himself. "Get a few close ups too. Why am I telling you this. Of course
you know what to do. Diego, can you date any of this ? If not, try anyway.
Perhaps Mateo can assist you."

"Frank!" Carlos said in a slightly raised voice.

Frank turned to him dazed.

"Take a deep breath, relax and calm down. We all know
how you feel, we feel the same way, but this is not going any where and yes
this is all real."

Frank burst out in a big smile and you could see the tension
leave his body. He watched us all still smiling.

"This is overwhelming, you know we should..."

Mario cut him short.

"No plans for now Frank, just look and enjoy with the rest
of us. One afternoon is not going to ruin this expedition.

Frank gazed at us again, he knew he was outnumbered,
smiled and gave in.

"Okay, I know you're right."

Chapter 45

"Okay then, as long as we're taking a break, I'm going to peruse some of this amazing collection." Diego offered walking to a large mass in the back of the chamber. As he disappeared the rest of us split up, each walking to a different stack. I also headed for a rearward shelving.

This particular stack was boxed in by hardwood logs. I had not seen this wood before. It was a very dark brown possessing tight grain with a polished look finish. It was constructed solid enough to climbon, which is what I did.

Once atop the treasure I reached in and pulled out a silver chalice, The bell portion about the size of my fist, the stem about six inches long with an octagonal base of four inches in diameter. The upper side of the base was inscribed with the same unreadable script on the scrolls. Who knows what age this could have been. Carefully setting it aside I reached for another prize. A blade and handle. This was not just any blade either. I recognized it immediately. It was Chinese of the Chou dynasty, about three thousand BP. (Before Present) *"Was there ancient trade ?"* I asked myself. *"This is a must discussion with the others."*

Returning it to a safe location I scanned again for something unique. I reached and pulled out an odd shaped object. It took a few seconds then it came to me. An ANKH. You know the symbol of life from the early Egyptian period.

A sort of long handled cross, but the upper most appendage almost shaped like a heart without the upper most dip, or an upside down tear drop, sometimes carried by those in power. It is most commonly seen in representations of King Tut holding such a device. There were even Egyptian Hieroglyphics inscribed on it.

This treasure wasn't just Mayan heritage; this was treasure of the world. The long ago world. I wondered if then others were running into the same thing.

"If you recall Eric, I mentioned, when my world was destroyed, our survivors dispersed around this globe hoping to share our advanced knowledge. We did manage to foster some trade but the rest of our teachings were not readily accepted."

"Then what you are saying is this treasure trove is truly authentic."

"What you have before you Eric is the original and the best. No price can be put on such things."

I was puzzled but asked Atal for guidance.
"Then how, my friend, does one go about protecting this art yet sharing its beauty. This should be something for the whole world to share, yet it is coveted."

"If I had the answer to that Eric we would not be having this conversation."

All was silent for a while, then;

"By the way Eric, I approve of your idea to share our experiences with your other friends. You may tell them I, too, trust them."

The sudden loud silence told me our time was over.
I continued treasure diving being repeatedly amazed at what

were probably one of a kind art works. Many pieces were, obviously, Mayan or pre Mayan works that showed sensitivity to their jungle surroundings and animals abiding there.

I heard Frank's call summoning us. It was just as well, I could feel a sense of melancholy creeping in which would have finished me for the day. I had not realized it but more than an hour had passed before Frank's retreating call. It was unanimously decided by Frank that we retire to the camp, attend to our journals, then during and after dinner we can proceed with our unabridged bull session. He almost appeared to be looking forward to it.

We followed through with the complete lock up procedure then leisurely strolled back to camp.

~ ~ ~ ~ ~ ~

Our latest discovery put a whole new light on our mission here. It was finally agreed upon by all that the discovery of uppermost importance was the new city. This in itself would rewrite a fair amount of history. The art and treasure finds should also do their part in understanding history and certainly contribute strongly in the reconstruction of history as taught today.

The first of these two will undoubtedly be easier to show the world. Even with the king's help, should he continue his association with me, the latter will be extremely difficult to sway the established academics. That will be the task we will have to undertake.

Dinner under the present joyous circumstances was quite good even though it was the same old MRE's and some leftover fish. It's a wonder how a person's mood can change the taste and scope of a meal as simple as an MRE.

As planned by Frank our bull session in relation to today's find commenced during dinner. At first the main thrust was to keep the treasure a secret from the world.

"But why ?" I asked. "This amount of artifacts and their origin will help our case for changing some history. It could lead to other areas, other countries and in turn change that history also. Is not one of our goals to reestablish the truth about world history ?"

"Okay, okay." Frank chimed in though with a smile. "I

never realized you were such a zealot."

I instantly took umbrage to his accusation and quickly realized he was joking. *"Or was he ?"* I thought.

Soon it was my turn to speak and as promised I began to tell my story of my relationship with the king. To me, they were the perfect accompaniment for my conceivably unbelievable tales.

I noticed immediately the doubt on Frank's face and with other questionable glints in his eyes. I could almost see the questions in his mind and his innermost thoughts of *(He may be a good photographer, and has helped on these expeditions but now his wacky side has really taken over.)*

I think the others noticed Frank's change also but so far they were with me. Their culture and heritage meant a lot to them. They believed in their ancient king and were trying to believe in my connections with him. I explained in as much detail as possible my conversations with Atal both before and after he died. I could feel the mental telepathy part was considered far fetched in their minds, though they continued to humor me. I went on with my present conversations with the king to an ever growing restless group.

Frank interrupted with his curiosity about the torch lights. I hesitated for a moment knowing my explanation would not be too readily accepted.

Perhaps if I included Mario, who was a early witness with me, the believability factor would increase. I started with the workings of the scepter which arrested their attention, to a point. Once I got on to its power and usage I could feel the doubt building. Not even Mario's not too convincing back up was of any real help. I was allowed to continue mt tale until the part of the small vial I had for personal use.

"Okay, Merlin the Magician, let's see this world changing magic powder, or is it a crystal ?" Frank said with extreme sarcasm and a sneering laugh.

The other four, harboring their own thoughts, were also taken aback with Frank's outburst.

I suddenly felt hurt. My whole positive world just crashed around me. I wanted to lash out at Frank but decided to be mature about it.

"Think what you may Frank. All I know is that I'm telling the truth. If you can't accept the facts before you then that's your problem." I answered calmly.

The change in expression on Frank's face proved he did not like my answer, or perhaps the way I said it. Frank abruptly stood up and without looking at me grumbled;

"I don't know about you guys but I for one am not going to listen to this theatrical hogwash."

He picked up his coffee mug and blatantly stomped away to the work tent. I sat back smiling to myself. Part of me, not too long ago, would have reacted the same way, though I believe I would have been more open minded about it. I returned my attention to the others.

With Frank now out of our gathering I could tell the apparent doubts showing just moments ago quickly disappeared. Mario became animated once again with his back up of my story. His account as a witness was wholly believable.

Mateo, too, expressed his belief in my story.

"How else would you know of the things you have led us to and shown us." he asked.

The next forty five minutes we were engaged in a question and answer session, the majority of which were about my conversations with the king. I even promised to ask Atal to attempt contacting one of the others. Personally I thought it possible considering that they were personally engaged with their heritage.

I was actually pleased when we broke for the night. It had been a long and hectic day and I needed my night time symphony. Carlos walked with me to my hammock. He quietly suggested we keep an eye on Frank.

"I've known Frank for a lot of years and have never seen him in this kind of mood. I've never known him to be like this. Just play it soft with him for a while. Maybe we can figure out what's bugging him."

I just smiled choosing not to answer. I was a bit perturbed by Frank's outburst.

At last I was alone and I welcomed my jungle orchestra taking over my mind and body.

Chapter 46

The night passed slowly. Too slowly for my taste. Something was nagging at me, enough not to let restful sleep overcome me. It was even more upsetting because I could not put my finger on the cause. I apparently dozed towards morning from sheer exhaustion most likely, because I suddenly realized my jungle orchestra had changed shifts and the morning sounds were filling the air. I forced my way out of my hammock, throwing water on my face trying at least to look awake.

I joined Diego at the coffee pot.

"You look like you've been out all night and are still suffering from a hangover." he quipped.

"I wish it was that good." I answered trying to put on a smile.

"I had some pretty dreams all night, about the treasure of course." Diego followed. "I can't wait to get a chance to sketch some of that beauty."

"I think you will have plenty of opportunity for that. It's not going anywhere for a while." This time I did smile.

"I was fascinated with that telepathy stuff. Do you think you could show me how sometime ?"

"I don't know if there is anything to actually show you but I'll try to explain what I do. Perhaps you can just pick it up from there."

"That would be great." Diego said with pure enthusiasm.

One by one the others eventually crawled out of bed. It was only then I discovered Frank was up early and had already gone to the tomb. That was so unlike Frank.

I made a few journal entries then made my way to the tomb with Diego and Mateo. They were both still captivated by my talks with the king. Once in the main chamber Diego went to the art hallway while Mateo made his way to the treasure room and Frank. Alone again I decided on one last check up on the scroll library.

Although I was alone with the scrolls I felt totally at home with the peace and quiet knowing the history they safeguarded in their ancient rolls. It was comforting for a change to know this small part of history was not destroyed by the European explorers as so much other history had been.

I stood there soaking up the knowledge of the scrolls wishing that I really could understand them. Someday, perhaps, depending on how long it takes for the translation.

"They are special to many of us Eric, and I am pleased to count you as one of our select few. I felt a disturbance in you last night. I can not account for that yet, but I feel deep inside you are correct in your uncomfortable feeling. Be watchful my friend."

I was going to ask Atal something more but I already knew it was useless. He had tuned me out.

Mateo found me in my semi dream state.

"I'm sorry to, disturb you Eric but Frank is acting very weird. It was quite obvious he did not want me in with him and the treasure. He had this strange look about him. It appeared he was making an inventory of the treasure yet something tells me it was more than that. I don't like what I was seeing."

"I'm not in his best standing right now, not after last night, so I suggest you get Carlos and explain to him what you just told me. I'll meet with you both later."

Mateo hurriedly exited to get back to camp and Carlos.

Why then, I don't know but I remembered something in the art hallway and directed myself there and to Diego. I found him sketching one of the murals. It was the one that encompasses ships of other nations. It was an intriguing piece. To think a people considered backwards by the Europeans, could know of ships of other nations, far and wide, have art and engineering beyond that of the discoverers and build cities to house thousands.

As it turned out the painting I wanted to view was the very one Diego was sketching. I explained to him my search which he instantly answered.

"You mean this." As he pointed to an Egyptian ship at dockside with a figure walking down a boarding plank holding a large cross like object.

"That's it." I almost shouted.

"What's it." Diego returned.

I relayed the story of my find in the treasure room, meaning the "Ankh". To me, anyway, this proved there was actual contact between the Maya and Egyptian peoples of long ago.

Diego and I discussed other aspects of the painting which would actually support my theory of early contact. I did not mention what Mateo had said about Frank. I was hoping that it was really nothing and Carlos would have it sorted out.

Diego wished to finish some art work, and I certainly did not want to see Frank right now so I decided some more alone time would suit my needs. I wandered to the main chamber and found the kings passage to the outside world. It felt good to be standing in the jungle again. I was at piece though short lived it was. Atal must have sensed I was alone.

"Eric, you are right to be alarmed. Something is in the air that is quite disturbing. Be cautious of Frank. He is no longer the person he once was. Be very cautious. I do not wish to see harm come to you or the others. They are sincere and you can trust them. I must go now, someone is summoning me."

I realized I had just been warned of possible trouble but what was foremost on my mind was the fact that Atal mentioned another being calling to him. I felt this was a major breakthrough in dealing with the king. He actually shared with me an inner most secret. The possibility could exist that one of my four Maya friends could make contact with him. Perhaps I'm not so crazy after all.

I forced my mind back to the king's warning. So I was right in my feelings about Frank. I don't dare mention this to him. He thinks I'm a nut job already by supposedly talking with dead people. I just may hold this back from the others also until I feel the time or situation is right. I'll find out what Carlos' assessment is later.

Rather than go back through the tomb I decided to walk around the complex on the outside.. I took my time enjoying my daytime serenade. About twenty minutes later I arrived at the first discovered portal. I admired the magnificence of the structure, its design and engineering even though I have seen it dozens of times. This whole city was just riveting.

Mario and Mateo were working at the campsite, the others had not returned yet. Mario was as concerned as I was about Frank, suggesting perhaps it was the pressure of the short study season. I hoped he was right though I had my doubts. I settled myself at one of the tables trying to concentrate on my journal to no avail. The Frank quandary was dominating my every thought.

I sat back attempting to clear my head when I saw Carlos returning. He was alone. He walked directly to me ignoring the greeting of Mario and Mateo. Before I could utter a sound Carlos stated.

"**T**his does not look good. Frank all but threw me out physically. He even went so far as to forbid me to enter the treasure chamber ever again."

"**Y**ou're joking of course ?" I asked not wanting to believe him.

"**I** wish I was." he answered. "It's as if he were under some kind of spell. He is suddenly obsessed by the treasure find. He denies anything is wrong with him."

"**T**hat's usually the first sign that there is a problem." I posited.

Just then Diego came running into the complex.

"**I** can't believe it. Frank just threw me out of the tomb."
He was yelling . "I was in the art hallway sketching. You know that Eric, that's where you left me. Frank entered the hallway calling out my name, or maybe I should say shouting my name. He even tried to grab my sketchbook. He said he wanted me out and right now. I never saw him like this before."

"**O**kay, okay, have a seat and calm down." Carlos offered.

He motioned to Mario and Mateo to join us.

A brief synopsis was relayed so we were all on the same page.

"**N**ow what ?" asked Carlos.

I took that as a lead.

"**I** almost don't want to say this, but Atal warned me a few days ago that I should be cautious around Frank. In fact he even said very cautious."

"**D**id he give you any details ?" Mario inquired.

"**N**o." was my answer. "He often talks in somewhat hidden riddles. Our talks are often quick and one sided, his side. I have tried on occasion to pursue things further but he just tunes me out and I have no idea why. It's almost as if he were doing the same thing he so often preached against, and that was control.

"**P**erhaps." suggested Mateo, "Atal is still carrying on as if he were king and not meaning his words for control but for guidance."

I thought about Mateo's words and conceded to his explanation because I did not find the king controlling up to this point in our relationship.

"**I**t appears the only controlling factor we should be concerned with now is Frank." Carlos put forth trying to keep us on track. I'll go back to my original question, now what ?"

A sudden lull came over the camp with everyone just staring at each other or into the jungle. Mario, in a take charge voice finally said what possibly we all were thinking.

"**W**e just have to talk to Frank and let him know what our concerns are. Tonight at dinner we can discuss everything in a sensible and logical manner. I'm sure he will understand our interest in the overall project."

The presentation of his thoughts made sense to us and all agreed. The air of serious concern was lightened somewhat as we relaxed with a change of subject.

Diego offered his ideas on a video of the art hallway that would present to the world the unique and heretofore unknown style of art. Carlos was about to comment on this when Frank appeared in the work area. Before a word could be uttered by any of us Frank seized control. His demeanor was aggressive, his face took on a red complexion, with his eyes squinted and teeth semi clenched. He started speaking almost shouting.

"**N**ow listen to me all of you."

On that word "you" his eyes went directly to me. He paused for a few seconds, all the time glaring at me. Frank then continued in his shouting manner.

"From now on, no one, and I mean no one will go to the tomb. I and I alone will conduct whatever research is deemed necessary and pertinent to this project. The tomb is absolutely off limits to all."

Frank's voice was downright nasty by the time he finished the sentence. Again, at the end his eyes were directly on me. I could not resist the impulse, so as I stared back I slowly smiled.

At last breaking contact with me Frank added.

"And there will not be any questions, that is my decision and you will abide by it.

The four Maya spoke in unison, each with different comments but all directed at Frank questioning his out of nowhere illogical remarks. It was obvious by his disgusted expression he did not want to hear anything. He stomped away heading for the supply shelter. After a few minutes he exited the tent carrying all the rifles, making his way back to the tomb. Carlos yelled after him.

"Wait a minute Frank, what the hell do you think you're doing."

Frank spun around eyes blazing.

"You heard my orders. Not you or anyone else will question them"

As he turned to the tomb I spoke out softly but firmly;

"You're wrong Frank. Whatever it is you're thinking, you're wrong."

Frank stopped, staying frozen in place.

"The treasure is not yours Frank." I continued. "It belongs to the Maya people, it belongs to the world, and it belongs to history."

By now I was standing. I took a few steps in Frank's direction but stopped as he turned towards me, a rifle pointed at me, his hand on the trigger. Both Carlos and Mario quickly jumped up and took a position between Frank and me.

"My God Frank, what's come over you ?" yelled Mario.

"Don't do this." added Carlos. "Let's talk about this."

Frank was now starting to shake, his eyes were glazed with his mouth straight line tight.

"There is absolutely nothing to discuss. You will continue your research until we leave and you will escort this *"Talk to the dead."* maniac out of my city."

As he finished talking Frank slowly backed away towards the king's pyramid. I moved forward but Carlos bid me stop and not aggravate Frank any further. I agreed, especially in Frank's present unstable condition. We all watched as Frank retreated, entering the tomb and closing the door behind him. Our breathing returned to normal and we gathered around the work table.

The sound of the jungle was all that was heard as we stared at each other unable to speak.

Chapter 47

Mario broke the silence when he started pacing.

"What the hell happened to Frank ? What has come over him ?"

"Greed." Mateo mumbled in answer.

Carlos shot Mateo an angry glance wanting to admit he was most likely right. I put in my two cents by adding that I've never known him to be this way. That was one fact we all agreed on.

"Let's just go talk to him." suggested Diego innocently.

"I don't think that's a good idea." answered Carlos. "Considering the state of mind that occupies him right now."

We all agreed with his answer.

"Let's let him have the night and possibly approach him in the morning." continued Carlos.

"But the door is closed and most likely locked. Won't he hear us when we try to open it ?" asked Mateo.

"I'm sure he will but what other choice do we have ?" commented Carlos.

Mario looked at me and I knew what was on his mind. I nodded my approval. Mario then quickly spoke of another way into the tomb. All heads snapped to him. That statement sure got their attention.

"How do you know that ?" Came a chorus of voices.

Hesitating with a touch of guilt, he told the story of our visit with the king and the demonstration with the scepter. I also filled in some details of that day that Mario overlooked. We both apologized for withholding the information of the scepter letting them know it was the king's wishes that we do so. Carlos then asked the next logical question.

"What about the scepter now ? It's in the tomb with Frank. What if he decides to use it ?"

"It's harmless now." I answered. "It no longer has any power."

"How do you know that ?" was the return reply.

Again I went into story mode and related my discussion with the king and how I witnessed its destruction. I did not, though, mention my little gift of the vial of the special sand, or the fact that I destroyed it also. There was again a period of quiet as our tales were digested. Mario went on to say no ill will was intended by our not divulging this information sooner.

Mateo suggested it was probably for the best that Frank was not privy to the story of the scepter what with his present mind set.

There was no anger or ill feeling held against us for which we were thankful.

Carlos took the lead in questioning the location of this other entrance and what kind of advantage would it give us. He was slightly taken aback when Mario spoke of the mural hallway, but let it pass. Another holdout we forgot to mention. We further discussed this option yet could not come up with a practical plan. We went back to Diego's original statement of just a direct approach but would wait till morning. We all agreed not much more could be done about Frank for now but busied ourselves with routine work until dinner. I thought about contacting Atol but chose to wait until tonight.

Much to everyone's surprise Frank reappeared at dinner time, weaponless. He cordially greeted us all as if nothing had occurred earlier. He helped himself to some fish along with one of our great MRE's.

"We should try for more of these fish, they're really quite good." he remarked without looking at us. We all sat there stunned, not knowing what to do or say. Out of the corner of my eye I saw Mateo and Diego whispering. Carlos addressed Frank attempting to be non aggressive.

"What's going on Frank ? Let's talk this out. WE're all in this together."

Frank answered quietly but firmly.

"You heard my orders Carlos as did everyone else. Us being in this together ends at the research stage. Now if you don't mind I will return to the pyramid."

As Carlos took a step toward Frank, Mateo jumped up moving to Carlos.

"Leave him be. He can do what he wants, it's his expedition."

Carlos was a bit taken aback with Mateo's action, even more shocked by his almost nasty tone.

"You go ahead Frank, I'll hold them here."

Now the rest of us were in disbelief at Mateo's words. Diego quickly moved to stop Frank, though Mateo moved faster. He pushed Diego aside and threw a roundhouse punch. Landing him on the ground. Frank had already started for the tomb with Mateo right on his heels. Mario rushed to Diego and before anyone else could react, Frank with Mateo at his side entered the tomb and of course closed the door. Mario helped Diego to his feet who now looked at us with a big smile spread across his face.

"Don't worry, I'm okay, this was all staged. Now we have someone inside with Frank. The plan is for us to enter via this other entrance early in the morning and hopefully surprise Frank. Mateo will see about negating the rifles to help our chances of success.

We had to give Mateo credit for such a quick thinking bold approach. Returning to our cold dinners we relaxed and discussed preparations for tomorrow.

Mario and I drew diagrams of the entrance by the mural hallway. Mateo was to keep Frank distracted and away from that part of the chamber. I hesitated for a moment, and then decided this was not the time for anymore holdouts. I told the story of the third entrance, which was accepted as no surprise by this time. We agreed to use both entrances to help our chances of a stealth visit. We hoped to peacefully curtail Frank to enable a quiet, sensible discussion to take place.

We were about to break for the night to get some rest when a commotion disturbed the quiet of the jungle. Looking towards the tomb we could see Frank, rifle in hand shouting at Mateo. He even fired a shot at his direction missing on purpose, we hoped. Mateo started running in our direction as Frank let go a second shot. You could see the dirt kick up near the running feet. The tomb door closed again as Mateo reached us out of breath. Mario helped him to a chair while I poured some water.

"He's gone completely mad. That treasure has totally taken over his mind." Mateo said between gasps.

"What happened ?" inquired Carlos.

"I thought he believed my sincerity at first." Mateo answered. "We settled down in the kings chamber while he ate his dinner and made small talk. He did not ask why I turned against you. When he finished eating he walked toward the treasure room. I quietly followed. When we neared the room he turned on me and went berserk shouting and screaming all sorts of obscenities. I didn't belong here, it's none of my business, and we are all out to cheat him. He actually ran me out with the gun pointed at me."

He sat back visibly trembling. It was then I decided to contact the king. I made known my intentions to the others and went off by myself to my sleeping area hoping the king would be receptive.

"I am here Eric, as I said I would be and yes I am aware of your situation."

I really did not know what to say so I made it as simple as I could.

"Can you help us ?" I asked almost pleading with the tone of my thought.

"The best was would be to get through to Frank yet his mental state makes that impossible. His mind is so filled with hate and jealousy at this point there is no room for telepathic reception. His disbelief in such matters also blocks intelligent connections."

Frustrated with his answer I rudely remarked;

"That's of no help to us and right now we need help before someone gets seriously hurt."

"Be patient my friend, I am aware of your plight. I did not say I would not help. Haste has never been a good virtue and should not be practiced, especially now. Franks reaction to the treasure is nothing new. I have seen this attitude many times before and the end result has never been good. This has been going on for millennium and will continue in the same mode for people such as you. We will continue this discussion another time, now we will address your immediate dilemma."

I understood the kings words but the here and now was foremost on my mind.

"Your idea Eric, of using the unknown entrance is correct. That will gain you safe passage, from there on out you must use your mind."

I was a bit confused by Atal's statement but before I could inquire further my thoughts were interrupted.

"Hear me out, Eric please, before you comment."

I remained silent.

"Just as you and I are now communicating, you must do that with Frank as must the others. It must all be done together; I of course will join in. Together we can blur Frank's mind which he will unknowingly accept as confusion. Our thought will be for him to leave the tomb. You must not let him see you or all will be lost. Letting his mind fix on reality will nullify our efforts. Once outside it will be up to your companions to carefully subdue him. Let us enjoin this exercise just before sunrise, perhaps at five o'clock. By that time he will be quite tired and more open to outside influence. We will converse in the morning after all goes well."

I knew the signs and I had been dismissed. I sat in my hammock a while longer trying to figure out how to sell Atal's plan to the others. I knew Frank was a disbeliever but I also had a hunch there were some doubters among the others. I felt I wasted enough time so I rejoined the group. Speaking as confidently as I could as I outlined Atal's plan I was looking at some questioning faces. I ended my little speech as positive as I could.

"Trust me guys, I believe this will work."

They did so hesitantly but they all agreed. We worked out a few details as to where to stand then called it quits for the night.

Chapter 48

I certainly did not get much sleep thinking and worrying about Frank and concerned about the whole expedition I guess. So much effort by all of us to have it all go up in smoke. To my mind at least the historical value of this city far out weighed whatever the treasure would bring.

The time was four thirty in the morning and we were all gathered at the tomb entrance. I reviewed the thought process once more before leaving the group to find my hidden entrance. I traversed the tombs passage ways reaching my destination with two minutes to spare. I was about to start my concentration effort when an outside thought interference surfaced.

"I'm pleased you are here Eric, now we can start this together."

I was about to answer then realized it would be useless. Atal sure had his own ways of controlling things. I set my mind to Frank as I slowly opened the wall to the great room. Pushing ever so slowly to maintain silence I was able to peek into the chamber. I saw nothing nor even heard a sound. All was silent. *"Where was Frank."* I thought. I immediately scolded myself for the deviation from my assigned task and pushed my thoughts back to Frank's movements.

I silently entered the chamber and secreted myself in a shadowed corner. I remained as still as the star at night till even my breathing was imperceptible. *"Frank you must leave now, come outside."* Became my repeated mantra. I felt a strong presence in the air which I attributed to the power of combined wills. A chill passed through me with the feeling of the king. I knew this had to work.

Within ten minutes I detected a presence from the direction of the treasure room. Willing myself to almost invisibility I waited with only the sound of my heartbeat disturbing my thoughts.

Frank appeared looking somewhat confused but on a definite mission. Approaching the entrance door he hesitated. My heart stopped. *"Go on Frank. You want to go outside. It is important to you Frank. Very important."* My mind repeated this a few times.

As if suddenly remembering something, Frank half smiled and continued to the door. Working the lever the door slowly pivoted allowing an early morning shaft of light to squeeze in running a path to the opposite wall. Frank breathed deeply and stepped outside. I moved as stealthily as I could to the wall heading to the opening. I stopped within inches of the threshold and listened. Only the distant sound of the jungle could be heard. I waited before going out just in case Frank detected anything and retreated to the tomb.

Five minutes passed, still not a sound. Inching closer I managed a quick peek outside. At first glance, nothing could be seen. I moved and stood in the full opening, it was then I saw all about forty feet away.

Diego, Mateo and Mario were surrounding Frank. Each had a hold on him. Carlos appeared to be talking quietly. To be on the safe side I closed the tomb making sure it was secured. Breathing easier I walked to the others. Frank was laughing and actually acting perfectly normal. I smiled with relief and felt good inside.

Nearing my colleagues I said "Hi Frank."

Whipping his head around to where he heard my voice his eyes went wild and with nostrils flaring, and started screaming,

"You son of a bitch. You did this. It's all your fault, you and your talking to the dead. You're the one who is crazy, not me. You've turned everyone against me. Well, you're not taking my treasure. Im worked all my life for this and I'm not going to let some nobody come along and usurp what is rightfully mine."

This violent outburst caught everyone off guard and the hold on Frank was unconsciously weakened. Taking advantage of this, Frank pulled himself loose and was running for the pyramid before we could react.

Diego was the first to respond taking off after him. We followed suit but were already being outdistanced. Diego was gaining but not enough. Frank reached the structure and as if he were part monkey scrambled up the side, all the time yelling.

"It's mine. It's mine. Stay away."

Mario joined in yelling,

Frank, be careful. Those outside stones can be loose. Take

care you don't slip.

His warning came too late. Frank gained the flat top but on his last step up the loose stone chipped off upsetting his balance and over backwards he went. We watched his body topple end over end down the length of the stepped pyramid bouncing like a rubber ball off the points of the steps. There was no scream of fear or pain, only the thud of the body impact.

The jungle was abruptly silent as if aware of death in its midst.

Diego was the first to reach the limp form that was once Frank. One could tell at a glance that almost every bone in the body had suffered some sort of fracture. Death was mercifully delivered with no undue suffering. We stood there, trance like, each in his own mind trying to make sense of this tragedy. Could it have been prevented ? We could rationalize everything yet this answer we will never know. We could not rationalize the inner workings of Frank's mind.

Chapter 49

A customary Maya funeral service was decided with the final resting place to be in the tomb. Arrangements for reburial could be made at a later date if family members wished it.

Mateo volunteered to notify Colonel Ramirez of the accidental death so that it was recorded officially.

A proper Maya casket was fashioned from local stone and was placed along a side wall of the king's chamber with appropriate Glyphs and dated recording the event. The body was adorned in its own period dress and out of admiration a few traditional Maya touches were added such as the red feathers and decorative colored stones. The final touch, agreed by all, was the Egyptian Ankh laid across his chest held by crossed arms. This was Frank's city after all and we vowed to see when the complex was officially named, his name could be somehow included. We ourselves would try to come up with a name.

As much of a damper Frank's death had on our work we felt obligated to finish out the season with our research. Work went on as normal, just at a slower pace. Two more outlying sites were found and plotted. Another stelae was discovered which of course required translation.

As for the treasure room we collectively went through and preliminarily categorized as much as we could. There were wonders from all over the world of long ago. A full and detailed inventory would take place next season cooperatively with the university and the Government Antiquities Department. Arrangements were to be made to have all four of Frank's Mayan team as a key part of the succeeding expeditions.

I personally chose to stay out of this from here on, turning over all my work notes and negatives, save a few special mementos, to the university.

The king understood my decision as we said our fair wells. He chose Mario and Diego to continue his thought communication. I was pleased to hear this. Both accepted the honor and were looking forward to new and future findings.

~ ~ ~ ~ ~ ~

I flew back to Vermont for a rest all the while thinking of the solitude of the jungle. Who knew within all that peace and quiet there would be such excitement. I was looking forward to some R and R.

It wasn't long before I was itching for some excitement again. The rainy season in the Yucatan sort of ruled out any more jungle treks, besides without my Mayan friends it wouldn't be the same. The thought of starting up my photo business again seemed rather dull by comparison. What to do with myself now was my present quandary I was still geared up for excitement and looking into the unknown.

The Anasazi always fascinated me, so I thought I would do some first hand research. The four corners area seemed like a good place to start.

I rented my house to a friend and before long I was flying west wondering what was in store for me there.

The End
(For now)

<u>References</u>

In search of the Maya
        By Robert L. Brunhouse
        Pub. by University of New Mexico Press

Ancient Maya Civilization
        By Norman Hammond
        Pub. by Rutgers University Press

Breaking the Maya Code
        By Michael D. Coe
        Pub. by Thames and Hudson Inc.